"Yes, I am quite alone
but for Gilles."

Lady Elise lifted her chin as she said it, her eyes adding, *So just try to do your worst, Englishman.*

He started to reassure her again, but just then her servant came through the door, bearing a goblet of wine that he extended to Adam.

Was this some new trick to slaughter the enemy?

"Ah, I see you fear our intentions." The Frenchwoman indicated that the goblet was to be given to her, took a sip, then passed it on to Adam with a challenging look.

Adam turned the lip of the goblet so he could drink where her lips had touched.

It was a gesture usually made by a lover. And he was pleased to see that he had startled her, for a faint color rose into her cheeks....

Dear Reader,

There is a lot to look for this month from Harlequin Historicals.

Sweet Seduction by Julie Tetel is the first of two intriguing stories set in Maryland during the early 1800s. Heroine Jane Shaw was raised as a Southern belle, but she is more than a match for the British soldiers who sequester her family's home. And don't miss the sequel, *Sweet Sensations,* coming in July.

Readers following the TAGGARTS OF TEXAS! series by Ruth Jean Dale will be delighted to discover the prequel to the earlier books in this month's lineup. *Legend!* is the story of Boone, the Taggart who started it all by turning the little town of Jones, Texas, on its ear.

Captured Moment by Coral Smith Saxe is set during the California mining days. Straight off the boat from the old country, the impish Rowen Trelarken stumbles into an immediate series of misadventures, dragging an unwilling Alec McKenzie along for the ride.

Frenchwoman Elise de Vire marries Sir Adam Saker as an act of revenge, but the force of the attraction between them places them both in mortal danger in *Beloved Deceiver,* a medieval tale from Laurie Grant.

Four new romances from Harlequin Historicals. We hope you enjoy them.

Sincerely,

Tracy Farrell
Senior Editor

Beloved Deceiver

LAURIE GRANT

Harlequin Books

TORONTO • NEW YORK • LONDON
AMSTERDAM • PARIS • SYDNEY • HAMBURG
STOCKHOLM • ATHENS • TOKYO • MILAN
MADRID • WARSAW • BUDAPEST • AUCKLAND

Harlequin Historicals first edition April 1993

ISBN 0-373-28770-4

BELOVED DECEIVER

LAURIE GRANT

combines a career as a trauma-center emergency room nurse with that of historical romance author; she says the writing helps keep her sane. Passionately enthusiastic about the history of both England and Texas, she divides her travel time between these two spots. She is married to her own real-life hero, and has two teenage daughters, two dogs and a cat.

For all of you who
"kept me sailing through the doldrums."
You are too numerous to mention,
but very much appreciated.
And, of course, to Michael.

Prologue

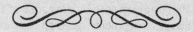

Paris, April 1417

"Help me! I am made of glass! I will break!" bleated the pitiful figure upon the gilded throne.

It was not one of the king of France's better days. Charles of Valois, clothed in ermine-trimmed purple velvet robes that were grease-spotted and threadbare, gazed with vacant eyes upon the young widow, then extended his dirt-encrusted hands with curling, untrimmed fingernails in a gesture of dismissal.

Elise de Vire stared at the monarch, aghast. King Charles had heard nothing of her carefully thought-out plea for revenge against the English. Had her long journey from Normandy to the French capital been for naught?

So the king was every bit as mad as he was rumored to be! She had hoped to find him in one of his lucid periods, but it was well-known that once he slipped back into insanity, he would be mentally incompetent for months. Elise did not have enough money to stay in the French capital indefinitely.

A lackey stepped forward, murmuring in soothing tones, and finally persuaded the king to be led from the room.

"Perhaps you had better speak with me, *madame*," said a voice from the shadows. "As you can see, my husband is indisposed, unfortunately."

Elise started as a figure stepped forward, sheathed in scarlet silk that strained with bulging rolls of fat as the woman settled her corpulent figure on the throne. She had three chins, one upon another, which bobbled as she inclined her head toward Elise. A grotesque horned headdress of stiffened red brocade, festooned with sheer veils, slipped slightly on her head, and Elise caught a glimpse of graying dark hair. The cloying scent of stale perfume and unwashed flesh wafted toward the young woman.

"Your Majesty," whispered Elise, sinking into a deep curtsy.

Isabella of Bavaria motioned her to rise. "I heard it all from behind there," murmured the queen, gesturing vaguely in the direction of the corridor that led from the royal apartments to the dais of the presence chamber. "I had a feeling that my lord was about to slip again." She spoke of the king's periodic insanity as casually as one discussed the weather.

Elise said nothing, not sure what was appropriate.

"So! You are a widow of Agincourt, and you would be revenged upon the death of your young husband, a knight," said Queen Isabella, studying Elise through pale eyes nearly lost in the folds of flesh.

"Yes, Your Majesty."

"Congratulations," the queen said dryly. "You are in a vast company, my good young woman, one of thousands of widows made so that day. Did your knight leave you no babes, then, to occupy yourself as a young widow ought?''

"Nay, Your Majesty," Elise said, bowing her head so that this powerful woman with her mocking voice and sardonic expression did not see her tears as the old hurt stabbed anew.

After seeing Sir Aimeri's mutilated body honorably buried, Elise had journeyed back to Normandy, hoping that at least she would be left with her husband's child. In a fortnight, however, she knew even that consolation was not to be.

She soon saw that she could not stay forever at Château de Vire. Aimeri's heir, his brother, saw Elise as a useless mouth to feed, while his wife found her sister-by-marriage a convenient nursemaid for her growing brood. And since Elise had no land of her own, unless she took the veil or accepted the suit of one of the several elderly, malodorous widowers her brother-by-marriage brought to the castle, a poor relation was all she would ever be. At eighteen years of age, it seemed to her but an endless death.

It was the English who had robbed her of the husband to whom she had been wed only two years. As the months went on Elise's grief was transformed into fury toward the invaders. And eventually her fury had brought her to leave Paris. She would be revenged against the English in any way she could.

"You have no family?" the queen persisted.

"A brother, Your Majesty, named Jean Jourdain. He is a gunner in the Duke of Burgundy's service. But he lives in a garrison, Your Majesty. There would...be no place for me there." Nor in Jean's heart... Elise thought of the distance that had been between them ever since she, a burgher's daughter, had married a knight while Jean remained but a soldier. No, she could not seek out her brother and expect him to find a place for her.

"You would serve France to achieve revenge against the English," the queen said. "You have no estate for which you must care, no frail mother or father?"

"My husband's estate fell to his younger brother and his wife. My parents are dead. Your Majesty, there is nothing and no one who depends upon me."

"Hmm," said the queen, rubbing her finger over her chins, as she considered the situation. "How old are you?"

"Almost nineteen, Your Majesty."

"And where could we place you to achieve this revenge, I wonder?"

"My husband said that I was very good at archery—perhaps I could be a sniper?" offered Elise. "I would not hesitate to draw my bow against an Englishman!"

Hoots of laughter from the courtiers present greeted her idea.

"Such an impassioned patriot!" said the queen with a chuckle, then she turned to the courtiers. "You lazy parasites would do well to copy her fervency!"

"Your Majesty, if I might make a suggestion..." came a voice from the back of the presence chamber.

Elise half turned, and saw the man making his way through the throng of splendidly dressed lords and ladies to the queen's side.

He was dressed all in black, from his sugar-bag hat with its brooch of jet, to the hem of his sable-trimmed gown with its scalloped sleeves. Below that, dark hose covered thick calves and disappeared into black kid slippers with curled, pointed toes.

"Your Grace of Burgundy, may I present Lady Elise de Vire?" drawled the queen.

Elise curtsied again, and arose to find herself being scrutinized by cold blue eyes. So this was John the Fearless, the famous leader of the Burgundian faction that strove to wrest power from the Armagnacs, whose hopes now centered on the Dauphin Charles. It was rumored that John and the queen, notorious for her *amours* despite her obesity, were lovers; now, witnessing the proprietary look Isabella bestowed on this man, Elise knew that it was true.

"Yes, she might well be a potent weapon against the English." The duke descended the dais to view the young woman from all sides. "Ah, a good figure, intriguing green eyes, beautiful hair, a sensual mouth..." he murmured as he walked around her.

What does he think I am, a mare on the auction block? Elise felt a rush of heat, fueled by anger, spread from the neck of her best gown of dark blue velvet upward.

"And she blushes, too—how enchanting," John the Fearless went on, but his eyes told her he knew she was angry, and enjoyed it.

"My queen, I think she might prove useful—with a little training, naturally—as a spy."

"You want me to go to England?" gasped Elise.

"Do you speak English?"

"N-nay...."

"Then that would hardly work, would it? However...the English will return soon enough to our shores, the greedy scoundrels! I remember that on his last campaign, Henry the Usurper married willing Frenchwomen of Harfleur to eligible Englishmen in hopes that they would form loyal colonies in his conquered territories. I would wager he will do so again. Our present intelligence reports that this time, Henry will endeavor to capture Caen as the gateway into the rest of Normandy," the Duke of Burgundy went on. "I propose that we place this patriotic young widow in Caen where she will be in a position to attract the notice of some bachelor of the English king's household, as highly ranking as possible, naturally."

"Why?" asked Elise flatly.

"In order to gain information about the intentions of the English, of course," the duke replied. "You did say you would do anything, did you not?"

Her heart had begun a mad, runaway pounding, but she should hardly be surprised, Elise reasoned. How better to make use of a reasonably attractive woman than to ask her to spy? Who would suspect a helpless young widow?

"Indeed I did," Elise said with a coolness she did not feel. "And is it truly necessary for me to marry this unsuspecting man? I'm willing to be a courtesan."

Duke John quirked a brow at her *sangfroid*. "Henry, royal prude that he has become, probably won't let you get close to his men without the benefit of matrimony. I hear that he forbids prostitutes among his soldiers, cutting off the women's left arms upon first offenses.

And a man will tell a *wife* things he would never utter to a whore.''

"What about my lack of English?"

"Never fear, I have no doubt you will pick it up quickly enough, sharing a man's bed.'' He sniggered. "And don't worry about the burden of wedlock. I have enough bishops in my pocket that it will be a simple matter to obtain an annulment—provided your Englishman survives the French army, of course!''

"Are you very sure you want to do this, Lady Elise?'' asked the queen.

Elise took a long moment to answer, mourning for that space of time the position of honor she had held as a knight's widow. She would be entering a shadowy world of intrigue, and after the dangerous chances she would take, doubtless she would no longer be considered quite a gentlewoman.

"If you are successful in achieving placement among the English, I will see that your brother is made captain of the Artillery,'' promised the duke. "And after the English are driven into the Channel, I will see that you marry a noble.''

After the English are driven into the Channel . . . it was but a distant dream, one that as yet had no substance to Elise. But Jean would be pleased, she thought, imagining her elder brother's pleasure at receiving his captaincy. Perhaps some day she could tell him that her influence had helped him gain that advancement, and of her own role in helping France. Perhaps then the distance that existed between them would disappear.

"I will do it,'' she said.

"Excellent," purred the duke. "I think your code name, in your messages to me, should be Vixen. Do you not agree, my queen?" he asked, lifting an auburn strand of Elise's hair and curling it about one of his fingers.

Chapter One

Caen, September 1417

Elise balanced carefully with her feet upon the high, narrow shelves, peering out through a crack in the shutters fastened over the small window.

"What can they be doing?" she asked aloud as the smoke from the cannon-fire and dozens of burning buildings cleared for a moment, long enough for her to try to see what was happening in the public square.

"My lady, what is happening?" called Gilles from below. Her servant had begged her not to take any chance of being seen, but being a dwarf, he was too short to reach the window, even if he climbed to the top shelf, and she *had* to know what was taking place.

"The English dogs have herded hundreds of towns-folk and men from the garrison into the square," Elise told him, glancing away from the window to answer the dwarf. Then the first screams reached them as the marketplace became an antechamber to hell.

"Oh holy Virgin, they're being put to the sword," moaned Elise in horror as she regarded the scene outside. "Women and children as well as soldiers! The scoundrels! Gilles, we must do something!"

"My lady, get down!" the dwarf insisted as Elise's vision blurred with the flood of tears. He tugged insistently upon the hem of her gown until his words reached her through the fog of terror mixed with rage in her brain.

"But Gilles, we can't just let it go on..." she sobbed.

"My lady, nothing we could do would affect the slaughter out there," he told her earnestly, wincing as a high shriek was borne on the breeze to their hiding place. "We would only suffer a similar fate. All we can do now is hope to stay hidden until their blood lust is sated. If we do that we may have a chance at staying alive."

Elise de Vire huddled in the corner of the tiny closet in which the familiar, homey scents of bread, flour and drying apples were in sharp contrast to the odor of flaming tow fired in hollow iron balls by the English bombards. She had been insane to leave the dull safety of the de Vire household! She would die here, either when the house was set ablaze or when some cursed Englishman found her, without having accomplished anything for French freedom! What had made her think she could be an instrument to save her country?

"They'll find us when they tire of easy prey," she said. "I don't think Burgundy envisioned anything like this when he set me in place here, do you?" Even to herself, her laugh sounded brittle, teetering on the brink of hysteria.

"Nay. Until now, the English king has always decreed mercy for honorable surrender, and that no civilians were to be hurt. But my lady, if you will remember, I—"

"Tried to dissuade me from Burgundy's plan, I know," she finished for him in a flat monotone. "Oh, Gilles, I should not have let you come with me from Vire. I never thought my need for revenge would result in your death, too, my friend."

"My lady, don't give up!" the dwarf said, patting her shoulder awkwardly. "Sir Aimeri would not have wanted you to lose courage now, would he?"

She gave a short laugh. "My late lord husband would be asking what I was doing placing myself in such danger, when I could be safe in a convent, if not at Vire tending Bertrice's babes. I... I don't think he ever understood my need to take an active role in the fight against the cursed English. That is for men, he would have said."

Gilles nodded. "He was a very lucky man to have had you to wife, even for such a brief time, *madame*."

Then they heard the door of the half-timbered house open, followed by the sound of running feet. They froze in the shadows, listening as the feet thudded throughout the house, upending furniture, throwing open cabinets, looking for anything of value. One of the intruders called out to another in the coarse, guttural tongue of the English.

The feet pounded closer.

So must the field mouse in the darkness feel while the hunting owl flies—knowing at any moment he will be discovered and seized in sharp talons, Elise thought.

Suddenly there was a blinding light as the pantry door was thrown open.

* * *

The screams had died away, and an eerie quiet reigned in the square now, broken only by the intermittent wail of an abandoned infant. The air in the marketplace was heavy with the stench of the blood that ran down its gutters. Already flies buzzed over the corpses of the French dead.

The Île St. Jean, the newer portion of Caen, had fallen only hours ago when the English king had decided to shift his attack to that quarter after spending three weeks besieging the Old Town, which was perched high on a hill and protected by thicker walls and the well-garrisoned citadel. Pouring through the breaches soon made in the New Town's wall, the English had attacked simultaneously from the west and east. The two divisions had fought their way to meet in the center, slaughtering indiscriminately as they went.

"Let the killing of innocents cease," King Henry had finally decreed, however, after coming upon the headless corpse of a woman with a baby still suckling at her breast. "Let the men loot and rape if they must, but no woman, child or priest is to be murdered henceforth."

Sir Adam Saker turned away from the scene of carnage, sickened. He had been among those who first poured through the breaches in the walls, and therefore his own sword was stained with French blood, but he had slain fighting men, not helpless innocents or those who had laid down their arms, believing their surrender would be accepted!

Then he had lost sight of Harry Ingles, his squire, in the thick smoke, and while searching for the young man, Adam had unwisely removed his basinet in order to see better. He had nearly lost his life when he was attacked from behind by a French man-at-arms who leaped at him from an alleyway. The Frenchman had landed one telling blow with a spiked mace before Adam gained the upper hand and ran him through.

Then he had found his way to the marketplace just after the massacre had stopped.

Why had King Henry permitted, nay, encouraged such mindless slaughter? Traditionally he protected women, children and priests by royal decree! Had the three-week resistance of the citizens of Norman Caen so outraged his pride that he felt such savage reprisal was necessary? Did the king feel he was now being merciful to authorize rape and pillage in lieu of killing? Adam thought he would never understand his sovereign, not even if he served him for a score of years....

Blast, where was Harry? When he had last seen his squire, the red-haired lad was leading the charge toward the center of the town, bellowing "God and St. George!" his sword raised on high. Ah, well, he was ever heedless of danger; it would be a miracle if the boy survived his foolhardiness long enough to be knighted.

"Sir Adam! Look what I've found!" shouted the selfsame Harry from the doorway of a half-timbered house that stood at the far corner of the square.

Harry stood just behind a struggling woman whose arms he held pinioned. In her efforts to free herself from the squire's grasp, the woman's coiled hair had come loose and partially covered her face, and all Adam could see was a heavy cloud of shaking auburn tresses.

Harry's companion, another young squire who had likewise strayed from his duty, emerged into the noon sunlight behind Harry. He was fending off the fists of the strangest little man Adam had ever seen.

As Adam's long strides brought him closer, he could see the man was a dwarf, surely no more than four feet high, with a head disproportionately large for his short body. The dwarf was shouting at the other youth in enraged, rapid-fire French. As Adam got within earshot, he was able to translate the little man's cries: "Unhand my lady, you bastard, you English dog, you limb of Satan! Me, I will gut you like a carp!"

"Cease your threats of violence, little man, and we will not harm you or the woman!" shouted Adam in French.

The dwarf turned, startled at the words spoken in his own language, enabling the other squire to get hold of his arms.

"She is a *lady*, milord—and why should we believe you, after what we have just witnessed in the square?"

"Because you have the word of a knight," Adam retorted curtly, not much caring if the strange creature believed him or not. He was hot, thirsty, and his head ached abominably. He felt something wet trickling down behind his ear, too hot to be sweat. . . .

Then the woman succeeded in freeing one arm and, brushing the coppery locks from her face, stared at him.

She was far from beautiful in the classic way praised by English troubadors, who favored blondes with blue eyes and milk-and-roses complexions. This woman was tall, probably only a handsbreadth shorter than his own six feet, and possessed a heart-shaped face with slanted, jade green eyes that reminded him of a cat. Her mouth was nothing like the rosebud pout praised by the same troubadors, being wide and red, forcing one to think suddenly of sensual things.

Her face was nothing like Anne's; yet involuntarily he thought of her, and how different this woman's features were from Anne's golden, perfect beauty. He felt a droning in his head, and an ache in his gut, and was not sure if the latter was the familiar ache of loss.

Elise looked at the English cur. He carried his basinet helm with him. Beneath the chain-mail coif, his face was that of a predator, with lean angular cheekbones bisected by an aquiline nose that must have been broken on some earlier occasion. His eyes were like polished bits of jet, and as impenetrable. His mouth was one hard, disciplined line amid the cruel features. She had heard his words, but could hope for no mercy from a man with a face like that.

She had to try, however.

"My lord, I am Lady Elise de Vire, and this is my servant, Gilles le Petit. If you have any chivalry in you, we claim your protection."

Something flashed in his eyes, but was gone before she could be sure of its substance, and was replaced by what was surely the devil's own light.

"Madame de Vire, I will repeat what I have already said—if you offer us no harm, you have naught to fear. Loose her, Harry."

The voice was as cold and sharp-edged as the steel of his sheathed sword, his French as faultless as the edge of his blade, no doubt, yet she thought she heard weariness underlying it. Why not? Murder was hard work, she told herself, straightening as she felt the young man let go the iron grip he had maintained on her wrists.

"Just as those in the square had naught to fear of you, sir knight?" she heard herself taunting him. Why had she said such a foolish thing? Her goal was to insinuate herself among the enemy, not anger them into slaying her! She could not help feeling satisfaction at seeing her bolt had shot home, however; he went white around the mouth.

"My name is Sir Adam Saker, Madame de Vire. Surely you have no cause to believe me, but I tell you that I took no part in the massacre of innocent civilians. I would not have, in any case, but in the event, I was too busy looking for my squire, who should have been at my side."

Oddly enough, she did believe him, watching as his eyes glared beyond her at the squire. She heard the young man behind her mutter something in English, obviously an apology in response to his master's stern reprimand.

"If you will come with me, Madame de Vire..."

All at once his voice seemed to fade and die away. She watched dumbstruck as he lost all color and crumpled at her feet.

Chapter Two

The first thing Adam felt when he came to his senses was the trickle of cool water down his neck from a soaked cloth, which had been placed on his forehead. Then the cool wetness, mixed with pain, spread to the side of his head.

"Lie still, Englishman, so that I may clean away the dried blood from your wound," came a female voice, speaking in French, maddeningly calm. When Adam finally managed to focus his vision, he saw that he was lying in a canopied bed in some chamber. His head felt light; his mail coif and arming cap had been removed, but he still wore armor. The auburn-haired French-woman—what was her name?—was sitting on a stool next to the bed wringing out a bloodstained clout over a basin.

Adam felt a wave of self-disgust as he realized that he had passed out in front of his prisoner. He, a knight of the realm, had swooned like a tender maid!

"That won't be necessary," he said, his voice curt, seeing that she was threading a bone needle with horsehair.

"But your wound, it needs stitching—"

"'Twill heal on its own. Where am I? Where is Harry, my squire?"

She shrugged, accepting his refusal. No doubt she was sorry he had awakened in time to prevent her from using her needle, which she had doubtless soaked in some deadly poison, he thought irascibly, as the headache resumed its pounding tempo.

"You fainted from loss of blood from this gash in your head. Your squire and the other one helped us carry you upstairs. 'Tis fortunate that they are such strong youths, no? Harry now guards the doorway downstairs, that none of your own brigands burn down my house over your head, Sir Adam." He noted the way her mouth shaped his name, making it sound like *Ah-dom.* "The other one said he would find your lord and let him know your direction."

The Duke of Clarence would probably laugh, thinking the tale improbable at best, for he had always said that Saker found it impossible to be injured, even though he had seemed to court death with carefree disdain. He would never believe Adam had swooned like a maiden from a mere cut on the head! No doubt Clarence, projecting his own shameless womanizing on his vassal, would accuse Adam of having found a comely wench to ravish.

"This...is your house?" he asked the Frenchwoman, aware of her clear-eyed emerald gaze. "Where is your husband, lady? Was he...is he of the Caen garrison?"

"My husband died at Agincourt, Sir Adam." She looked away, and rose, busying herself with emptying the basin of bloodied water out the open window onto the street.

A muttered oath below told him she had succeeded in dousing Harry Ingles. She came back to him, her face a study in innocence. Adam was hard put not to smile, in spite of the circumstances, imagining his squire's discomfiture. Harry's dignity was very important to him.

"I am sorry for your loss, *madame*." Probably this was not the best time to mention that he had been at Agincourt, as well. "He left you no keep, no manor?"

She twisted her mouth wryly, and looked him in the eye. "As I was childless, the small castle of Vire went to my brother-by-marriage. We...I...decided it would be best if I lived elsewhere."

He wondered if the brother-by-marriage had had roving hands, and she had left to escape his lecherous attentions. Probably, he thought. If she was a widow she obviously was no virgin, but there was something about the young widow that was so guilelessly earthy. "You live alone here?" he asked, to banish the sudden image he had of this woman, her eyes closed, her head tilted back in passion.

Her look became wary, a forest creature scenting a trap. "There is my servant, Gilles le Petit."

"Just the dwarf? No woman to wait on you?"

"I had a serving wench, Agathe. I haven't seen her since just before the siege. She was afraid of the English—with cause, you see," she said, nodding meaningfully toward the marketplace outside. "I imagine she has gone back to her family's farm outside of Caen. So yes, I am quite alone but for Gilles." She lifted her chin as she said it, her eyes adding, *so just try to do your worst, Englishman.*

He started to reassure her again, but just then the dwarf came through the door, bearing a pewter goblet of wine that he extended to the surprised Adam.

Adam hesitated. Was this some new trick to slaughter the enemy?

"Ah, I see you fear our intentions," Lady Elise said. "Gilles?" She indicated with a gesture that the goblet was to be given to her, took a sip, then passed it on to Adam with a challenging look.

He turned the lip of the goblet so that he could drink where her lips had touched. "After that gracious gesture, lady, how can I be laggard in drinking?" he drawled.

It was a gesture usually made by a lover. He was pleased to see that he had startled her, for a faint color rose into her cheeks before she looked away.

He wondered why he had done it. "I thank you for your nursing, Lady Elise," he said. "Even with Harry downstairs, you could have slit my throat while I lay insensible and escaped with that young fool none the wiser."

"You must not feel shame that you fainted," Lady Elise told him, her composure regained and amusement lurking in those feline green eyes. "Wounds of the scalp bleed much, but they are rarely fatal."

"Thank you for your kindly assurance!" he retorted, irritated that she had understood his embarrassment. He was aware that his show of temper only amused her more. "I shall be leaving now."

"I cry pardon, milord. I did not mean to offend your manly pride," she said with suspect mildness. "Let us change the subject. I was about to ask what would happen to us now?"

''You are free to do as you will, lady.''

From below them, the distant shouts of an army bent on pillage reached them.

''Please, milord,'' spoke up the dwarf, ''how long before a not-so-chivalrous Englishman comes upon this house, and ravishes my lady? Before you fainted, you said, 'Come with me.' Did you not intend to escort her to some sanctuary where she might be safe, Sir Adam?''

He turned from the pleading of the dwarf to find Elise de Vire gazing at him imploringly.

He had been so intent on escaping the impact of that emerald gaze that he had forgotten the suggestion he had started to make before passing out. Some faint distrust stirred within him still, reminding him of her defiant taunts, so different from her entreating, trustful expression now. *Remember that she is the enemy.*

''I was merely about to offer you escort to sanctuary, Lady Elise. Surely there is some church, some convent where you would be safe?''

''The Abbaye aux Dames, the Trinity, is in the hands of your Duke of Clarence,'' she reminded him.

The convent, originally founded by Matilda, wife of William the Conqueror, was outside the city walls and had been been seized by the duke as his headquarters. ''The nuns are still there,'' he told her. ''His Grace has only taken over some of the larger chambers.''

''Then would you please take me there, Sir Adam? Doubtless they can find some work for my servant, Gilles, as well.''

He fought a battle with himself—*her problems are no concern of yours! But she helped you! Nay, how could she have harmed you with Harry looking on?*

*Easily, after he went below, while you were still un-
conscious*—and lost. In any case, he needed to report
to the duke, since he was Clarence's vassal, and perhaps he would find him there. Telling himself he was
merely performing a chivalrous duty and doubtless
would never see Lady Elise de Vire again after turning
her over to the care of the abbess, he said, "Very well,
make ready, and I shall take you there."

"Oh, thank you, Sir Adam! Our Lord will reward
your kindness!"

He thought for a moment she would kiss his hand,
and took refuge in brusqueness. "Send my squire to
me," he told the dwarf, "then assist your lady to gather
her belongings."

Elise felt the English knight's eyes upon her as she
moved about the room, first removing and folding a
few garments from the clothespress, then reaching into
its depths to pull out the small casket containing her
modest cache of coins and the garnet brooch Aimeri
had given her. Placing them in a small, ironbound chest
at the foot of the bed, she turned back to Sir Adam.

"Could your strong young squire carry this chest for
me, do you think, milord?" she asked, giving him what
she thought was a winning smile.

"I am sure he would not want a lady to be without
her comforts, especially if you flutter your lashes at
him that way, Lady Elise," came Saker's retort as he
worked at pulling on the second of his metal gauntlets
without his squire's help. "And please, I am no lord,
just a knight. 'Sir Adam' will do."

She stifled the urge to make a sharp reply, saying
mildly, "I did not mean to offend, Sir Adam. Perhaps

you should know that before my marriage, I was only a burgher's daughter. Matters of etiquette and protocol are still somewhat new to me.'' That, at least, was the truth. Her background was a fault of which Aimeri's brother and his wife had always managed to remind her.

So Sir Adam thought her a coquette, did he? What a confusing man he was—drinking where her lips had touched the goblet, then acting prickly as a monk after a long fast! What experiences had shaped him, this English knight with his fierce, dark, suspicious eyes?

Was he naturally distrustful, or had she gone too far with her last words? She must not overplay her role! Had she convinced him that she was but a terrified young widow in need of succor? Had she aroused anything beyond his chivalrous instincts? Now she was not even sure whether he liked or despised her!

The ironic part of it was that after witnessing the enemy running mad with blood lust in the square, it was hard to remind herself that she *was* anything more than just a terrified widow seeking protection! You are an instrument of revenge, she told herself. Then she looked back to see that he was still studying her, his gaze thoughtful.

Elise congratulated herself on suggesting that he escort her to the Trinity. There she would be safe among the good nuns, yet very much in contact with the English since it was the royal duke's headquarters. Surely that was an advantageous position from which to gain useful information. And Sir Adam's squire had told her that Thomas, Duke of Clarence, was Sir Adam's liege lord—which would mean Sir Adam would probably be at the abbey frequently....

Bah! If Sir Adam Saker thought her only a silly, fluttering female, she was sure there would be others among the English army who would find her appealing—to their cost!

Chapter Three

By tacit agreement, Adam and Lady Elise went up the rue Exmosine, a route that led past the quais to the Abbaye aux Dames without taking them through the marketplace area.

Even so, there were signs of carnage every few yards: fallen French men-at-arms, ghastly wounds outlined by congealed clots of blood; women, their skirts thrown up about their dead faces, lying on their backs with legs spread; crying, wandering children, looking for parents who were probably dead.

The air was still thick with drifting smoke; there were houses ablaze everywhere, often with shouting, booty-laden English soldiers running out of them. Several of these, sighting Adam and his female companion, gave cheers of approval, obviously thinking the copper-haired Lady Elise had agreed to give herself to him in return for protection. They called insults to the dwarf trotting alongside her, but when Sir Adam stared them down, they offered no further mischief.

By the time they had reached the safety of the abbey, the Frenchwoman was trembling, her green eyes dilated and enormous, her face drained of color. Adam

noticed her hands clenching and unclenching among
the folds of her gown—with fear or rage? Picturing his
sisters, or Anne, if Saker Castle had been taken . . . he
did not blame her.

Taking her to the main part of the convent, still occupied by the Benedictines, Adam sought out the abbess's chamber. The abbess opened the door at his
knock, her austere face wearing a distrustful expression as she saw that it was an Englishman standing
there. Then she saw the face of the young woman behind him, and stepping around Adam, held out her
arms to her. "My very dear Madame de Vire, I worried about you, even more than most others, knowing
you were alone—"

With a sob, Lady Elise threw herself into the abbess's embrace, collapsing against the woman's spare
frame and weeping loudly.

"My poor child! There, now! You are safe! It will be
all right!" she soothed, stroking the Frenchwoman's
disheveled tresses, all the while scowling at Adam.
"This man, did he harm you in any way?"

"Now why would I bring her here if—" Adam began indignantly, but the abbess silenced his protest with
a peremptory hand as she waited for the young widow
to answer her.

"Nay, Mother, he did not," Lady Elise said finally,
her voice muffled against the black serge bodice. "He
has offered me only kindness, and has brought me here
to sanctuary, if you have room. I brought my servant,
Gilles, also. He would be happy to do whatever work
you might set him to."

"But of course, you must stay—and your servant
too—though you are not the first to seek safe haven

here. We harbor everyone from serving wenches to merchants' wives, to knights' ladies, and soon we shall have to start doubling up! But we shall give shelter to all who beg it. 'Tis an evil day, an evil day indeed," she said, glowering anew at the English knight. "You may go now, Sir Knight—it is good to know there is one English knight who has not forgotten his honor," the abbess told him grudgingly even as she waved him off with a dismissing gesture.

Harry Ingles set down the ironbound chest. Adam started back down the corridor with a sigh of relief, planning to cross the cloister garth and see if the duke had yet returned to his quarters.

"Sir Adam?"

Adam turned to find Lady Elise had freed herself from the abbess's embrace, and was facing him with eyes glowing like rain-wet jewels. "I . . . I thank you, too, for what you have done. . . . I will pray for you always."

"'Twas nothing," he muttered, embarrassed, wanting to leave, yet somehow wanting to gaze into that upturned face longer.

She glided forward, and stood with her back to the abbess. "Mayhap . . . since your lord is quartered here, I shall see you again?"

Now the abbess was looking daggers at him. "Mayhap," he said, surprised. He did not know what else to say, and after gazing at her for another moment, left her standing there.

As it happened, the duke had not returned, but a lackey tidying his chamber—the one the nuns reserved for visiting ladies of nobility—was able to inform

Adam that Clarence could be found in a large house of gray stone just off the marketplace, a building that had been set aside by King Henry to collect all booty of great value.

Adam groaned, for it was now late afternoon, and he had hoped to avoid going back into the conquered city with its grim sights and smells. He longed to shed his armor and the sweat-soaked tunic beneath it in the relative peace of his tent, which was pitched among the other knights' pavilions outside the abbey. But there was no help for it. Leaving the Trinity behind, he and Harry reentered the Île St. Jean.

They found the gray stone house without difficulty, for he had noted it when passing by only an hour ago with Lady Elise. Going in, Adam saw his liege lord strolling among piles of carpets, rolled-up tapestries, chests of coin, gold and silver plate, and casks of wine, directing the placement of plunder that soldiers were still bringing in from the fallen city. Adam noticed many muttered remarks and resentful looks as the men left behind the items.

The duke had a ring on every one of his plump fingers, and as Adam entered, he was holding up a ruby necklace to the light.

"Ah, Saker! 'Tis a veritable treasure trove, is it not? And Henry says 'tis all mine, but for a French history book he fancies! Caen is a rich town, is it not?" Thomas of Clarence crowed, practically capering in his glee.

"*Was,*" corrected Adam with a sardonic quirk to his brow that the duke missed in his absorption.

"Was, indeed! I'd say we showed them who's master, eh, Adam?" Clarence snorted. "Those still left are kneeling in the streets, begging my royal brother for mercy as he passes by! What do you think of this bauble, my friend? It would adorn Mavis's neck to perfection, would it not? Inspire her to even greater heights of skill in bed?" Clarence was referring to his latest mistress, a well-endowed widow of one of the few English knights to fall at Agincourt two years ago.

"No doubt, my lord."

Clarence looked up. "You're mightily gloomy, for one who's been dallying with a comely Frenchwoman all afternoon, from what young Tom Barrington tells me. What's the matter, did she not please you? You're one of the conquerors, Saker—take what you want!"

The second son of the late Henry IV had all of his kingly brother's handsomeness with none of Henry's restraint and little self-discipline. Already, a taste for rich food had given the Duke of Clarence a thickening belly and hints of jowls in his cheeks. Both his and Henry's exploits among the fair sex had been legendary before Henry became king; upon assuming the throne, Henry had become solemn and dedicated to kingship, while Clarence saw little reason to alter his course.

It was impossible for Adam to find the man's words offensive, however, because as usual they had been delivered with a charming grin. Adam found himself smiling back.

"I fear the report of my success with the Frenchwoman in question has been greatly exaggerated, Your Grace," he told the duke ruefully. "I woke up in her bed, true enough—but only after I had swooned on her doorstep like a lovesick damsel," he admitted.

"Say you so? I did not believe it when the lad told me they'd had to carry you upstairs! Got bashed in the skull with a morning star, did you? Lucky you're possessed of such a thick pate! No matter, go back to her—I hear she's comely, if you like redheads. I prefer blondes, myself. Tell her that her beauty made you swoon, and that you can't forget her!"

"No, I don't think so...I'm sure she thinks of me as one more English devil, complete with a forked tail and cloven hoofs!" He did not add that the cinnamon-haired Frenchwoman was not his sort, either. There was only one woman for him, golden Anne...and he couldn't have her. "I'm too weary to be interested, in any case."

"Have a rest and a good meal, and you'll feel more like carousing," the duke said sagely. "Perhaps I'll go look her up, then, if you're not so inclined. A woman to warm my bed would be most welcome tonight! She lives on the square, the lad said?"

Adam could not have said why a little shaft of anger lanced through him then. He was no monkish prude, but he was glad to be able to tell the duke, "I fear you will find the house empty, my lord. I escorted her to a convent before coming to you here." He did not add that it was the very abbey in which Clarence was staying; with luck he would never see her, hidden back among the nuns' quarters as she was. Adam told himself he merely wished to spare Elise de Vire the importunities of the royal duke. After her recent harrowing experiences she would not be looking for a liaison with the hated enemy!

Clarence shrugged. "There are others. But it grows late. Let me appoint guards here, and then I want you to accompany me to supper in my royal brother's chambers in St. Stephen's. Henry specifically asked that I bring you with me."

"Supper? With the king? But Your Grace, I . . . I'm hardly dressed to attend the king!" Adam protested, indicating his armor. "Beneath this steel I'd wager I stink like a goat that's been dead a week!"

"No matter," Clarence said, waving an airy hand. "Henry's steward will see you bathed and appropriately appareled before you enter the royal presence. Come now, won't supping at the king's table, with the finest captured vintages, be preferable to a cold joint and ale in your pavilion, Saker?"

Adam knew when he was beaten, and gave in with good grace. When the king commanded, one obeyed. "Of course—even assuming I could *find* a cold joint. I would be honored to attend you, my lord, but I must confess myself mystified. You say His Grace asked *me* to attend? Why me?"

He had met Henry on many occasions, of course. Adam had been one of the young squires knighted in honor of Henry V's coronation, and now that he had taken service with Thomas of Clarence, he and his lord attended the king frequently. Of course Henry knew his name, but then the king had an astonishing memory for names, and could have named most of those who had fought at Agincourt, right down to the the lowest man-at-arms. Why did Henry want to speak to him? Could he have heard the same rumor that the duke had, that Adam had spent the afternoon in dalliance with a young French widow, rather than in securing the city for his sovereign?

His apprehension must have showed on his face, for Thomas chuckled. ''Oh, no, my brother doesn't intend to upbraid you for lustful behavior—'twould hardly be fair, would it, after he authorized rape and pillage? But I think I'll let him tell you what he wants you to do,'' the duke said tantalizingly.

L'Abbaye aux Hommes, also called St. Stephen's Abbey, was situated beyond the western wall of Caen's older quarter. The monastic twin to the Trinity, it had been William the Conqueror's portion of the penance required after he had married his cousin Matilda in defiance of the pope.

The king was as good as his promise. While Clarence was ushered elsewhere, Adam was shown into a guest chamber where a large oaken tub and a manservant awaited. Adam had dismissed his squire to return to his tent, but the servant adeptly disarmed him at the same time as a pair of lackeys were emptying buckets of steaming water into the tub. Moments later, Adam was left alone to luxuriate in the steaming water, feeling his aching muscles soothed by the heat even as he sponged away the grime of battle.

Deliberately he banished the shades of those he had slain in the forenoon during the attack through the eastern wall. It had been a fair fight, and had he been less skillful, he could as easily be lying dead tonight rather than the desperate French defenders who had sought to turn him back.

There's nothing lacking here but the services of the castle chatelaine, he thought, lathering his hair with the cake of soap that had been provided, then rinsing it with the bucket sitting ready for the purpose next to the tub. It would be nice to have a woman scrubbing his back, even if 'twas only walleyed Edyth, the scullery wench, who had never concealed her lively interest in the young Adam when he'd been home at Saker Castle.

But thinking of home made him think of the lady of Saker Castle—his brother's wife. With a stifled oath he finished his bath and grabbed for the length of toweling. One mustn't keep the king waiting.

Also according to his promise, the king had ordered that a knee-length *houppelande* of finespun, soft wool and a linen shirt and slippers be left hanging in the room for Adam. Wondering if they were his to keep, Adam dressed in the garments, enjoying the soft, clean feel of the fabrics after the rough, dirty clothes he had worn for months on campaign. Now more than ever, he wondered what the king was softening him up for.

King Henry, with his love of austerity, was said to sleep in the common cell of a Benedictine monk here in the abbey, but the room into which Adam was ushered showed no sign of asceticism.

It was a large chamber with Turkish carpets on the floor, tapestries on the walls and real glass in the windows. A fire burned merrily in the grate, shedding light and welcome warmth on the crisp fall evening. King Henry and his brother, Thomas of Clarence, sat at a long table with an inlaid enameled design, drinking wine from jeweled goblets.

"Ah, Saker, there you are," said the duke in greeting, raising an arm to beckon him forward. "Come and sup with us."

Adam bowed low to the king, and then to his brother. "Your Graces honor me deeply," he said.

King Henry looked fatigued, but his mood was expansive. "Welcome, Sir Adam! As Thomas says, come and join us." With a gesture he indicated to servants waiting at the back of the room that the first course was to be brought in.

As coneys stewed in clear broth were set before them, Henry said, "Thomas tells us you suffered a mace wound to the head today, Adam. Are you feeling all right?"

"I'm quite recovered, thank you, Sire," Adam said, giving a shake of his still-damp black hair as if to prove it. "Even the headache has disappeared after the pleasure of a bath." As always, Adam was touched by the sincerity of the king's interest—and amazed, he reminded himself, that this was the same man who had permitted a massacre today.

"He also tells us you were aided by a beautiful young Frenchwoman, whom you later assisted to sanctuary," Henry continued. "You are to be commended, Sir Adam. Would that more of my men were so chivalrous, since these French are rightfully our subjects too," he added piously, and bent his head to sip a bit of broth.

Adam did not know what to say. Apparently no reply was required of him at this point, however, so he began to enjoy his food as dish after dish was brought forward for their selection.

Following the rabbit stew, there was roasted venison in pepper sauce, fish jelly, *blancmange* of chicken and almonds, apple tartlets and boiled vegetables, accompanied by the finest burgundy Adam had ever tasted. He noticed that the king ate sparingly, taking only small amounts of the plainer dishes and watered wine, but Clarence more than made up for his brother's abstemiousness, heaping his trencher with large helpings of everything on the table.

While they ate, the two brothers talked, and Adam listened, watching each as he spoke. "It was a great victory today, a great victory—even though the citadel and the Old Town have yet to surrender," Henry said, his eyes gleaming.

"They will, brother. The dauphin's promise to come and relieve them is a farce, and everyone knows it."

"Yes . . . I think I shall wait a few days before setting a deadline for their surrender. Let them hear the horror stories—and see the benefits of my mercy afterward. The burghers penned up behind the walls will be demanding that the garrison surrender."

"Naturally," agreed Clarence.

Henry stopped eating long before either his brother or Adam was satisfied, but courteously urged them to continue when Adam noticed and would have stopped. "Go on, sir knight, enjoy your food. I have found that my stomach punishes me if I do so, but there is no reason why a fighting man should not eat his fill.

Finally, however, even Clarence had belched noisily and wiped his face with a linen napkin. King Henry leaned forward.

"You have no doubt heard, Sir Adam, of the unfortunate death of Sir Edmund Springhouse today?"

Adam nodded, his face grim. "He was a brave knight, Sire. It was a horrible death." Sir Edmund had fallen into a ditch while going through one of the breaches in the walls, and the French had set the knight afire by throwing down flaming bales of straw on top of his helpless form. Remembering, Adam could still hear the man's screams of agony.

"His death is a great loss, Adam, just as that of any of my knights, but in this case more than you know. Sir Edmund was in charge of our intelligence network."

At first, Adam could only stare, trying to make sense of the king's words. "Sir Edmund? But he always seemed so... ordinary, Sire... that is to say—"

"That you didn't suspect Springhouse to have any capabilities other than being a doughty warrior, eh? That's exactly as it should be, Saker. For if you didn't see through his bluff exterior, neither did the spies of the Armagnacs and the Burgundians—and believe it, they are everywhere. Fortunately, my clerk has kept detailed records of the information Springhouse ferreted out for me, so his successor won't be entirely starting from scratch. That's where you come in, Saker. You're an excellent knight, and have no other apparent interests—to your credit, you're no womanizer—but I think you're capable of more. I want you to be my spymaster."

Chapter Four

"You want me to run your espionage network?" Adam repeated incredulously. "But why, Sire?"

"Why not?" King Henry said, leaning back in his large, carved wooden chair. "You speak French excellently, and read and write it as well, we are told," he said with a nod toward Clarence, "which is a vanishing skill even among our nobles. Just two generations ago a baron spoke English only to his servants, but times have changed."

"Yes, but, Sire—"

"And after what happened in the square today, we think you will have a very good disguise."

"Sire?" Adam repeated, puzzled.

"You came after the... let us call it the *unfortunate* incident in which we let our temper get the best of us and *allowed* many innocents to be slain—and we saw the expression on your face. Oh, don't bother to deny it. You were disgusted, weren't you?"

The king's hazel eyes bored into Adam's, and Adam could only say: "Your Grace has... always shown mercy before... at least to those who surrendered, and always to women and children. I . . . I did not understand, but I do not presume to judge you, Sire."

King Henry looked away. "It is well to leave that to Our Lord, but I shall tell you that I will do penance for today's massacre forever." His voice was flat and lifeless; only by his omission of the royal pronoun *we* could Adam begin to suspect the depth of the king's feelings.

"But since I noted your expression," the king went on, "it is probable that others did, as well. And then there is the matter of your good deed with the French girl today. You behaved with great chivalry when you could have forced yourself on her." He waved away Adam's attempted protest. "Don't you see, your apparent sympathy for the French provides the perfect screen for you? I want you to continue to act very pro-French—even if it appears that you disapprove of what your king does. Only Thomas and I will know it is a pose. By doing so you may put yourself in a position to hear certain...information...from those who think you a French sympathizer, as well as from the spies we already have in place. Who then would suspect that you are working against them?"

"Is it possible that I would have to go behind the lines myself, Sire?" He was as brave in battle as the next man, but something in him chilled at the thought of going without armor, in disguise, pretending to be something he was not.

"Spying is a dirty business, hardly fit for a gentleman.... Nay, I do not think such a course would be necessary."

But he did not, Adam noted, absolutely rule it out.

* * *

Elise thought she would go mad with boredom. She had been a guest at the Benedictine convent for a week now, and although she was safe, there was little to do besides eat, sleep, gossip with the dozen women who had also sought sanctuary and, of course, attend some of the daily cycle of services that punctuated the Benedictine day. There were bells at midnight, bells at dawn, at midmorning, noon, midafternoon, dusk and bedtime! Elise had never had the slightest inclination to be a nun, though she admired their devotion, but now she attended one or two of the daily Offices out of sheer frustration. How was she serving France here, behind convent walls?

She had watched for some sight of Sir Adam Saker, spending sunny afternoons out in the garth, which was accessible both to the nuns and their English "guests," but she had caught no glimpse of the tall, dark-haired knight. She had, however, stitched on an altar cloth for the abbess until she had nearly gone blind! She had attempted to make conversation with other English knights and nobles who passed by, hoping to glean some information, but many of them spoke little French, and one actually thought her conversation an invitation to fondle her!

Gilles had come into the garth just in time to see her slap a red-faced, portly baron. Seeing the dwarf, the nobleman had stalked off, muttering imprecations about Frenchwomen's teasing ploys.

"What did you expect, my lady?" Gilles asked bluntly as she paced in frustrated anger. "You spoke to him and smiled, when all the other women cower and flee their presence."

"Apparently that is all it takes for an Englishman to be encouraged," she said, smacking one fist against another. "Ah, Gilles, I'll wager you wish you served a real lady, rather than a scheming hussy like me."

"I serve you gladly, Lady Elise," he insisted, "but I would remind you that you offered to obtain information for the queen and Burgundy by any means you could. Is it realistic to wait for your source of information to be young and handsome, and must he offer marriage? One who is less than an Adonis might be more willing to tell you all, just to gain your favor!"

"Of course not—why would I want to be locked in marriage to any English cur, handsome or not!" She turned away, then back to face her servant. "I know I must not be too...uh, demanding. But that one was so grossly fat, Gilles, and his breath stank! His hands were like—like huge red hams!" Elise shuddered.

Just then, in the distance, the English cannons roared in unison, and the dull thud of exploding stonework reached them.

"For the love of Jesu, Gilles, when 'tis not the tolling bells, 'tis the damned cannon. I vow I suffer a perpetual headache here, do you not?" Elise asked ruefully. "If something does not change soon I shall run mad."

She had tried to leave the grounds once, just to go into the New Town and see what was happening, and if anything more might be salvaged from her house, if indeed it still stood! Elise had been turned back at the gates, politely enough, it was true, by an apologetic guard who did not appear to understand her pleas but who firmly prevented her from leaving.

The other women, for the most part, did not appear unduly alarmed when she brought the news to them that they were virtual prisoners. A few, who had lost husbands in the fighting, were actually contemplating taking the veil, while the others were merely more philosophical about taking each day one at a time.

"The abbess has asked to see you," Gilles said, interrupting her pacing. "Perhaps that will serve as some diversion."

"More likely she means to reprimand me for my 'unseemly behavior,'" Elise said darkly. "No doubt Goodwife Matilde has been expressing horror at my 'shameless flirting' again."

"Ha! That one would take any man who looked twice at her, and her husband scarce cold in his grave!" Gilles said, causing her to smile at his vehemence.

The abbess, however, had apparently not intended to upbraid Elise for her behavior.

"Madame de Vire, I hope you have not been unhappy among us?" Mother Marie du Sacré Coeur asked her, her serge skirts rustling as she came from behind the table to take Elise's hands in hers.

"Nay, Mother, 'tis just that I . . . chafe at inactivity," Elise said, scanning the abbess's expression for disapproval and finding none.

"You do not aspire to a life of contemplation?" The abbess looked amused.

"I'm afraid not," she admitted. "I do not have any holy vocation."

"There are other vocations, other uses to which Our Lord puts us," Mother Marie said.

Now she will urge me to find a good man to be my husband, and to give him babes, thought Elise, for

what other use has a woman if she is not to give her life
to God?

"There is also, for example, the calling of patriotism," the abbess said, to Elise's surprise. "Surely
freeing our country of English influence is a holy task,
too. My noble patron, the Duke of Burgundy, knowing that 'the Vixen' has not been able to communicate
with him because of the English siege of Caen, bids me
to tell her to take heart, and to pass along any messages she might have through me."

Elise felt her mouth drop open. "You know...that
I am a spy, Mother?"

The abbess nodded briskly. "I do. I was curious, in
any case, when I heard of a young widow who had
moved into Caen at such a time. Though I live behind
convent walls I maintain an interest in what happens
outside them, you see. And then, when Caen became
blockaded, I got the message from His Grace of Burgundy, saying that you were his agent, and expressing
some concern as to your safety in the event Caen was
sacked, as of course it was. I believe your goal is
to...develop a *relationship* of some sort with an Englishman, hopefully a gentleman close to King
Henry?"

"Yes, Mother. The duke thought the English king
would be encouraging his unmarried men to marry
Frenchwomen again, to colonize his conquered areas.
But I do not necessarily have to marry the man, if I can
obtain valuable information...without doing so...."
Elise's voice trailed off, and she was unable to look at
the abbess. She wondered what the elderly, celibate
woman, who presumably had never known the touch

of a man, thought of her for being willing to use her body to help France.

"You are a daring young woman," Mother Marie du Sacré Coeur remarked cryptically. "Surely Our Lord will bless your intention to help France, even if you must commit sin to do so."

"Thank you, Mother. It's...good of you not to condemn me. But I confess I have been unable to obtain any sort of information to pass on to the duke. I find I am unable to leave the convent, and I do not even know what is going on in Caen!"

"At least I can bring you up-to-date about Caen, my child. The English have given the citadel a deadline of the nineteenth of September. If the dauphin has not relieved them by then, they are sworn to surrender to the English, who have pledged that they will harm no one."

Elise allowed herself an unladylike snort. "Can we trust the bloodthirsty thieves in that? Do you think the dauphin will come, Mother?"

"The dauphin? Bah, Our Lord will make His second coming in glory sooner! Nay, child, I think we shall see the rest of Caen surrendering on the appointed day and I believe the carnage is over—at least for Caen. Then, if King Henry does as he has before in marrying Englishmen to Frenchwomen, you will have your chance to place yourself among the enemy, if not before. Have you any particular Englishman in mind?"

The question caught her unaware. Elise felt a blush stealing up from the high collar of her woolen gown. "Nay, Mother, it matters not to me, s-so long as I can fulfill my vow of revenge," she stammered. "The English killed my husband at Agincourt, you know."

"God rest him," the abbess said, crossing herself. "But I thought I caught a hint of, shall we say, *interest* in the eyes of that tall, dark Englishman who brought you to us the day they entered the New Town. And I could swear you did not find him entirely... displeasing."

Elise leaped up and began to pace. "'Tis merely that he had acted honorably, the first Englishman I have known to do so. But I have not seen him since, Mother. It makes no difference to me which of the enemy whose lust I use to France's advantage," she said, and wondered if it was a greater sin to lie to an abbess than to a layperson.

The bell tolled, indicating the hour of None. "Do not let your patriotism turn you into a hard woman, my child," cautioned Mother Marie du Sacré Coeur. "I shall see if there is aught I can do to... bring you in contact with that knight, or another suitable Englishman. Meanwhile, perhaps you should use this chamber to draft a message to Burgundy," she said, indicating parchment and a quill pen at one corner of the desk. "I am going to attend the Office now, so you may write undisturbed, and leave your correspondence here."

The very next morning Elise, sitting in the cloister garth and enjoying the crisp autumn sunshine, saw the abbess fulfill her promise. Harry Ingles, his carroty-hued hair blazing like a firebrand, stood at the far end of the grassy enclosure, having been halted in his progress by the abbess, whom Elise saw point in her direction. A moment later the young squire turned down the path that led directly to the stone bench on which she sat.

Elise hid a smile as she watched the young man approach. *I don't think a squire would be able to aid me in my goals, Mother, especially one barely able to grow peach fuzz on his chin as yet, but one never knows.*

"Madame de Vire, good day!" he said in enthusiastic, if execrable, French. "I have not seen you since that day I found you hiding in your house—I hope you do not hold that against me?"

"Nay, of course not. It is war, after all, is it not?" she asked with a very Gallic shrug, favoring the youth with a big smile. "And you did not hurt me…it is good to see you again, Monsieur 'Arry."

She enjoyed watching the blush of pleasure that flooded his face. This one, at least, had not yet learned to hide his feelings, to look superior and bored.

"Yes…well…I appreciated your helping Sir Adam—he's a great fellow, isn't he?"

"He is lucky to have such a brave, loyal squire," Elise said, allowing her eyes to glow. "I understand you led the charge into Caen!"

The blush deepened, and Elise was reminded of a hound puppy she'd had that became ecstatic with joy whenever she tickled his belly and praised him.

"Yes, *madame,* I did. Though Sir Adam said I was a foolhardy young bull with nothing between my ears!"

"Nonsense! You were as brave as Roland himself, and so they shall sing of you one day! And what have you been doing, these past few days? Does your master keep you busy, running messages and such?"

"Oh, he's just concerned for my safety—and he was right—I'm very lucky some crossbowman didn't use me for target practice! My father is the sergeant at arms at Saker Castle, you see. He wouldn't want to tell him and Mam I was killed. And yes, I've been busy! I was chosen to ride into the citadel up there on the hill," he said, pointing behind her, "riding a white horse and carrying a white flag, to convey the terms of surrender to the garrison."

"Ah, you're very brave indeed! They might have hanged you from the ramparts as a message of defiance!" Here her admiration was totally unfeigned; messengers often paid the supreme price when the besieged weren't ready to parley.

Harry looked as if he might die of bliss. "'Tis naught! Someone has to do it, don't they? And I wasn't in any danger. I think they're going to give in—beggin' your pardon, *madame*."

"You need not apologize, 'Arry," she assured him warmly, allowing her sooty lashes to flutter. "I think it would be best if they did, too. No one can stand against the mighty English army. And how does your master pass his time?"

"Sir Adam? Oh, he's been attending the king a lot . . . but he doesn't say what they talk about . . . I'm here lookin' for Sir Adam, actually. You haven't—"

Elise had started to shake her head, when a voice came from behind her. "No, she hasn't, but now you've found me, Harry. What did you want?"

Startled, Elise turned around, to see Sir Adam Saker lounging against the door to the outside stairway that led to the Duke of Clarence's quarters. How much had he heard? She felt the heat rising on her own cheeks.

As Harry recovered himself and mumbled his message in English, her eyes met those of Sir Adam. His dark gaze was hooded, enigmatic, giving nothing more away than the dark brown waters of the river Orne, and just as cold. He muttered some terse words, obviously instructions, and the youth took off in the opposite direction after a hasty farewell to Elise.

"Practicing your wiles on my squire, Madame Elise?"

Chapter Five

Sir Adam stood there in a dark blue velvet *pourpoint* that strained to cover his broad, muscular chest. The design of a falcon in flight was embroidered in gold over the breast of the garment—the family emblem, she realized, for a saker was a type of falcon. The skirt of the doublet was short, drawing the eye to legs clad in well-fitting black hose and short boots of soft leather with dagged cuffs. His head was bare; a capricious breeze ruffled raven hair that gleamed in the sunlight.

All these things she noted before she let herself gaze back into the eyes that were studying her with deliberate thoroughness.

"Your squire Harry is a nice boy," she found herself saying as she fought to keep the irritation from her voice and turn the conversation to her advantage. "But it is not gallant in you, Sir Adam, to suggest that a woman needs to practice," she added, looking obliquely at him in a flirtatious style totally foreign to her.

"Just a figure of speech, Madame Elise. Of course all Frenchwomen are born knowing how to captivate—

or they suckle the knowledge in with their mothers' milk." He looked displeased at the thought.

"And is 'Arry captivated, do you think?" she asked, allowing herself one more jab and pleased to see his jaw tighten.

"No doubt he will start singing your praises all over again as he did that first day. 'Tis a cruel thing to collect striplings' hearts carelessly, *madame.*"

"Such was not my intention, Sir Adam. I was merely asking him what he had been doing, to pass the time. I have been bored to distraction here, with nothing to do but stitch and pray, sleep and eat—yet they tell me I may not leave."

"'Tis for your own safety, Lady Elise. There is still much unrest. But doubtless you will be released soon. The surrender of the garrison is expected very shortly."

"You're so very sure that is what will happen," she said, pretending great interest in her sewing. "Tell me, are you always so sure?" She gazed at him again, forcing herself to enter the dangerous depths of those dark eyes.

"Not always, Lady Elise. But the failure of the dauphin to rescue Caen seems a sure thing."

"And then what, sir knight?"

Looking faintly uncomfortable, he pretended to misunderstand. "Then we shall move on, leaving the garrison in English hands, of course."

"Of course," she said lightly. "Nay, I meant, to me."

"I'm sure there will be no restriction on your leaving then."

"I wonder if my house still stands? Do you know, Sir Adam?" she asked, moistening the thread in her mouth, then smoothing it between thumb and forefinger.

He looked away from the sight. She could see the pulse beating in his neck. "It stands," he said at last. "But that's all. There's very little left inside that hasn't been stolen or burned."

She guessed he had not wanted to admit that he had checked on her house. For a moment she allowed herself to feel the panic that a woman alone, gently reared, must feel at the prospect of homelessness. She turned tear-wet eyes upon the knight standing before her, and clutched the altar cloth desperately. "But where will I go? I have very little money.... I will have to become a servant—or take the veil!"

He scowled, thunderclouds darkening his eyes to black. "Surely there is no need to overdramatize your predicament, Lady Elise. A comely woman like yourself can always find some fool to twist 'round your little finger. I give you good-day."

Sketching a bow, he stalked off without a backward glance, leaving her alone with her fury. Damn the blackguard for his mocking insolence, his scorn, his wary avoidance of the tender trap she was trying to set!

Many minutes passed before she realized that the encounter had not, after all, been a failure in her terms. She bothered Sir Adam Saker, and that, after all, was much superior to indifference.

With the nineteenth of September came the expected surrender for, as expected, the dauphin had failed to come to the aid of the besieged garrison. The burghers of the Old Town, unwilling to be slaughtered like their fellows in the New Town or starved out, had made their wishes known: They were willing to surrender in order to survive.

Promptly at noon, the Caen garrison formally surrendered, and rode or marched out of the citadel. Those who had armor were allowed to wear it, but they were required to add any swords, maces, pikes, lances, crossbows and handguns to the pile growing beside the castle's two bronze cannons.

"I would have thought they could hold out longer," Adam heard King Henry say to his brother. They were sitting on their horses in the castle bailey, watching the sullen-faced soldiers leave. "They had a well with good water, still a goodly quantity of wine, they weren't out of foodstuffs yet...."

"You mean that we English would have fought on," Thomas concluded for him, "until we starved to death. Quite right, Your Grace. But the little frogs aren't English, are they? And we broke their spirit by breaching the supposedly impregnable walls of the New Town—or perhaps it was the fickle dauphin who broke their hearts."

Such a lack of resolve was incomprehensible to Henry, just as it had been incomprehensible to him that his small army might win against overwhelming odds at Agincourt two years before. He shrugged, then brightened as he looked at the fine, strong walls of the castle.

"Whatever the cause, thanks be to God. We are well pleased with the result. I think I shall want the chapel royal to be...there," he said, pointing to the southeast tower. "See to it, would you, Thomas?"

Thomas made a bow from the back of his destrier, then rolled his eyes at Adam on his other side, obviously finding Henry's piety amusing. Adam was careful to keep his expression neutral. It was one thing for the duke to laugh at his elder brother, quite another for a mere knight to do so. Adam found King Henry's religious fervor mostly admirable, though it was not something he felt able to emulate. Who could say the English successes had not been brought about by prayer?

"We shall have a banquet tonight at the Trinity, to celebrate the great victory that has been vouchsafed us," King Henry announced suddenly. "My nobles and as many of my knights as possible, the rest to be fed at long tables set up in the garth."

"Very well, Brother, but why at the Trinity?" Thomas asked, surprised. At Henry's uplifted brow, he added hastily, "You're welcome, of course...I simply thought you would want to have it at St. Stephen's, and not put yourself to the trouble of going around or through the town."

"It will be no trouble, nay, perhaps wise for us to show ourselves garbed in regal splendor, the conquering king, and all that," King Henry said. "'Tis just that your headquarters are where the women are—the brides, that is."

"Brides?" asked Thomas.

"Yes." Henry smiled at his brother's blank look. "I have decided it would be wise to do as we have done before, and offer willing French brides to unmarried gentlemen in my train who would be willing to settle here, so that we may know there is a core loyal to us among those who are willing to say anything if we will only leave them in peace. A notice has gone out, both to the town and to those women who sought sanctuary in the convent, announcing our generous offer of five pounds' reward and the awarding of available properties to any Englishman who takes a French bride. They may meet and select one another at the banquet tomorrow.''

"Well, Brother! You've been very busy, haven't you?'' Thomas murmured in admiration. "It sounds as if it will be fun to watch...and mayhap I will be able to convince some lusty *demoiselle* that I am panting for a French bride myself. At least long enough to provide an interesting end to the evening.'' The duke chuckled. Henry pretended not to understand.

So the little coppery-haired French widow would not starve or go into demeaning servitude after all, Adam thought, conscious of a perverse wrench of pain at the thought. *All she has to do is go up to the first unmarried gentleman who suits her demanding tastes, flutter those sooty lashes and—voilà!*—a respectable English bride with a husband to provide for her needs. The idea left a bad taste in his mouth.

"No doubt there will be many takers among our bachelor gentlemen,'' drawled Thomas, with a sidelong glance at Adam. "Why don't you wed one, Adam? Time you were providing yourself with an heir, isn't it? What about that toothsome redhead you rescued? I've seen her about the cloisters—she'd keep you warm at night!''

"No, thank you, Your Grace. When I'm ready to wed I'm sure there'll be an English lady or two left,'' Adam retorted.

"See, I've ruffled his feathers already! Only jesting, Adam,'' Clarence protested, aiming a playful punch at

Adam's shoulder that caused the knight's black destrier to half rear, baring long teeth.

The king looked thoughtful as Adam concentrated on controlling his stallion. "Hmm, 'tis an idea worth considering. Yes! I think you *should* wed a Frenchwoman, Adam. It would be the very thing to set the seal on your pro-French pose. You're not betrothed, are you? Not promised to some sweetheart back across the Channel?"

Adam felt the blood drain from his face. "Nay, Sire," he answered, wondering if he dared protest. A vision of his lost love rose before him: Anne, her soft pink mouth curved in a smile, her gentle blue eyes shining with love—*for his brother, John*....

Another face took her place in his mind, that of Elise de Vire, with her high cheekbones, those exotically tilted jade green eyes, that mouth too wide for beauty, but that made him think of kissing... that cinnamon-hued hair, which reminded him of a vixen fox slipping through a sun-dappled woodland, just as stealthily—and just as sly?

"Very well, 'tis settled," King Henry said, taking Adam's stunned silence for assent. "And if you fancy the young woman you aided, why not, indeed, make her your choice, as Thomas suggested? She's a knight's widow, is she not? I assume she would be willing. Why not seek her out before the banquet and ask her? You'd make a handsome couple." The king smiled, very pleased with himself.

"As you wish, Sire," Adam murmured, his mind whirling. It had been voiced as a suggestion, but he had no doubt it was a royal command. He toyed briefly with the idea of selecting another of the women refugees within the convent. There were others, he knew, whose background was gentle enough not to make the match a mockery, whose faces were pleasant, and whose temperaments were likely to be a lot more docile than the fiery Elise de Vire's!

But he discarded the idea as soon as he thought of it. Uncomfortable as she made him, he could no sooner see her claimed by some red-faced, beefeating baron from Yorkshire than he could fly. He didn't love her, he reminded to himself. His heart had already been given permanently to Anne, no matter that she hadn't claimed it. And in his new capacity as master of intelligence for the king, it would be as well to have the slippery French widow under his control. He could not imagine the woman who condemned all Englishmen would suddenly turn gentle and tender to one in particular. Nay, it was best she be where he could keep an eye on her.

Adam had actually intended to speak to Elise that same day, to give her twenty-four hours to get used to the idea, but events dictated otherwise. The arrival of one of his agents from the south—the soon-to-be taken direction of the army—and the need to consult with that spy at length kept Adam busy until well after dark.

It was the same the next day, with Clarence and the king requiring his attendance on various matters just as if they had not suggested earlier that he approach Lady Elise.

He was not at liberty to go and seek out Elise until just before the banquet. What if someone else had already claimed her? Unconsciously Adam quickened his steps through the corridors of L'Abbaye aux Dames so much that Harry, grinning, had to run to keep up. The young squire knew better than to tease his master, however; Adam had been as prickly as a hedgehog all morning, and as the day had worn on and he had been further delayed, Harry could almost see by the tense set of his jaw that Sir Adam's control over his temper was tenuous indeed.

The banquet was to be held in the hall of the guest quarters, the only room in the abbey big enough to hold the rows of trestle tables even now being set up, with lackeys scurrying about laying out white linen cloths and plate borrowed from St. Stephen's. Apparently uncaring that their presence hampered the work, lords, knights and ladies milled about in the aisles between the tables. The babble of voices had reached Adam long before he reached the hall, and now as he stood in the entranceway the din rose up to meet him. Everywhere he looked men were speaking to women, smiling, winking, laughing; some had already joined hands and were speaking only with their eyes. Apparently the state of war between France and England was no barrier to romance here!

Having already searched the faces of the couples who had spilled out of the crowded room into the corridor around him, his eyes roamed restlessly up and down the aisles of the hall, seeking the copper-haired French-woman, but not finding her. Perhaps she had joined the lesser folk in the cloister garth, where tables had been set up on the grass?

Dismissing Harry with a curt reminder to stay out of trouble, and not make promises he couldn't keep to some French *demoiselle,* he retraced his steps and went back out to the garth, but had no better luck there.

He told himself that Lady Elise had decided for him. Whether she had left town, or found that she did indeed have other legitimate, or *illegitimate,* opportunities within Caen's walls, it was of no import to him. He'd go back up to the hall, look over the available ladies of suitable quality, and if none pleased him he'd forget the whole matter. What could the king do—try him for treason for refusing to make a marriage of convenience?

He could not have explained why he found himself asking the abbess herself if she knew where he could find Lady Elise de Vire.

Elise was kneeling at the altar rail in the Lady Chapel of the Church of the Trinity. From the mulish expression Adam saw on her face before alerting her to his presence, he warranted she was not praying, even though her eyes were trained on the bland features of the Virgin. He coughed.

"What? You! You're not supposed to be here in the nuns' precincts—this is not the chapel for guests—"

He held out a hand in reassurance as she jumped to her feet. "Do not trouble yourself about it, Lady Elise. I am here with the Reverend Mother's knowledge and permission. She thought I might find you here."

"Oh... I see." Her eyes darted from his intent gaze, and fell to her hands, which were clasped restlessly together.

"You do not attend the banquet?" he asked her at last.

"I... was going back eventually. It was just so noisy... men and women everywhere, making marriages as if picking partners for a dance, or as if the

Last Trump would sound tomorrow.'' She made a gesture with her hands as if to explain how that atmosphere had affected her. ''I just needed to get away for a few moments.'' How to explain that she just wanted to escape long enough to give him time to arrive if he were going to come? Elise hadn't known, until she saw the first Englishman, grinning fatuously as he approached her, how much she had counted on being chosen by Sir Adam Saker. Why, she didn't even know if he was already wed or betrothed!

''It does sound like a chamber of madmen up there, does it not?'' he said, trying to ignore the profound relief he felt to have found her here. ''You . . . you're looking very well, *madame.*''

It was the truth, even a sweeping understatement. She wore a gown of peacock blue *checklatoun* caught under her breasts by a belt of black, braided cord trimmed with tiny silver folly bells that tinkled as she moved. The long, trailing sleeves were folded back at her wrists to show close-fitting sleeves of creamy silk that had tiny silver buttons to the elbow. A heart-shaped headdress and fine mesh crespinette hid all but a few fine, curling tendrils of her auburn hair. Why did the current fashion keep women's tresses out of sight when they were one of their most attractive features?

''Thank you, Sir Adam,'' she murmured while he was wondering what made him ponder the absurdity of clothing styles. Still, she kept her eyes modestly downcast—so he could not see the triumphant flash in her eyes?

''When I did not find you in the hall, I thought perhaps you had joined the procession leaving Caen,'' he remarked, then mentally kicked himself for admitting he had been searching for her. "You *are* free to depart the abbey now, you know, and those leaving the city have been permitted to take jewelry and a small sum of money with them."

"How *gracious* of King Henry, to be sure," she said, her voice dripping with irony as she raised her eyes to him at last; in the dimness of the chapel, the light of a score of votive candles was reflected in their depths. "A few who elected to leave have already made their way back to Caen. They say just a league or two beyond the southern gate the men are being relieved of the two thousand gold crowns they were supposedly allowed to keep, plus any fine clothes they might be wearing, and the women of their jewelry. One woman was even taken off into a grove of trees and relieved of her honor. So much for the king's mercy, Sir Adam," Elise said coolly. "I can't afford it, and so I remain here."

"I am sorry to hear of it—I will report it to the king immediately and those involved will be punished," he promised her, dismayed that his question had led into such a negative path. How was he to penetrate her cool hauteur and propose marriage? Even now she was practically glaring at him, unmoved by his promise, composedly waiting to see what he would say next.

"So—you are willing to marry an Englishman?" he asked. His voice sounded abnormally loud in the silence of the chapel.

She looked back at the altar with its rows of candles, their flames wavering in the draft. "It seems my best option at the present time, as I have no desire to enter the convent, go into service or go back to Vire to accept the *charity* of my brother-by-marriage."

"No doubt there will be many unwed knights, and possibly even a baron or two who will scramble to wed you, once you return to the hall," Adam said, watching her reaction.

"Oh...do you think so? Yet I may only wed one, may I not?" She gave a nervous little laugh.

"I'm afraid so. Shall you like being the wife of an Englishman, Lady Elise?" he asked in an affectedly casual tone.

"That very much depends on the Englishman, does it not?" she riposted.

"I suppose so." Suddenly Adam was tired of the game, of the uncertainty of not knowing what she would say. "Though perhaps you are looking forward with joy to being besieged by would-be suitors, I would like to forestall that, if you are agreeable. Lady Elise, would you do me the very great honor of becoming my wife?"

Chapter Six

"Why, Sir Adam, you surprise me," Elise said archly, but he would have been surprised to learn that astonishment was what she was genuinely feeling. "I thought you believed that I was looking for a 'fool to twist 'round my little finger'—is that not what you said?" She tried to breathe normally as she waited for his reply, afraid that he would somehow take back his offer at her teasing, yet needling him to conceal the warring emotions within her breast.

"I'm not such a fool as to pass up the chance to gain a French estate of many *hectares* in such an easy fashion," he told her with studied carelessness. "I had to marry sooner or later, in any case, and in this way I'll have more than a meager knight's fee in Leicestershire." But she saw that for all his offhandedness, his gaze swept over her avidly.

"Well, I am relieved to hear there would be *something* in it for you," she flashed back before she could stop herself. Would he always affect her this way? Whenever they spoke she always had to smother the urge to slap his face!

"Nay, lady, pardon me. I . . . I'm but a warrior, better with a sword than with words," he apologized stiffly. "I do want to take you to wife, and no other." His eyes had once again gone black in the dim candlelight.

Elise let him wait for a long minute, studying his mouth, set in a tightly held line until a tiny muscle jumping in his temple distracted her. "Then I accept, Sir Adam. I will wed you." Then, avoiding the fierce light that now sparked in his eyes, she went on as if discussing the weather, "I must confess I am relieved, not disappointed, to know that I will not be among those being courted with unseemly haste at the banquet tonight. We shall amuse ourselves in watching them from our table, yes?"

"Perhaps. Shall we return to the hall?" he asked, extending his arm.

"Give me but a few moments, if you would, Sir Adam. Now that this has happened, I . . . would seek Our Lady's blessing." She needed a few moments to herself in order to discipline the spiraling excitement within her at the thought of being wedded to this man. She genuinely intended to pray, and ask the Virgin— and St. Denis, patron saint of France—to bless the sacrifice she was making for France. And to teach her how to keep her heart.

"Certainly," he said, his eyes hooded again. "I shall await you in the hall, my lady." His mouth descended on the hand he had somehow captured in his. And then, after bowing to her, he was gone.

Elise felt in every cell of her body the warm brush of his lips upon the back of her cold hand. The chapel was unheated, except for the radiated warmth of the votive candles, but now she felt consumed by flames.

It was too long since she had known a man's touch, she told herself. She would have to conquer the delight that surged within her if she was to be effective in achieving her revenge. *Remember Aimeri, and the pleasure you used to feel in his caress, you silly wench.*

She told herself she was happy because she would now be able to accomplish her goal. Sir Adam Saker seemed well ensconced in both the Duke of Clarence's and the king's favor; surely that would make it easy to obtain information that would aid France in driving the English usurpers back across the Channel. And if she could obtain it by sharing the marriage bed of an Englishman who was not unattractive, so much the better!

"Well, well, my lady! It seems you have accomplished the first stage of your plan! Are you pleased?" Gilles le Petit asked, stepping out from behind the broad pillar just outside the Lady Chapel.

"Eavesdropper," she accused, caught off guard by the dwarf's sudden appearance. "You're lucky he did not think you an assassin, and run you through."

"In the church?" Gilles asked in mock horror. "Even the English have more honor than that, my lady. Well?"

She put him off no longer. "Yes, I believe I am pleased. Who in my position would not be? It seems I will not have to steel myself to wheedle secrets from some fat, ill-smelling *chevalier* after all."

"Have a care, my lady. Methinks this knight is no one's fool," warned Gilles, his face twisted with worry.

"At least with an ugly, unpleasing lord you would not have to guard your heart."

Elise turned from her servant, disturbed that he had voiced the very same concern that she had about herself and Sir Adam. "Oh, there's no danger of that, believe me, my friend. I left my heart in the grave with my husband. I shall not forget that this devilishly handsome knight might have been the very one who killed him."

"As you say, my lady." It was plain he was not convinced, but as a servant he would say no more at present.

"And now, if you would excuse me, I was about to pray." Kneeling again, she turned her back on Gilles.

Rules of precedence decreed that Sir Adam and his lady be seated at one of the long trestle tables among other knights, rather than at the high table with the king, the Duke of Clarence, the earls of Salisbury, Huntington, Warwick, and other nobles, yet Elise took note of the pleased smile Henry gave Sir Adam as the king made his way, after all others were seated, to his place on the dais.

"The king—he seems approving of you?" Elise ventured.

Sir Adam made a self-deprecating gesture, but his eyes gave nothing away. "He has encouraged me to wed. Better to marry than to burn, as St. Paul says in Holy Writ."

"Yet he himself is not married," Elise pointed out as the servers began to proffer heaping platters of roast chicken, *viand royal* and beef.

"He waits for Katherine of Valois." Adam placed several choice pieces of meat on her plate, and poured some muscadelle into the goblet they shared.

"He must conquer France first, before he can have her," she insisted stoutly, then realized how argumentative she sounded.

Unoffended, Adam nodded, using his eating knife to carve off a pair of slices from the loaf of *pandemain* at their table. "He will do so, eventually. He knows it, and so do the Valois—else why would they keep their princess unwed? She will be their bargaining piece when all else is lost."

"How sad for the princess, to know that is her fate."

He looked at her oddly. "'Tis not an unusual fate for a princess, is it? And surely 'tis blessed rather than sad to be the means of making peace between nations? I would wager Princess Katherine does not fret at the prospect of marrying such a handsome warrior-king," he said, with a nod toward the dais, where King Henry sat in regal splendor, in his tunic of cloth-of-silver and a purple velvet mantle.

"But she must wait on events, perhaps for years," Elise pointed out.

"Some things are the sweeter for waiting," he said, impaling her with his dark gaze.

Something within her thrummed to life at his words, and warmed her more than the sweet wine she had sipped. To cover her momentary confusion, she looked away, studying the variety of couples sitting around her.

Across from Elise and Adam, Thérèse Montelieu, a widow somewhat older than Elise who shared her small cell-turned-bedchamber, seemed well pleased with the

short, heavyset knight who was even now paying her
assiduous court. Down the table, a black-haired
woman Elise only knew as Angelique, wearing a becoming dress borrowed from one of the ladies, seemed
to have snared a genial if walleyed gentleman who appeared entranced as he stared at the generous bosom of
the woman he had chosen. Elise smiled, hoping he did
not find out before the wedding that Angelique had
been one of Caen's more successful whores. The
Frenchwomen had made a pact not to disclose Angelique's previous status, and it looked as if all were
keeping their promise, though from time to time they
exchanged amused looks with the girl. 'Twill serve him
right if she gives him the pox, Elise thought with glee.
Even two of the women who had vowed to take the veil
seemed to have changed their minds and were now
paired off with Englishmen.

Lust was almost tangible in the air. Everywhere Elise
looked, sly glances were being exchanged, and little
kisses; from the expressions on some faces she gathered that more than a few of these matches would be
consummated this very night, if some private place
could be arranged.

She looked back to find Sir Adam's eyes on her. We
will be man and wife within the next few days, she
thought. Is he thinking about *that?*

The meal went on, course after course, until finally
the sweet wafers and wine were passed, to signal the
end of the feast. Just then the king, who had eaten but
sparingly, Elise noticed, began to speak.

"We are told that this convent is the one our ances-
tress, Matilda, was required to build in penance for
marrying William the Conqueror, as they were near in

blood, just as my present headquarters of St. Stephen's was William's penance. I say to all of you assembled here that 'tis fitting a religious foundation built by such a devoted and faithful wife should now witness the unions being formed here this night between our subjects, once natural enemies, now united in love."

Elise saw that there were smiles all around at his words, some a little sheepish—because they would be marrying for other motives? How many of them would truly love their partners, whether right away, or as time went on? How many, like herself, would wed for some other, less hallowed reason?

"For those agreeing to wed, a priest will be performing weddings in St. Etienne le Vieux, in Old Caen, all day tomorrow, so that the good nuns will not be distracted from their religious obligations by having their chapel used for such a purpose. Unfortunately there is not time for long honeymoons, as we are an army on the march and winter is drawing near. We will depart from Caen on the day after tomorrow, leaving our city in the capable hands of Sir John Popham, who has been selected our bailiff for this area." He indicated a solemn, hatchet-faced Englishman sitting near the dais.

A collective groan, only partially suppressed, went up from the English soldiers at this announcement, for many had anticipated that King Henry would make Caen his winter quarters. Already the winds blew with chill precision through chinks in the stone walls at night.

What kind of a king continued his campaign in winter? Elise wondered. And where were they headed? It was vital that the Duke of Burgundy learn of the army's direction as soon as she could learn it!

"We would now retire for the night, but you need not cut short your merrymaking. My minstrels will play in the gallery for your entertainment."

All stood as the king departed, looking haggard and drawn in spite of his genial mood. It was rumored that he had been fasting all week in preparation for the day that Caen had surrendered.

"Sir Adam, a word with you, if you please," the king said as he passed by them. "I do apologize, Madame de Vire—I will not keep him long," he added, to Elise's amazement.

Elise was so surprised that she had been spoken to by King Henry himself—and called by name!—that she did not hear Sir Adam's murmured words as he left her side. Evidently he had been promising that Harry Ingles would attend her until his return, however, because the redheaded squire materialized beside her as in the gallery above, a trio of lute players struck up a sprightly tune.

"Allow me to be the first to extend my...felicitations upon your upcoming...wedding, Lady Elise," he said, struggling for the correct French word. His eyes ran with frank appreciation over her peacock silk gown. "Sir Adam is very fortunate to take you to wife. I only hope that he realizes...just how fortunate," Harry added.

Elise was wise enough to see that she was the object of the calf love shining in the young squire's eyes, and she was touched, but she had to find out what Harry had meant.

"Thank you for your kindness, 'Arry," she said, "but I am sure I am the lucky one to be marrying such a handsome, puissant knight, is it not so? But what did you mean, you 'hope he realizes how fortunate'?"

All around them, couples were again chatting and laughing, moving out of the way as the dishes were cleared and the trestle tables were taken apart and stacked against the walls.

Harry Ingles blushed self-consciously and looked away from her curious gaze. "Ah, my lady, I fear I've spoken out of turn again. 'Tis just that...that it seemed Sir Adam could only love one woman, and so would never wed...."

Elise knew, from her conversation with Sir Adam in the chapel, that he had never said anything about love, merely land, but Harry's words further whetted her feminine curiosity. "Sir Adam loves another woman?"

Harry looked alarmed, realizing his explanation in an unfamiliar tongue had only dug him in deeper. "In God's truth, *madame,* I *shouldn't* be telling you this— I meant just to tell you I was happy for you both—"

"It will be all right, 'Arry," Elise said soothingly, patting his hand. "I swear I will not say a word to milord. I would understand him better, that's all, and you know he is so—so maddeningly silent at times," she said. "*Please,* 'Arry, you would be doing us both a service, I swear."

The carrot-topped youth didn't look at all certain, but finally he said, "He loves—*loved*—the daughter of a baron whose land marches with Saker Castle, Lady Anne Stratham. But the Lady Anne loved Sir Adam's brother, John, Earl of Saker, and wed him."

So the woman Sir Adam Saker loved had not only married another, but that other was his very own brother, making it necessary for him to see them to-gether as often as he visited Saker Castle! What tor-ture for a proud man. Elise began to understand a little of the pain that must be fueling his sardonic looks, his prickly manner.

"Is she . . . is she very lovely, this Anne?" she asked, trying to mask her eagerness to know that she was not.

"Aye," Harry said with a sigh, unknowingly dash-ing her hopes. "All gilt and pink she is, with blue eyes like the Virgin's robe. But Lady Elise," he added, be-latedly catching sight of her crestfallen features, "I think you're very lovely, too—in a French sort of way—that is, if I'm not being unpardonably bold...." His voice trailed off in dismay.

"Never mind, 'Arry, a compliment is always appre-ciated. And it pleases me to know that my lord did not pick me for my resemblance to this...Lady Anne." She could hardly bring herself to say the name, she real-ized with a sense of disquiet. Could it be that she was *jealous* that some other woman already had laid claim to Sir Adam's heart? Nay, 'twas only that she could carry out her mission the better if the Englishman who wed her was smitten with *her*, not merely replacing some lady he had failed to win!

Had Sir Adam actually selected her because she bore. *no* resemblance to his brother's wife? Bah! Why tor-ture herself with wondering? She was only marrying him to help achieve victory for France, and she should not let her silly feminine pride be affected.

A strolling servant, carrying a trayful of cups of *ozey*, a sweet French wine, stopped in front of them.

Harry took a cup and offered it to her; when she declined, he drained it himself. From his garrulity Elise thought he had already drunk quite enough, but perhaps she could take advantage of the fact.

"'Arry..." she began, flashing him her most brilliant smile, "the king has said we shall leave Caen the day after tomorrow. I'm just curious—do we head straight for Rouen? I know someone there, you see..."

"Nay, my lady, 'tis due south we're headed, I'm told. In the direction of Argentan and Alençon, actually."

How easy it had been! "How very odd," she murmured. "Everyone knows Rouen is King Henry's eventual target, being the capital of Normandy."

Harry shrugged. "I'm just a squire, Lady Elise. 'Tis not for me to understand the reasons of the king."

Neither of them paid much attention to the wine server, who had stopped very near them and was busily rearranging the cups on his tray. Then he resumed his circuit about the room.

An hour passed, and Adam did not return. She wondered, as Harry strove valiantly to amuse her with witty remarks, what the king had for him to do that was taking so long. There was much she did not know about her husband-to-be.

"'Arry, I believe I have the headache," she said at last. "Too much wine and food and noise, you know. Would you be so kind as to escort me to my chamber, and make my excuses to your master? He may send word as to what time our ceremony will be held."

It was the truth. Her head *did* throb abominably. She longed to reach the peace and serenity of the cell and take refuge in sleep before Thérèse Montelieu

returned. Thérèse, she knew, would be bubbling over
with excitement, eager to exchange girlish confidences
and sly remarks about their respective bridegrooms.
Elise wanted none of that. Before she slept, she needed
to write a message to Duke John about the army's intended path through Normandy, and get Gilles to deliver it to the abbess's office. There might be no time on
the morrow, and the sooner John the Fearless knew
King Henry's plans, the better. The need for action on
her part would have the added benefit of keeping her
from being tortured by uncertainty—at least until she
was finished with the letter.

Chapter Seven

The altar was ablaze with candles. The dancing light was reflected in the golden gleam of the candelabra and the bejeweled pyx set in front of the crucifix. Altar cloths of red velvet and gold brocade competed with the magnificence of the English bishop's robes.

Darkness came early to Normandy in September, preventing the witnesses in the magnificent Romanesque church of St. Étienne le Vieux from seeing the full glory of the stained-glass windows, but those who required more visual splendor needed only to look at the couple now standing before the bishop, thought Harry Ingles.

In a burst of hero worship, the squire decided that his master had never looked more handsome, or more like a figure from a romance, than he did at this moment. Sir Adam's liege lord, the Duke Of Clarence, had lent the knight a *houppelande* of crimson velvet, with long, flared sleeves that revealed the tight-fitting sleeves of his gold silk shirt. His massive warrior's shoulders strained the seams, for Thomas of Clarence had not spent the hours swinging a battle sword and hefting a lance that Sir Adam had. There was a black velvet sash from his left shoulder to his right hip, embroidered in gold thread at the center of his chest with the figure of a falcon—a saker falcon, Harry corrected himself, remembering the origin of the family surname.

He had shaved Sir Adam himself, making idle chatter in the face of his master's saturnine silence, and trimmed the newly washed hair that now gleamed like midnight moonlight in the candle glow. The knight had borne his ministrations in mute patience, but had called a halt when Harry suggested that he crimp his hair in the latest fashion.

"I'm no French *mignonne,* to be wearing girlish curls and essence of roses, Harry," he had growled, running a hand through his damp black hair. "Let Lady Elise de Vire see that she is getting a true Engl*man,* and if she considers me a barbarian compared to these pretty fellows, too bad."

The result was that Sir Adam Saker was the most magnificent male presence there, a fact that did not seem to be lost on Lady Elise, though the king and Clarence had honored them by attending. She was looking up at her splendid bridegroom as if bedazzled. Sir Adam was now placing his signet ring, with its engraved falcon emblem, onto the French girl's finger. Of course, it was much too large for her, but the unprepared bridegroom had nothing else as yet. The squire saw Elise smile in a bemused fashion as the ring nearly slid back off her slender finger, saved from doing so by Sir Adam's quick grabbing of her hand.

He seemed curiously loath to release her, but at that point the bishop bade them kneel and receive his blessing, and the clasped hands were hidden among the folds of crimson velvet and the emerald green silk of the bride's dress.

Harry heard the dwarf, standing beside him, sigh.

"Are you thinking that they make a handsome pair, as I am?" he whispered to Elise's odd little manservant.

"Nay," shot back Gilles le Petit. "I am thinking that if he does her ill, I will cut out his heart."

As sonorous Latin phrases washed over Adam, his mind roamed free, trying for the sake of his sanity to banish the image of Elise as he had first seen her only an hour ago.

She was a siren in the emerald silk gown worthy of a Valois princess, her exotically tilted eyes echoing the hue of the fabric, that too-wide, too-red mouth faintly smiling at his astonishment. Elise wore her hair loose, as was fitting for a bride, curling in fiery splendor against the jewel green of the gown's bodice.

Knowing that his eyes had already given him away, he had stopped her when she would have covered the gown with a cloak. "Nay, I would have Caen see that the most beautiful bride has been kept for the last."

"But...I have heard that others have been pelted with filth as they rode to their weddings."

"You will not be, my lady. Wait and see." He sensed his mysteriousness annoyed her when she was already tightly strung, but said nothing more as he helped her onto a borrowed palfrey.

"We shall return here after the ceremony," he told her. "His grace has given me a private chamber in the guest quarters for tonight. We will be served supper there before we retire."

"How very kind of the duke," she had murmured, sweeping gold-shot coppery lashes over her eyes. Just now her face showed all the maidenly, modest delicacy of a virgin, in spite of the fact that she was a widow.

The doubts had been there, but after the banquet last evening, when Denis Coulet had joined them, the doubts had blossomed into poisonous black flowers giving off an evil scent.

"Your betrothed is a toothsome woman," the agent had said to Adam as he slid into his seat beside him, taking advantage of the momentary lull as the king left the room to answer the call of nature.

"Oh? And when did you meet her?" Adam asked, an eyebrow raised, since Coulet had only just returned from Chartres, where he had been spying on the queen and her lover, Duke John the Fearless.

"I heard that the king had 'suggested' you marry one of the Frenchwomen, and saw you leave her side to come up here. Thought I'd get a close look without her noticing me. I borrowed a linen cloth," he said, pantomiming laying it across his arm, "and a trayful of wine cups and *voilà!* I am an invisible servant."

"How clever," Adam drawled. "So?"

"As I said, a toothsome morsel," Coulet continued, grinning, picking his teeth with the edge of his dagger. "But perhaps you had better keep her close when the army nears Rouen."

"What's your meaning, Coulet? My head aches, and I've no time for riddles. If you have aught to tell me, spit it out." Coulet had given them valuable information already, but there was something about the man that set his teeth on edge. Had he just noticed it when the man began talking about Elise?

"My meaning? I walked up just in time to see her flutter her lashes at your squire and ask him if the army was headed next toward Rouen. She 'knew someone' there, she said." He raised and lowered his brows twice in rapid succession, and succeeded by that gesture in wordlessly implying that Adam would not be happy to know about that "someone" in Rouen.

"I hope you don't make a practice of creating something from nothing in that manner when it comes to espionage," Adam had retorted. "She could well mean a spinster aunt, you fool!"

"Very likely," the man said in soothing tones that did nothing to calm Adam's raised hackles. "Perhaps I spoke out of turn. 'Tis just that my countrywomen can be very... ah... devious, and I would hate to see you cozened, my lord."

"Thank you for your concern," Adam had said, trying not to grind out the words. "I assure you your fears on my behalf are groundless." They had been speaking in French, and the foreign tongue made it possible for Adam to conceal the sarcasm that might have surfaced in English. Just then the king had returned, cutting short their private speech, and Adam had striven to forget the poisonous seeds that the agent had planted.

But the acid had roiled in his stomach as Coulet rose to give his report on the status of the royal court in exile, and suspicion had taunted Adam last night in his dreams.

Many of those who had jeered and shouted insults as they threw rotten vegetables and worse at the other French brides had gone in for their suppers now, but the urchins he had paid to spread the word had been successful in lining the streets between here and the church.

"Vive le chevalier anglais!" they had shouted, and "Long life and happiness to the friend of the French and his beauteous lady wife!" as he threw showers of *sous* to them.

She had stared at him, her green eyes mirroring her astonishment, as the cheers went up, and he realized that she had feared receiving the same ill-treatment her fellow brides had.

The crowd's reaction had only made him feel more cynical. He'd always suspected the French could be bought, as long as the price was right and the money held out. But they were a fickle lot and would desert as soon as the coins stopped flowing. But he'd accomplished two goals by his "generosity": he had protected Elise from a potentially unpleasant ride, and he had furthered his image as a sympathetic, pro-French Englishman, just as the king wished him to appear.

"It was most kind of their graces the king and the Duke of Clarence to attend our wedding."

"Aye, it was quite an honor," responded Adam, but he did not look up from the seethed pike in claret he was toying with.

They were alone at the small round table in the chamber that had been provided for their wedding night. Outside, it was fully dark; inside, the room was lit by two sconces near the table and a fat hour candle on the nightstand. The fire in the grate had burned down to glowing embers.

Their wedding supper lay in front of them; in addition to the fish, there was a freshly baked manchet loaf

and sweet butter, dried apricots, jellied eggs and cus-
tard flans. They should have been hungry, for neither
had eaten since breaking their fast after their individ-
ual sessions in the confessional, but neither was.

For Elise, at least, confession had been a travesty, for
what could she safely confess? The seal of the confessional was supposed to protect all penitents, and the
priest was French, but who knew where his allegiance
lay? With the Armagnacs, who favored the dauphin,
or the Burgundians? Or perhaps the cleric owed some
debt of gratitude to King Henry, for not destroying the
abbeys. She dared not trust her life to priestly integrity
in these days when dukes such as Burgundy boasted of
"their" bishops!

So Elise was forced to confess trivial sins, such as
being cross with Thérèse Montelieu when she had
damaged a borrowed headdress, and not being dili-
gent in her prayers, when she longed for absolution for
the sin she was about to commit this very day: partici-
pating in one of the holy sacraments, matrimony, for
less than holy reasons.

"Well!" she spoke brightly into the well of silence,
"we are wed now, and yet I know scarce anything
about you or your family. Would you tell me about
yourself, and your background, my lord?"

For a moment it looked as if he were going to ignore
her question, and she wondered what to do. But then
he looked at her with a half smile that told her he was
perhaps as glad to have something to talk about as she
was. "Very well, I suppose you have the right to know
whom you have married. I am the second son of a Leicestershire earl who died four years ago, leaving my
brother, John, the Earl of Saker. My lady mother fol-

lowed my father within a twelvemonth. Saker Castle is in that part of England known as the Midlands. The Sakers began as falconers to the king in Henry I's day, were ennobled by Henry II, and have continued to be known for our falcons ever since.''

"You remind me a little of a falcon," she said consideringly, her head tilted slightly to the side as she regarded him. "So very alert you are, and with such a fierce eye. And your nose... it is so proud, like a falcon's beak—"

She reached out a finger, and before he realized what she was about, Elise ran it down his nose, tracing its contours.

"I cannot decide whether you just insulted me or not," he said wryly, "comparing my nose to a beak."

"Oh! Such was not my intent, my lord!" Had he trembled at her touch?

"So formal? Surely in private I can be 'Adam' to you."

She took encouragement from that. "Adam, then. But please, my lord, tell me more—did you have no sisters?"

"Yes, there were three. Mary-Claire, who became a nun; Cecily, who is a widow now, her knight having died at Harfleur; and Amicia."

"Is Amicia old enough to be married?"

"She will never marry. She still lives at Saker Castle. She was born...crippled. Not deformed...she just cannot walk. Everyone loves her, though. I suppose she's something of a saint," Adam said musingly.

"Ah, too bad. I can see that you love her, and it must be very hard for you to see her suffer."

"She's in no pain, but yes, 'tis hard to see her sit all day in her padded chair in the hall. She insists on being where she can see what is going on. Someone must carry her downstairs in the morning, and up to her bed in the evening.

Elise noticed he had sedulously avoided mentioning Anne. She had to know how he felt about Anne *now*. Did Anne still hold that same place in his heart, now that he had been joined by the rites of the church to another woman?

"And are you still your brother's heir?" It was an oblique way of asking if his brother was married, and she felt proud of how she had phrased the question so as not reveal that his squire had been talking about him to her.

Was that a quick intake of breath? Elise was not sure, but she saw the reflex tightening of his mouth, and did not imagine the sudden bleakness in those rich brown eyes.

"Nay," he said. "That is to say, I probably shall not be much longer. He married Lady Anne Stratham, an advantageous marriage for them both. She's a lovely woman."

How much had it hurt to say her name? He gave no clue, other than a slight tightening of his lips.

"Do you mean that she has not yet given him an heir?"

"Not yet, but she is raising the baseborn son that John got on a peasant woman before they married."

"But what an exceptional woman, to care for her husband's lovechild!"

"Yes..." he said musingly. Then, "Thank you for not calling my nephew a bastard. 'Tis such a mean, stained word for an innocent child."

She gave a Gallic shrug. "What about you, my— Adam? Tell me of your life before you came to France with King Henry."

"There's not much to tell, I assure you. I was knighted when I was twenty-one, one of several knighted in conjunction with the king's coronation, and I entered the service of Thomas, Duke of Clarence. He did not come to Agincourt, but sent most of his vassals."

It was as near as he would come, evidently, to admitting he was there. So he could have been the one responsible for Aimeri's death, she told herself, stubbornly ignoring the voice that told her that it had been men-at-arms, not knights, who without regard for chivalrous rules had pulled knights from their horses and slain them.

As if sensing the direction of her thoughts, Adam spoke. "And what of you? I know you are a widow with a brother-by-marriage of whom you are not fond, but little else. Is there no one else to care that you were widowed, or that today you have wed an Englishman?"

Only that last, sardonic phrase saved his words from being so thoughtful and caring that she might have given in to tears. Braced by that, she responded as lightly.

"Only a brother, who serves Burgundy as a gunner. We are not close, so... his opinion does not matter, I suppose. My father, a burgher of Paris, and his goodwife died a decade ago."

"So you are quite alone."

But for me, she expected, nay hoped he would say. *And once my family meets you, they will love you, too.* But he did not say those things, merely kept looking at her.

She was drowning in his eyes, unable to look away from the deep pools so dark brown they looked black in the flaring candlelight. Sir Adam's nostrils flared, and an artery pulsed steadily in his forehead as his eyes locked with hers.

She loved him, Elise realized in that instant just before Adam looked away. She was married to this tall, dark, English knight, and tonight she would be his in their bridal bed. Suddenly, she didn't mind; in fact, she could hardly wait, Elise decided, her pulse accelerating and her lips curving in a smile. For in spite of the secret reasons for which she had agreed to marry an enemy, flying in the face of her need for revenge, was the fact that she had fallen in love with Adam Saker.

They realized at the same moment that the other was finished eating, and had been for some time.

"I think we had better retire now, my lady," Adam said to her. "With our departure scheduled for the morrow, we shall need our rest." Standing, he blew out the sconces, leaving the room in shadows relieved only by the hour-candle's flame and the faint glow from the hearth.

She stood, uncertain as to how to proceed.

"Come, I will play tiring woman to you since you have no maid," he said, indicating with a gesture that she was to turn around so that he could unfasten her gown. "I hope you did not mind the lack of a bedding ceremony."

"Nay," she said on a laugh, heat coursing through her veins like strong wine. "Once was enough for that nonsense." She remembered the drunken guests at the wedding at Château de Vire, their ribald remarks as her tipsy bridegroom had been brought to their blossom-strewn bed, and her embarrassment as the covers had been pulled back to show Aimeri's naked thigh touching hers. In the morning, the bloodstained sheets, betokening her lost virginity, had been proudly displayed. There were some benefits to being a widow, after all.

Silence greeted Elise's remarks, and she wondered if she had done right to remind him that she had been married before. She had meant to relax him by reminding him that she was no nervous virgin, but had she instead raised the specter of the past? Was Adam, like many other men, resentful when he could not be the first?

She felt the cool night air caress her back as the silken gown, a relic of her days as Sir Aimeri's bride, slithered off her hips to the floor and she was left in her chemise. Now he would pull her to him, and kiss her before removing the rest. . . .

"There now—I think you can manage the remainder, can you not?"

He stepped away from her, and, grabbing up his cloak from a chair, spread it near the fire. Next he cropped a folded-up blanket from the bed. In front of her astonished gaze he sat down on the cloak and began pulling off his soft leather shoes.

"I bid you good-night, Elise."

Chapter Eight

"Good night? You 'bid me good-night'?" she asked, incredulous. "You...you are not going to...to consummate our marriage?"

Adam stopped in the act of pulling off the silk shirt that had been under the *houppelande.* "No. At least, not at the present."

"But...I don't understand..." she said, her eyes beginning to spill over with tears. "We are married! Why did you marry me, if you did not desire me?"

"'Tis not that.' *If I could only show you how much I desire you, my copper-haired beauty. I want you so much that this aching may well kill me.* He turned away from the figure crouching on the bed so that she could not see the evidence of his arousal, and so that he would not be further inflamed by the candlelit outline of her lush form in the sheer chemise.

He wished he could convince himself that Elise had become his wife only by royal command, but he knew it was not true. The fact was that he could not help himself.

But marrying her, putting her beyond the reach of other men legally, at least, was one thing; trusting her with his love was quite another. He could feel the magnetism, the shimmering silver cord between them, but who could say that if he put faith in their union, he would not be betrayed? He did not dare make himself vulnerable to her without even knowing if he could trust her!

"Then it is Anne, is it not so? You still love the Lady Anne—" She clapped a hand to her mouth. Only minutes ago she had been congratulating herself for not revealing that knowledge, and now she had been so frustrated that she had taunted him with it!

"Vixen! Who told you that?" He was on his feet now, standing there in his shirt and hose, the veins in his neck standing out, his eyes glittering with rage.

Vixen. Her heart began to hammer. "Why...why do you call me that?" Did he know? Had he intercepted the letter she had left in the abbess's office? Oh, Holy Virgin, why had she ever agreed to spy for Burgundy?

He cleared the space between them in the blink of an eye. "Because of this, you red-haired fishwife—" he said, grabbing a thick strand of her curling auburn hair and twisting it about his fist, his furious face only inches from hers. "In my country, a vixen is a woman with a shrewish temper such as yours. 'Tis apparent that Harry has been gossiping with you."

He was talking about her hair color, not her code name as Burgundy's spy. Relief made her dizzy—or was it the fact of his nearness? She could feel his hot breath, wine-scented, on her face.

"You mean *la mégère,* then, a word that comes closer to your meaning, I think, not *la renarde,*" she said, her eyes never leaving his. "And yes, Harry did tell me, but only while explaining why he was glad we were to wed. It sounds to me as if you finally learned to give up what you could not have," she went on recklessly. "And don't you dare to reprimand that boy—he worships you, whether or not you deserve it!"

"Thank you for the language lesson, my little French shrew-wife! And now I have a lesson for you—" His lips descended on hers with punishing force, his hand, twined in her hair, preventing her from wrenching away from him, or from escaping the tongue that forced its way past her teeth to brutally claim possession of her mouth.

He kissed her until they were both breathless. Elise had sagged against him, afraid of his sudden violence at first, then beginning to hope as the kiss went on that it would mellow to passion.

In a moment, however, he pushed her from him, his face flushed, his eyes still wild. "Do I kiss like a man still in love with another woman, vixen?"

The tears spilled down her cheeks now. "Yes...yes, you do. And I'm sorry for you in that, milord, because loving your brother's wife must be a constant misery to you."

"I *don't* love her anymore, damn your eyes! But that doesn't mean I'll couple with you just because you've been too long without it and the king has ordered us to marry!"

She felt the blood drain from her face at that. "You are pleased to be insulting, milord," she said icily. "I did not believe the reputation Englishmen have of being cold fish. But I see now 'tis well deserved."

Elise thought for a moment he would strike her, and she steeled herself not to flinch, but he did not.

"Nor did I believe the French reputation for being fickle! But I hear that you have a special 'someone' in Rouen, and it happens that I don't give my love lightly to an inconstant wench who may decide to rejoin her lover when we reach that city!"

So Harry gossiped to his master, too, Elise thought bitterly. "There is no lover in Rouen," she said in a voice heavy with scorn. "There is only my brother, Jean Jourdain, whom I mentioned to you at supper."

"Your *brother*. How gullible you must think me, *wife*. You said he was with Burgundy. The last I heard, John the Fearless was at Chartres, not Rouen." His voice lashed her with scorn.

"He is Captain of the Artillery at Rouen," she protested. "He was given the post by Duke John!"

"What a convenient story. Perhaps my squire will believe it."

"It is the truth!" she insisted, pounding the bed with her fist. "I will swear it on any holy relic!"

He gave a short, mirthless laugh. "I would not imperil your soul on such a little matter, Elise, for the sake of your pride. And don't worry about your wedding night. 'Tis not as if anyone will know on the morrow—since you are a widow we need not worry about bloody sheets, after all."

He didn't believe her! He thought she'd perjure herself to convince him! She had been ready to lie, of course, to carry out her spying, but here she was telling the truth and *he didn't believe her*. He thought she only cared about the blow to her pride. Her mind reeled with shocked anger and hurt.

"Again, I bid you good-night." He lay down on the cloak and after covering himself with the blanket, turned on his side away from her.

Yes, her pride was involved. She had gambled by throwing it at his feet, by virtually begging him to make love to her, and lost. For the moment making him love her besottedly for the sake of gaining information was totally forgotten.

Elise turned on her side also, facing away from him, and concentrated with all her being on controlling her breathing so that he did not know she was weeping.

Dawn had streaked the sky in orange, lavender and salmon pink when Elise awakened, conscious that the other side of the bed was still empty and that her head throbbed with a dull misery. She wondered where Adam was, and how long he had been gone. She was just sitting up, pulling the blanket around her against the chill when the door opened.

It was Adam, dressed in the quilted *aketon* that went under his armor, and carrying hunks of bread and cheese and a cup of watered wine, which he set on the nightstand.

"I give you good-morrow, Elise. Break your fast, lady, and dress as quickly as you can. The army leaves Caen this morning."

She had not forgotten, of course, but she had assumed that such an assembly would take hours of preparation. But now sounds reached her through the wooden shutters: horses stamping and neighing, harness creaking, men shouting and swearing, cart wheels creaking.

Adam's eyes swept over her, and she was acutely conscious of her tousled hair, and the tops of her breasts visible through the sheer chemise that showed above the blanket. She felt herself blushing.

There were hollows under Adam's eyes. He looked as if he had not rested any better than she had. He turned back toward the door. "Come down as soon as you are ready, my lady. G-Gippetty awaits outside the chamber to carry anything needed."

In spite of herself she smiled at his fractured attempt to pronounce Gilles le Petit, then said, "My lord, will you not break your fast with me? Surely you should eat, if we're to begin traveling so soon." Elise gave him what she hoped was a dazzling smile, in spite of the ache in her head and the pounding of her heart.

"I thank you, but I have already broken my fast. I'll see you below, my lady." Then he was gone, and she heard the clink of his spurs as he made his way down the stone corridor to the winding staircase.

Adam had steeled himself against the appeal of the sleep-ruffled curls that formed a fiery aureole around her face, and against the slumbrous jade of her eyes. But he was totally unprepared for the ache in his heart as he pretended to be immune to the wounded-fawn expression that had come over her face before he could excuse himself from her. It was a genuine look of disappointment, he'd swear—though the daughters of Eve possessed such skill that it might have been deliberate and practiced, for all he knew. Grinding his teeth in frustration, he struck the wall with his fist as he strode angrily down the hall. What sort of hell had he taken on?

It would have been so easy to turn to her last night and take her in his arms, and let the morrow take care of itself. He knew that she had wept, and had tried not to let him hear. But that had only been wounded pride, hadn't it? He wouldn't let desire conquer his better judgment, just to salve her feelings!

Adam had lain awake the better part of the night, gritting his teeth in his effort not to weaken in his resolve. He wouldn't let his heart become a woman's possession, as he had with Anne, only to have her discard it without ever really knowing it was hers!

He'd be damned if he was going to make love to Elise, and let himself care, if she was going to leave him when they got to Rouen. Her brother, she had said! Perhaps she had truly thought he was as naive as that, he thought, trying to forget how relieved he had felt at that moment when she said it, and how much he wanted to believe her.

Though he heartily disliked the agent Coulet, the fact was that Coulet had reported that Elise demonstrated intense interest in going to Rouen—more than she would feel if she was just anxious to see a brother. No, it was better not to be a fool.

By the light of day, Elise had been even harder to resist, he thought as he strode angrily out into the courtyard with its milling soldiers and stamping horses. She'd been so beautiful, even with the marks of a poor night's sleep, and the sadness clouding those exotically tilted green eyes! Saints, he was only human! How was he going to resist Elise's charms all the way to Rouen? They were newlyweds, and everyone would conspire to keep them together as much as possible, thinking it was what they both wanted! He swore aloud.

It would be torture—but only for him! Adam reckoned that Elise, piqued at his apparent lack of interest, would soon recover with her *amour propre* intact. She'd leave him somewhere on this campaign, and he would know that he had been wise to protect his heart.

In the meantime, however, he would have to seek the purchased ease that was offered by the whores who managed to make themselves available despite the king's strictures.

"For me? This beautiful creature is for me?" Elise exclaimed in disbelief as Gilles led forward a snow-white palfrey, caparisoned in red leather. Then she turned to Sir Adam. "My lord, do I have you to thank? Is this a wedding gift? If so, I thank you with all my heart—"

"Nay," he told her brusquely, "'tis a wedding gift from King Henry. He found out you would have nothing to ride, and he bade me give you this mare. He said I should say it was from me, but...I will give you your morning gift when I have the opportunity to purchase something suitable."

Determined not to let her facial muscles reveal her disappointment that the gift was not from Adam, she caressed the palfrey's arching neck, saying, "Oh, she is so lovely!" She stroked the mare's soft muzzle. "I shall call you Belle," she crooned to the mare, who regarded her with calm interest, "and we shall be good friends, yes?"

Elise had wondered, descending the steps from the abbey's guest quarters into the courtyard, what her new husband had arranged for her, for she knew he had no spare horses. He could hardly have her riding pillion with him, since he rode in full armor, ready to protect his liege lord at a moment's threat. Elise had assumed she would have to ride in one of the carts, along with the laundresses, the only other sort of female allowed in Henry's army.

With the help of Gilles's clasped-hand boost, she settled herself in the sidesaddle, hooking her leg into the holder provided and decorously settling her skirts about her. This was a finer mount than the lady's palfrey she had left behind at Vire. Elise felt like a queen, or a duchess at the very least! Belle's ears pricked up alertly as her new rider gathered up the reins, but she did not prance or curvet, standing quietly and awaiting the signal to move.

As Elise had feared, having a mount of her own did not make her any more able to ride alongside Sir Adam. As the English army formed up and prepared to move out of Caen, Sir Adam told her that she was to ride at the rear, near the baggage wains and carts, a sensible precaution in case of attack. "Gippetty" and the other two French brides who were coming along with their husbands—the remainder had married men who would be staying in Caen—would bear her company, he told her. Her face wooden, she turned Belle and headed for the rear of the procession, followed by Gilles.

"'Gippetty,'" she repeated to her servant once they were out of Adam's earshot. "How drolly my lord pronounces your name."

Gilles, mounted on his piebald pony, agreed, covertly studying his mistress's face for some clue as to what had taken place last night. Had Sir Adam Saker truly made her his wife after they had retired to their chamber? Gilles didn't think so. There was a lingering discontent on both his mistress's face and Sir Adam's that did not speak of sexual satisfaction.

Had Lady Elise, intimately alone with her first man since Sir Aimeri, found herself unable to pretend the passion needed to fool the knight? He didn't think so. She had truly loved Sir Aimeri, but it had been two years since his death. And he had seen the occasional unguarded look on Lady Elise's face when she gazed at Sir Adam Saker, which told him that perhaps her passion would require no pretense.

That thought made him worry. Gilles was no idealist; he knew that many women, as well as men, were able to separate the cravings of the body from the needs of the heart. But he did not feel that his mistress was one of those pragmatic females. He sensed the aching need lying buried deeply within her, and had worried that the wrong man would discover and exploit it.

Wasn't Sir Adam Saker, an enemy Englishman, the wrong man? Still, Gilles had sensed the animal attraction between the English knight and the French widow from the moment they had met.

Gilles did not give a damn about who sat on the throne of France. They were all thieves, anyway. But he did care about Lady Elise, who had always been kind to him …and the English knight *would* pay dearly if he harmed one hair on her head. But unless Saker found out that his bride was a French agent, Gilles did not think physical harm was what he had to worry about.

At supper last night, after their master and mistress had disappeared upstairs, a somewhat wine-flown Harry Ingles had confided in the dwarf about Sir Adam's lost love, the Lady Anne. In the loquacious manner of a tosspot, the squire had waxed eloquent about Lady Anne's golden beauty and his master's broken heart, though he had become positively lyrical in praising Lady Elise. "She's just what he needs," he had said. "He'll soon worship the ground she walks on."

It was very apparent that such a transformation had not yet happened. And if the English knight took advantage of the adoration shining in Lady Elise's green eyes, and carelessly broke her heart after easing his needs on her, Gilles would see to it that Sir Adam Saker never reached England alive.

Chapter Nine

"Ah, and here is the last of the blushing newlyweds," purred Thérèse Montelieu from the cart carrying four of the French brides as Elise drew up beside them on her new palfrey. "When you did not come down, we grew worried about you, did we not, Angelique?" she asked the other woman sitting with their baggage piled around her. "After all, you had been wed to that tall, *formidable* Englishman with such cold, fierce eyes.... But I see we need not have fretted, judging by the quality of her morning gift, eh, my friend?" She pointed to the mare.

So Thérèse and Angelique were the two brides whose husbands would not be staying in Caen as colonists. Elise was not entirely happy that one of the women was the talkative, sly Thérèse, but it might certainly be fun to watch the evolving relationship of Angelique and her unsuspecting spouse.

The prostitute-turned-wife smiled and yawned, stretching like a waking cat. "It would seem not indeed, dear Lady Elise. Tell me—is he as fearsome in bed as he is in armor?"

Elise flushed, feeling at first that they mocked her, but a second glance showed her only naked curiosity on the women's faces, rather than scorn. Occupied with their own wedding nights, there was no way they could know that Adam had not consummated the marriage last night, and they were too far away to have over-heard Adam admitting the mare was a gift of the king's rather than his own.

" 'Twas a pleasant night," Elise lied at last. "And yes, I am very pleased with Belle. Is she not pretty?" She'd sacrificed enough of her pride last night—she'd not admit to these women that she had slept alone, virtually untouched, on her wedding night, and that her mare reflected the king's thoughtfulness rather than her bridegroom's!

"Ah, look at her blush!" teased Angelique. "You'd think she had been a maiden, not a widow. It must have been quite a night!"

Apparently her reaction satisfied the women. Elise had no desire to make enemies of either of her coun-trywomen, for she would need their companionship on this journey, and who knew when she might need their aid? It was no concern of hers what compromises with their self-respect the other brides were willing to make for their English husbands. "And did all of you pass the night well, also?" she asked carefully.

" 'Twas nice to have a lover in my bed, after such a long while—even an Englishman," said Thérèse, sigh-ing, "and even if he is dull as mud he will be faithful, unlike a Frenchman."

"Ha! 'Tis only because the English have not the en-ergy to be otherwise!" Angelique laughed. "Me, I find my Ralph's slavish adoration ... amusing. I wonder if he would think me so wonderful if he knew I was a whore?''

The other woman seemed to find the black-haired Angelique's remarks very comical indeed, while Elise inwardly thought it ironic that circumstances had made a burgher's widow ally to a common harlot, the sort of female she would never have acknowledged before. Ah, well, and what was she, Elise, but a would-be prostitute, albeit for a good cause?

Sir Adam made a point of checking on Elise when the army made its stop at noon, cantering back on his destrier to where she and Gilles were eating their midday meal of bread and cheese washed down with ale.

"How are you faring, my lady? Is the mare well behaved?" he asked her as she sat cross-legged on the blanket the dwarf had spread out. Behind her the other brides and the laundresses stared and giggled behind spread hands.

"Her manners are perfect, my lord," Elise replied, shading her eyes against the sun. "Why not dismount and have something to eat, and quench your thirst?" With the visor of his helm raised, Adam looked so hot and sweaty—how he must be baking in that steel shell under the sun's rays! She could not have said why the sight of his flushed face made her feel warm in such a pleasant way....

He hesitated, eyeing the space on the blanket next to her longingly. "I'm sorry, but my meal will have to be eaten elsewhere, I fear. His Grace said he needed to confer with me when we stopped. I shall join you at supper this even, Elise." With that, he wheeled his destrier and cantered back to the front.

"Well! Milord seems to be a very important man, for a knight," she said thoughtfully to Gilles, who was standing at the edge of the blanket.

"*Madame*, might I offer myself as an unworthy substitute?" came a shy voice from nearby. It was Harry Ingles, still on horseback, and he had waited until his master had ridden away to approach. Obviously Sir Adam had reprimanded his squire for gossiping with his wife.

Elise shot a look full of mischief at the dwarf.

"But *of course*, dear 'Arry! I would be only too glad for you to bear us company, if milord does not need you.... And there is a favor you could do me, if it would not be too much trouble."

"Anything, my lady, anything," said the squire, sitting down with alacrity.

The army had gotten a late start at midmorning, so they had not made a full day's march of twenty miles by the time they stopped that evening. The king had found reason to summon his brother and Adam again while the royal pavilion was being erected, but Adam found his own tent already set up and dinner roasting over a spit when he was finally through with his duties.

"Harry, thank you for managing on your own," he said, pointing to the tent. "And that looks—and smells—very good," he told Elise, indicating the golden brown fowl turning on the spit. "What magic did you use to obtain it?"

She smiled, but touched the dwarf's shoulder. "'Tis he you must thank for it."

"Gippetty, you're a wonder indeed," he murmured, and saw the little man beam. The dwarf had probably stolen the poultry from some farmhouse they had passed, but Adam knew better than to ask.

"My lady assisted me in the preparation," Gilles said modestly, and Adam's gaze went back to his bride.

Elise had changed into the peacock blue gown and bathed the clinging dust from her face, and her cheeks glowed with dewy freshness. She had also removed the concealing headdress and had brushed out her dark auburn tresses, confining them with the gold fillet again as she had last night for the wedding.

"My lord, Harry will disarm you, and then won't you sit down and take your ease? I shall serve your supper," she said slowly and carefully.

She had spoken in English!

Elise chuckled at his startled response, her laughter deep and womanly. "I had Harry teach me how to say those things," she said, taking refuge in French again, "and I practiced until you arrived just now, isn't that so?" she asked the grinning squire, who gave a confirming nod, a teacher proud of his pupil. "Since I am to be the wife of an English knight, I should learn English, no?" she continued as Harry began to remove the pieces of armor. "As we eat I shall learn the names of everything we touch, yes?"

After filling their wooden trencher with pieces of roast chicken, stewed onions and baked apples, they sat down to eat. In between bites she was as good as her word, learning the English words for the food they ate, and going on to ask the English for *spoon, trencher* and *cup,* then, looking about her for ideas, *tent, campfire, pot* and *blanket.*

"And how do you say in English, 'will my lord have more wine?'"

He told her, and held out his cup to be filled after she had repeated the phrase in her heavily accented English. She was damnably adorable in her determination, he thought, and felt his loins tighten as he looked at her in the failing light and saw her tooth catch on her lower lip as she said "'ave" and corrected it to "have."

He had to break the growing spell of enchantment.

"You're doing very well," he said, "but surely there's no need. 'Tis no trouble for me to speak French to you." Was she just amusing herself, learning to parrot his tongue to beguile the tedium, until she could rejoin her lover, Jean? Adam was aware of how churlish he sounded, but didn't care.

Elise frowned momentarily. "No, I want to learn English! I will astonish you with my progress by the time we camp tomorrow night!"

"Very well, then." He shrugged. "If it pleases you." Then he said, "My lady wife, thank you for a most pleasant meal."

Was it a prelude to leaving? He had seemed increasingly restless. But he must not leave—she had to keep him here! She asked a question that had been on her mind in an attempt to draw him out.

"Tell me, my lord, did you never mind being second? Did you ever envy your brother, John, and wish you were the heir?"

He was startled by her bold question, she saw with a quick glance through her lowered lashes, but he answered it. "Not really. Oh, I wouldn't mind being an earl, but I never resented my brother. John's not perfect," he said with a wry face, and she knew he was referring to his baseborn child, "but we were always close."

Were. Was the use of past tense significant? Could he no longer feel close to the man that had claimed his beloved?

"And when did—"

"Perhaps we can continue this later, my lady." He could see that Elise was eager to ask him more questions, but he cut her off. "I had better go see to Alastor, for sometimes he is fidgety in camp," he said, rising to his feet.

Adam could not have said why he felt he had to bring their evening together to a close, but he felt exposed and vulnerable before Elise's seemingly innocent but very potent charm. He had never talked so much to a woman before, even Anne, he thought. Whores never asked more than how much they would be paid, and what he wanted them to do.

He purposely spent a long time currying the warhorse and checking his hooves for stones, tasks he normally left to Harry. It had been a long day over dusty, uphill roads. Surely Elise, unused to such marches, would be asleep by the time he returned.

She had not sought her pallet; instead, she was waiting by a kettle full of fire-heated water. "I thought you might want to bathe, my lord. Surely you are sweaty and muscle-sore after so many hours a-horseback."

"Yes...well, I..."

Obviously she intended to assist him herself. If she touched his bare body, lathering the soap, washing his hair, he would be lost. "Actually, some of the men-at-arms are bathing in the stream over there beyond that grove of trees. It's a warm night...so I thought to join them. I just came back to let you know. But go ahead and use the water yourself, if you want," he added, looking away so he would not be further tempted. "And you'd best go to sleep as soon as possible after that. King Henry will be eager to break camp at first light after our slow start today."

"Yes, my lord," she said dully, and went into the tent. She was asleep, or pretended to be, when he returned an hour later.

Elise had cursed his horse before, and now she cursed Adam himself as he walked away into the night. How was she to succeed—in espionage, if not in love— if she could not get close to him? He seemed as wary as a forest creature!

Ah well, there would be other nights.

At least she was very satisfied with the results of her first day's tutoring. Elise only wished that she had begun her language lessons earlier during those endless days of waiting in the convent. What an effective spy she would be, indeed, if she understood the enemy's speech, and better yet, if she could decipher things written in English!

That's seizing the initiative, she commended herself. Though Burgundy had sniggered when he told her that she would learn English very quickly in her husband's bed, she would not wait for that!

Gilles le Petit had placed his pallet outside the tent, and knew that Sir Adam, upon his return from bathing, had made no use of the privacy thus afforded to get to know his bride any better. Nor did matters change the next night, though again Sir Adam was careful to inquire about Elise's welfare and to take his supper with her. He had listened encouragingly to Elise's animated efforts at speaking her husband's tongue and had praised her progress, but when it came time to seek their rest, Sir Adam had again made a transparent excuse—something about green apples griping his belly—and had gone off until he thought she might be asleep.

The dwarf trotted his pony forward the third morning out of Caen, ignoring the amused gibes of the men-at-arms he passed, and found Sir Adam upon his black destrier, riding just behind the Duke of Clarence.

"A word with you, Sir Adam?" he said, motioning the knight to the side of the road so that their words would not be overheard.

The English knight looked surprised, then worried. "Is aught wrong with my lady? Is she ill?"

"Your concern does you credit, sire. Nay, she's not ill. But I hope you will forgive me for speaking bluntly?"

"Say on," Sir Adam said, but he looked wary.

"You may dismiss me from my lady's service when I'm done speaking, but I must say this. Madame Elise is well enough, but she looks like a bruised flower. Why have you not…" He hesitated, then went on in a rush. "You are wed—why haven't you made her your wife?"

Sir Adam's jaw clenched, and Gilles held his breath, expecting to be struck by a clenched mailed fist.

"I won't dismiss you, but you go too far, little man! What is between me and my wife—"

"Your coldness hurts her," Gilles interrupted doggedly. "She does not understand why you spurn her.

Can it be you are still in love with that English lady?
She will not return to you, Sir Adam!''

Sir Adam Saker's eyes blazed. "I'm going to cut out
my chattering squire's tongue, as the saints are my
witness! And if you were not so dear to my lady, I
would knock you off your pony, you meddlesome
frog," Adam snarled, his fists clenching reflexively so
that Alastor, his sensitive mouth responding to the
suddenly tight reins, half reared.

"Hear me, damn you, once and for all—not that it's
any of your business—I am *not* pining for anyone. 'Tis
merely that I do not wish to throw my heart at the
French girl's feet, only to have her trample it in her
haste to get to her lover!''

"My lord, he's *not*—''

"Not her lover anymore? Nay, not until we get to
Rouen!'' Adam said with a cynical snort. "Then I
doubt she'll even tell him of the marriage before she
spreads her legs for him!''

Gilles, of course, had been about to reiterate that
Jean Jourdain was Elise's brother, not her lover, for
Elise had told him that Sir Adam had not believed her
about that fact. The English knight's crude remarks,
however, made him stiffen in offense on Elise's behalf. Let the stupid oaf pass up the unbelievable gift
that belonged to him, then! He would only regret the
time lost when he found out his error!

The dwarf wheeled his pony and headed back toward the rear.

Chapter Ten

Leaving the flat plain of Caen behind for the hilly part of Normandy, the army had reached the first potential stumbling block in its path, the fortress of Argentan.

Ignoring the gay chatter that flowed around her, Elise pretended to eat her midday meal among the other ladies as she watched the English assemble around the stout castle walls in preparation for a siege. Adam would not be joining her, she knew, for he had gone into the castle as the royal envoy to demand surrender.

Much she cared, Elise told herself fiercely, her spirits still stinging with humiliation after his rejection of her—for rejection *was* what it amounted to, no matter what flimsy excuses he tendered. A bath in a cold creek! Green apples griping his belly! What kind of an innocent fool did he take her for? Very well, she would not lay her pride in the dust for a damned Englishman anymore, she told herself, then added fiercely: *I hope the Argentan garrison makes an example of him!*

Elise repented of that thought almost as soon as she had uttered it in her mind. Though his heart was no doubt as black as his hair, she loved Sir Adam Saker, and she certainly did not want any harm to come to a hair on that arrogant head!

She saw that Harry and Gilles had erected their tent, so Elise made her excuses to Thérèse and Angelique and fled to its concealing shelter. There she spent the next hour on her knees praying for her lord's safety.

A shadow filled the open flap of the tent. Elise jumped to her feet, bumping the ironbound chest in front of her that had held her eating dagger propped up before her to form a cross. It fell to the ground with a thump.

"My lady, I beg your pardon for my intrusion...." A man stood before her, dressed in the livery of the king, but the words he spoke to her were in Burgundian-accented French.

Elise was all at once acutely aware of her solitary surroundings. Even the laundresses had deserted the beginnings of the campsite to watch the artillerymen move their cannon into position against the castle. Everyone wanted to see the first shot fired into the French castle should the envoy's mission prove unsuccessful. Everyone, that is, except this slightly built, olive-complected man with drooping mustaches. He wore the livery of the king, yet he sounded Burgundian....

"Has...has aught happened to my husband?" she asked, a cold chill spreading upward from her stomach. Had the king sent this servant to let her know that the defiant men of the fortress had hanged Adam from the ramparts? She had heard no outcry from those outside, who would have surely reacted to such a sight.

"Nay, lady," he said, continuing to speak in French, "I know of nothing that has gone wrong since Sir Adam Saker trotted under the portcullis on his war-horse carrying the white flag of parley. I—I merely wanted to introduce myself to you."

"Is there a reason you should be known to me?" Elise asked him. He was an utterly unremarkable sort of man, the sort who would be absolutely unnoticeable in a crowd.

Her last thought proved ironic when he began to talk, after first backing out to make sure no one stood near the tent. "Other than the fact that we are both French? But yes, *madame*. I am Denis Coulet, and the reason that you must know me is that I am a courier. You are the Vixen, is it not so? 'Tis through me you will send your messages to Burgundy and the queen, Vixen."

As a courier, he could make use of his anonymous-looking features as part of his disguise.

"But you wear Henry's livery...."

Coulet shrugged. "When I am in the English camp, I am a servant. A Breton, I tell those who ask, and everyone knows that a Breton's only allegiance is to himself. The English cannot tell a Breton from a Gascon, the fools. And if I am absent from the camp for many days while I am carrying messages, who will notice the lack of a man such as me?"

She had to smile at the truth of his words. "So you are to take my messages to the duke? I had wondered if I would have to send Gilles, my servant. He is not exactly so... unnoticeable as you."

The man gave a short laugh. "The dwarf? I would have to agree with that, Lady Elise! Nay, you may send your messages by me with complete trust. Have you aught to tell John the Fearless since you communicated last, Vixen?"

"Nay... but how will I find you if I do?"

"Hmm..." He bent and scooped up some stones from the rocky ground outside the tent. "Leave some stones piled up, like this—" he piled the stones into a sort of cairn "—at the back of the tent, where Sir Adam will not be apt to see them when he comes in and out. I shall make it my business always to know where you are lodging."

"Yes, that will work, I suppose...." She smiled at him. "I am glad to make your acquaintance. 'Tis good to know you are there, Denis Coulet."

He flashed a smile that showed two or three blackened teeth. "And Madame Elise, it is a pleasure to meet such a brave Frenchwoman." Then he bowed and was gone.

As if in answer to her prayers—or perhaps because the story of the savage treatment of Caen had spread southward—Sir Adam returned by dusk from the castle, carrying the news that Argentan would surrender without so much as an arrow being loosed in its defense.

Elise was limp with relief at seeing him stride up to their tent, leading Alastor and carrying his basinet, but she tried to greet him as casually as if he had not spent the day risking his neck.

"Good even, milord," she said, standing just outside the tent. "I trust all has gone well, since I see you before me."

His smile was almost boyishly triumphant, making little crinkles at the corners of her eyes. "Aye, my lady,

I told you there was little to worry about. Argentan surrenders on the morrow, and will be treated full honorably. Have you seen Harry? He was supposed to await me, to take Alastor.''

"You would have him wait all day, Adam? You know Harry, he must have become distracted.''

"It doesn't take but a butterfly to distract that carrot-head,'' he said wryly, and turned his attention to her. "I hope the day was not too tedious for you, my lady? And dare I hope your marvelous Gippetty has been able to forage something delicious for our supper?''

She was on the point of telling him that Gilles had, indeed, managed to procure a hunk of not-too-tough beef—by paying for it rather than stealing it—and that they had turned it into a delicious stew with turnips and onions when the aforementioned Harry came running up the path toward them.

"I'm sorry I missed you, Sir Adam—they told me you'd come across from the castle! Here, I'll take Alastor!'' he said, reaching for the reins.

"How very kind of you, Harry,'' Adam said with an ironic quirk to his brow. "And where have you been?''

"I...I'm afraid I got into a dice game with a couple of the wain drivers.'' panted Harry, obviously winded from running, for the camp lay on a hillside overlooking the rocky mount on which Argentan was built. "And once I finally stayed long enough to win my coins back, I heard that you'd left the castle and gone to the king's pavilion...but you had just left it.''

"So here you are. Take the horse, Harry, and be about your duties.''

"But Sir Adam! A messenger arrived just after you left His Grace the king. 'Tis wonderful news and King

Henry bade me to tell you. His Grace the Duke of Brittany has agreed—there is to be a truce! They meet in Alençon to finalize the details!''

They had been speaking in English, but Elise had caught the words *truce* and *Brittany*.

"What is it, 'Arry? I'm afraid I do not follow your English so fast," Elise said, smiling up at the panting squire.

"Nay, 'tis not necessary—" Adam began, but Harry, dazzled by the Frenchwoman's smile, was already translating his news.

"Brittany makes an agreement with the English!"

"And is that so important? Surely the mighty English can conquer with or without that?"

"'Tis important, Lady Elise, because it means our right flank is protected and we can turn eastward without fear of attack from the rear."

"Ahh," breathed Elise, "I see now. Thank you for explaining it to me, 'Arry...Harry." She beamed up at the squire, then at her husband, who looked anything but pleased.

"If you are done chattering like a rook, *'Arry,*" Adam growled, "do be so kind as to take my mount, if you please?"

Crestfallen, not understanding the reason for his master's harsh voice, Harry quickly complied.

"Adam, I do not understand. I was only happy to hear good news...." Elise began hesitantly.

She had only acted like any woman, eager to hear the latest information after a day spent away from her husband, but Adam had felt *frisson* of uneasiness about her excited interest. But how could he explain that to Elise, whose upturned face reflected only puzzlement?

"There may be spies about the camp, my lady," he managed to say at last, "so 'tis not well to be bawling news like a town crier."

She turned her face away as if rebuked. "I . . . I suppose you are right. I should not have meddled, milord. But come, we shall disarm you and then you will see what Gilles has found for the pot!"

Ignoring the fatigue born of a tension-filled day, Adam made the effort to be an amiable supper companion, praising the *ragoût de boeuf* and continuing Elise's English lessons. But he made time afterward to speak to Harry alone and reprove him in no uncertain terms about his flapping tongue.

When he returned to the tent he did not notice the small cairn of stones piled up just in back of the tent.

The parchment gave a dry, rustling sound as John the Fearless, Duke of Burgundy, broke the red wax seal and unfolded it, holding it to the light shed by a fat beeswax candle on the table at which he sat.

"Excellent, excellent," he said to the man standing next to him. "This letter sent by the abbess in Caen, which reached me only this morn, confirms what you have told me. The Vixen is in place, she tells me, having married an English knight in Henry's train. Henry's army is heading south, rather than eastward as we might have expected."

"Yes, Your Grace," answered the man before him, whose garments still showed the dust of hard riding. "I believe he means to control the south before heading for Rouen. The castle at Argentan surrendered without a shot, and I make no doubt Alençon will do likewise."

"Bah! They let Henry's reputation defeat them, and he can save his cannon for Rouen," Burgundy sneered. "Still, 'tis an interesting course Henry takes, with winter coming on."

"But the Vixen sends more recent news," the man continued. "The English king and the Duke of Brittany are agreed upon a truce, to be finalized in a meeting at Alençon. Henry's flank is now safe, and his rear, should he turn upon Rouen."

Burgundy's fist clenched. "I was expecting it, though not so soon. Brittany sells himself cheaply—but then he *is* the son of Henry's stepmother, Queen Joanna. Family loyalty, and all that—something we know little about, eh, your majesty?"

But Queen Isabella ignored the gibe, knowing her lover was irritated by the Vixen's report. Lolling in a cushion-padded chair, she was more interested in the young widow than in English Henry's conquering path.

"And Lady Elise—is she fortunate enough to have snared a handsome Englishman as her unwitting dupe?"

"He's Sir Adam Saker, Your Majesty," the man told her. "As to handsome... I couldn't say! He certainly does nothing to speed *my* pulse, of course!" He laughed hugely at his own joke.

"Of course," the queen said, allowing her annoyance to show just enough.

"That is to say... I *suppose* he would be appealing enough to a woman. He's passing tall... has black hair and dark eyes—rather a grim visage, though. I'd guess he'd be no soft, indulgent mate, Your Majesty."

"Hmm." The queen's brow was furrowed in thought. "Sounds as if our little Vixen may not be able to rule him easily with her favors. But perhaps when such a one as that becomes besotted the fall is all that harder. I wonder how he is in bed, this grim English knight...."

The man standing before the queen and the duke tried not to look shocked, shifting his gaze uneasily to Burgundy. John the Fearless merely rolled his eyes, and looked amused.

"Ah, my queen, you wonder that about every man."

Queen Isabella just smiled her feline smile. "You may scoff, my *dear* duke, but consider...our Vixen has been without husbandly *attention* since Agincourt—"

"As far as you know," interrupted the duke.

"Oh, I think she's been chaste. Revenge was her only concern when you recruited her, my heart." She used the endearment as if the courier were not standing right before them, and her husband the king not still alive, though hopelessly mad, in a chamber elsewhere in this very castle. "I wonder whether her resolve will remain intact when faced with such strong temptation."

Duke John shrugged. "If she becomes more of a liability than an asset, she can be dealt with. I am sure our friend here will assist us in that, should it become necessary."

The man inclined his head. "Of a certainty, Your Grace. You have but to command me, and it is done." He had other information concerning the Vixen's English husband that he knew the duke would be interested to have. But he would judge the right time to tell him...and if such a time ever came, Burgundy would first have to pay him well.

Chapter Eleven

Alençon, November 1417

His mouth had the sulky droop of a disappointed angel. His eyes held a darkling glare as he gazed across the room at his wife.

The watcher was studied by yet another. *Would that I had seen this Adonis before he found Elise de Vire,* thought Thérèse, now surnamed Pilcher, as she gazed at the tall English knight leaning with deceptive ease against a pillar in the great hall of Alençon Castle. *Perhaps I would not now be bound to kind, dull Sir George, who slumbers over the remains of his supper.*

"Your wife is in good looks tonight, is she not?" Thérèse inquired, gliding over to where Sir Adam Saker stood.

For a moment it was as if he had trouble remembering there was anyone else in the great hall but the woman he stared at so hungrily.

"Good even, Lady Pilcher. Yes, she is. How kind of you to say so." The dark eyes flicked over her briefly, politely, before returning to Elise, now laughing delightedly at some remark made by the Duke of Brittany. Henry's newest ally, learning that Lady Elise was French, had made a point of seeking her out and engaging her in conversation in French after dinner.

"'Tis her wedding dress she wears, is it not?"

"Aye—'twas to honor the duke and the treaty that she wears her finest."

"Ah, how emerald green becomes her, don't you think? It turns her eyes to jewels."

"Indeed."

Now was the time, Thérèse mused, a French courtier would turn the compliment gallantly to her, seizing the chance to praise the perfection of her crimson velvet gown, which clung to her full figure so lovingly that despite the modest neckline little about her figure was left to the imagination. A French *chevalier* would likely whisper to her that he could see the outline of her nipples in the clinging velvet, a tantalizing sight that made him want to steal away with her somewhere to touch what the cloth merely hinted at. But perhaps Sir Adam merely needed a little guidance along the path.

"Do you not mind that the duke monopolizes your wife, flirting with her so boldly?"

His eyes were cool, assessing as they returned to her. "'Tis natural that she would enjoy conversing with a countryman. She is still very unfamiliar with English, yet no one sitting near her during the long banquet spoke French but myself. Have you been trying to learn your husband's tongue, *madame?*"

It was a veiled rebuke. Thérèse pouted. "I fear my lord is but an indifferent teacher of English when we are together. And as to what else we study, well ... in that I must confess *I* am the teacher, Sir Adam." Thérèse managed to convey much about the subject matter she taught by thrusting her breasts forward and licking her lips.

"How fortunate for Sir George," Adam said, quirking a brow.

Thérèse shrugged. "But I *would* like to improve my English," she said, laying a hand on his wrist, "and I sense that in this area of knowledge, Sir Adam, *you* would be an excellent instructor."

His cold gaze impaled her. For a moment Thérèse felt a dart of fear. He said nothing, however, and she felt emboldened to continue.

"Your wife is obviously occupied, and since you do not mind, why should we not obtain some wine and seek a quiet alcove in which to pursue our...lessons?"

A Frenchman who was for some unusual reason unwilling to respond to such a patent offering would have at least pretended regret that he could not act on such a generous offering. He would have sighed and groaned, the picture of agonized self-denial, but Sir Adam Saker was, of course, not French. He did not even hesitate.

"No, thank you, Lady Pilcher. Perhaps you should wake Sir George and see that he reaches his bed safely," Sir Adam said, and then he bowed, adding, "I bid you good-even," before he moved away.

Thérèse's eyes narrowed as she watched his retreating figure. She had never felt such envy of another woman.

Adam did, however, make good on one part of Thérèse's suggestion. Gesturing toward a passing lackey, he commandeered a flagon of wine and seated himself in the gallery where only an hour ago minstrels had serenaded the diners. From here he had an excellent view of Elise and the duke.

He had lied through his teeth to Lady Pilcher, the would-be temptress. He minded mightily that Brittany had swept Elise away after supper with his sympathetic mouthings. "Politics are important, yes, and we are determining the fate of nations here, are we not?" he had murmured in his thick Breton French. "But I have talked treaties and wars and so forth all through dinner with His Grace the king, and now it is a pleasure to speak my native tongue to a countrywoman. You do not mind if I borrow her for a little while, do you, Saker? We would not bore you with talk of Paris and those things only the French care about...."

As if he, a mere knight, could refuse a duke such a seemingly innocuous favor! Adam took a long draft of the potent *ozey*.

Evidently "those things only the French care about" centered on the bosom, thought Adam with rising anger as from his gallery seat he watched the duke chattering gaily with Elise. For whatever Brittany was saying to the copper-haired Elise, whose back was turned to Adam, the duke's eyes seemed to be riveted on Elise's breasts. All at once the modest décolletage of the gown, in which an inch or two of cleavage was veiled by a filmy lace insert, seemed positively shameless.

His thoughts continued their sour tenor. Elise seemed to be enjoying the lecher's attention well enough, he noted, seeing her high color and shining eyes. Once, her merry laughter at some sally of the duke's reached his ears, causing a reflex clenching of his fists.

Yet 'twas his own fault that he was up here, suffering the fiery pangs of jealousy as he watched another man flirt with his bride, was it not? The damned dwarf had said as much a few days ago when he had sought him out on the march, saying that Lady Elise was hurt by his coldness.

His *coldness?* Adam gave a snort at the irony of it. 'Twas certainly not cold blood that coursed through his veins now, as he spied upon his wife! Nor had it been so this afternoon when he returned early to the chamber which had been assigned to them after the castle had made its surrender and chanced to find Elise bathing.

He closed his eyes, shutting out the noisy scene in the hall below, remembering the spellbinding sight.

Steam still rose from the water in the borrowed oaken tub. Elise had half stood, startled by his unexpected arrival, and then, blushing as she realized how much of her nakedness was revealed, had sat back into the water with a splash and a squeak.

"Oh! I...I did not expect you so soon, my lord. But 'tis well that you have come. You can use the water too while 'tis still hot. Why not join me now? There's plenty of room...."

The heat of the water had caused tendrils at her forehead to curl, forming fiery accents to the high color in her face. Its level disturbed by her sudden movement, the water lapped around her breasts, tantalizing him with glimpses of rosy areolas. He felt his groin tighten and beads of moisture break out on his forehead.

Adam took a step toward her. Her blush made her seem embarrassed to be found like this, but her green eyes met his avid gaze directly.

She stirred the water invitingly, sending a wisp of steam floating up. "It feels so *good,* Adam."

Suddenly he had known that her surprise was feigned. Elise had wanted him to find her like this, hoped he would come in time to see the tempting sight of her naked. He felt resentment at being treated like a forest creature to be snared, and perversely avoided the noose.

"Nay, don't trouble yourself, I'll wait till you are finished," he'd said, and turned to warm himself at the brazier that burned near the bed.

She wouldn't give in easily, though. "But won't you pour the water over my hair to rinse it?"

It was a dare, one he could not refuse without acknowledging some sort of victory to her. So Adam had gritted his teeth and tried to ignore the way her tilted-back head had exposed the white creaminess of her throat and more of her breasts than he had seen before.

His manhood rose at the sight, protesting its long denial of satisfaction, a denial that was becoming more and more painful in these weeks of constant proximity to the woman who bore his name yet who was not in truth his wife. She wanted him, he knew. At any time he could turn to her and cross the painful impasse between them, and Elise would not refuse him. He had lain next to her night after night since they had left Caen, hearing the small noises she made as she settled into sleep, feeling her radiated warmth and smelling the clean scent of her hair—and yet he had not availed himself of her. Nor had he done as he had promised himself by coupling with the numerous whores who found their way into the soldiers' tents despite Henry's prohibitions. It seemed like too much bother to obtain something that would not in the least resemble, he knew, what he could experience with Elise.

He could not have prevented the hands that stole out of their own accord to grasp the wet, slick smoothness of her shoulders. Dropping the empty bucket and kneeling, he laid his face against hers, reveling in her cheek's softness against the scrape of his beard. He heard her moan as he turned to kiss her at the angle of her jaw.

In another moment he would have pulled her from the bathwater and laid her down in the rushes, plunging deeply inside of her as soon as he could pull aside his clothes.

Then suddenly the door behind them had been flung open and walleyed Sir Ralph Eppingham stood there, blinking owlishly at the sight, one eye staring at Adam, the other seemingly diverted to Elise.

Adam had jumped to his feet and instinctively moved in front of Elise, partially blocking the other man's view.

"What...what are you doing with Angelique?" Sir Ralph had quavered, the picture of outrage mingled with fear at having to challenge such a powerful warrior as Adam.

"'Tis not your lady, you purblind fool! Your chamber is the next one over! Now begone!"

"Oh! So 'tis! So 'tis! Beg pardon, Sir Adam, Lady Saker!" he gasped, backing from the room with scuttling haste.

Adam turned to Elise as the door slammed in his ears. She now sat watching him, her mouth twitching with amusement, though desire still made her eyes heavy-lidded.

But the spell had been broken for Adam. He had come so close to falling into her trap...yet now he saw it for what it was. He tossed her a length of toweling.

"There you are. Now I'll bathe while you dress, my lady, for we are expected at the feast within the hour."

Her eyes had told him how little she cared if they were on time for the supper celebrating Alençon's surrender and the treaty with Brittany, and it was those eyes that haunted him now, shining for another man. He emptied the flagon.

Gathering her emerald silk skirts, Elise climbed the stairs to the gallery, hoping that if she did not find Adam, she would at least find no other prowling nobles with lecherous eyes and roving hands.

Her senses still tingling from the encounter in their chamber, she had enjoyed sitting by her husband at the banquet, accepting the choice tidbits of meat he cut for her with his dagger, drinking from the same goblet as he did, feeling the brush of his knee—accidentally?— against hers as he leaned forward to make some comment to one of the other diners.

She knew the emerald silk gown made her the cynosure of all eyes, complementing the hue of her eyes and her coppery tresses, but she had worn it for Sir Adam Saker alone. It would be tonight, she had thought, sitting next to him. *It would have happened this afternoon, if not for Sir Ralph's accidental intrusion, but tonight after the banquet, when we are alone*

*in our chamber, he will no longer resist the attraction
that is there....*

Elise had not minded overmuch when the Duke of
Brittany had taken her away for a while after supper.
One was expected to enjoy mingling with the other
guests at such a gathering, and the duke was in fact a
thoroughly charming conversationalist. It *was* pleasurable to speak French with a fellow Frenchman—and
it was not impossible that she might pick up some valuable tidbit for the Vixen to pass on to Burgundy.

Besides, the enforced waiting to be alone with her
husband lent a certain added anticipation to her feelings. Did Adam feel the same? she had wondered, only
half paying attention to Brittany's suave compliments.
At last, however, she became aware of her companion's bold stare focusing upon her breasts and the increasingly salacious slant of his remarks. Did he
imagine Sir Adam Saker was a complaisant spouse,
perfectly willing to lend her to any important noble?
Pleading a headache, she finally escaped the duke, his
plaints at her going following her as she walked away.

Where was Sir Adam? It was growing late, and most
of the celebrants had left the hall. Was he angry about
the length of time she had spent with the duke? If so,
once she found him she would prove to her moody,
difficult Englishman that his were the only eyes she
wanted resting upon her with such bold intimacy, his
the only daring praises she wanted to hear!

Yes, there he was, lounging on a backless bench in
the far corner of the darkened gallery, a flagon dangling from his fingers, watching her as she walked rapidly toward him.

"Ah, there you are, m'lady." Lit by a single torch at the end of the walkway, his features were hard, his eyes unreadable.

"Yes . . . are you ready to go? I vow, I didn't want to be rude, but I thought I'd never manage to courteously leave His Grace's presence!" She was chattering, she knew it, but Adam's mocking voice had made her uneasy.

"So His Grace of Brittany is done with you, is he? That damnable lecher! How very *kind* of him to entertain you! And how kind of you to return to your humble knight while there is still something left of the evening." He sneered.

"Nay! We only talked. I admit, I became uncomfortable the more we talked, so I made my excuses, but no doubt the wine made him overbold."

"'Overbold'?" he mocked. "I saw him reach out and tuck a stray curl back off your bodice. Had I not been but a knight, *I'd* have been bold enough to run him through!"

The duke's gesture, accompanied by a whispered query as to whether she was as fiery as her hair's hue indicated, had indeed annoyed her, and it had not been long afterward that she had left the man's company.

She now became aware of two things simultaneously: that Adam had spent the time since supper's end drinking steadily, and was now well-flown with wine, and that there was a coiled fury within him. He sat unmoving, coldly assessing her response to his scornful words. From his high vantage point, she realized, her polite smiles and laughter must have looked very different. Sinking to her knees in a swirl of emerald silk, she said, "I'm sorry. I swear that I never said anything to encourage him, my lord."

"Nay, do not apologize, wife!" he said, pulling her to her feet as he leaped to his. Seizing her upper arms, he pulled her with cruel force against him, backing her into the wall next to them. "Share what you will with whomever you will! Just say that you have saved some of that honey for me—I need but a trifling taste, after all."

His mouth descended onto hers at the same time as his hips ground into hers, the wall at her back and the hand twisted into her hair preventing her from moving to avoid the pressure of his jaw forcing her mouth open. At the same time as she felt the punishing savagery of his kiss, Elise felt Adam's hard arousal as he rocked his hips suggestively against hers. His other hand had found its way inside the flimsy lacy barrier of her bodice and was roughly massaging a nipple. He groaned, closing his eyes.

Despite the words meant to hurt, in spite of the ferocity of his lovemaking—if it could even be called that—she wanted him.

"Let us go back to our chamber, Adam," she whispered into his ear. Surely the night air would cool his fevered brain enough that his anger would be transmuted to passion.

"Nay, why so shy all at once, wife? After having to watch you with the duke, I've a mind to sample your delights without further waiting—" His hand was wrenching up her skirts, the cold glitter in his eyes leaving no doubt as to his intent. "You sought to lure me into the bath for just this very thing, did you not? You were disappointed when you didn't get what you wanted, weren't you, Elise? I say it will be *now,* wife, and right here!''

''Not like this, Adam. Don't let it be like this....''
The rough stone at her back scraped into her shoulder blades, little tempered by the thin satin barrier. She felt as if she were caught in a nightmare from which she could not waken. Was he actually going to take her right here, standing against the wall, as if she were a town harlot? Yet, incredibly, she felt the flame of her own need rising to meet his lust, weakening her will, and she knew she would soon cease struggling.

''So prim and proper, Elise? Did your lover, Jean, never take you like this?'' Adam grated, his hand at last finding the warm, moist center of her. With his other hand he began to fumble with the ties of his *chausses.*

His accusation, penetrating the haze of the desire that suffused her, was like a bucket of cold water thrown on her senses. Instantaneously she was furious—and damned if she'd allow Sir Adam Saker to take her up against a wall in a darkened gallery where anyone might chance to stroll!

''Get away from me, you drunken *débauché!*'' she snapped, boxing his ears and pushing at him with all her strength.

If he had not been intoxicated, and in the midst of unfastening the points that held his *chausses* to his shirt, Elise would have never succeeded, but the combination was sufficient to overbalance him. Her last sight of Adam before she fled down the stairs was of him lying on his back, propped up on his elbows, his *chausses* around his ankles, his dark eyes bleary with confusion.

Chapter Twelve

Troyes

"Ha! Listen to this, my love," said Burgundy. Denis Coulet had just handed him the Vixen's latest communication, which he now read aloud to Queen Isabella: "'Since the banquet celebrating the bloodless submission of Alençon and the treaty with King Henry's stepbrother the Duke of Brittany, I have become a great favorite of the king, through no effort of my own, I must hasten to add. I was merely courteous to the duke, as a fellow countryman, yet apparently His Grace spoke so glowingly of me to King Henry that the king himself has condescended to thank me for my efforts in diplomacy!'"

The queen interrupted with a snicker. "Courtesy, indeed! If I know Brittany her courtesy was shown best on her back!"

"I believe not, Your Majesty," Coulet murmured. "If the Vixen has cuckolded Saker yet I've seen no sign of it."

"Perhaps not with Brittany, but what about Henry? He sounds as if he's rather taken with our foxy widow," retorted the queen.

"If I may dare to correct the queen, Henry's much too proper to do such a thing, even assuming her lord were willing to wear horns for the king's sake. Saker's like a bear with one cub around his wife!" Coulet mused with a twisted smile.

"'He has even invited my lord and myself to sit with him on occasion at supper,'" Burgundy continued to read. "'A great honor, is it not? If he only knew!

"'We tarry a few days at Alençon at present, as King Henry is ill with the mysterious fever and flux that Sir Adam tells me plagues the king intermittently. I suspect it is more due to his austere way of life, his frequent fasting and denial of the most routine comforts in bedding and clothing, than any infirmity of his bones.

"'I must tell you that English rule has not been entirely unpopular in conquered towns we leave behind us, if only because King Henry has greatly reduced the *gabelle,* or tax on salt, to one-third of what it used to be. Since everyone must use salt to keep meat through the coming winter, King Henry's name is blessed.'"

"Bah! The English dogs would win the people through bribes!" scoffed the queen.

"'You will be interested to know that our next objective is Falaise, the fortress we bypassed on our initial southward *chevauchée* from Caen. It is rumored to be well fortified, but the English troops are hale and in good spirits after so many easy victories and are troubled with little sickness. They have lost few men to the dauphin's snipers hiding in the woods, and have captured not a few of those, drowning them in icy streams if they do not feel like troubling to haul them off to dungeons.'

"She closes with that," concluded Burgundy, rolling up the vellum. "By the saints, I can't believe the English are contemplating a siege—in December! Are they mad?"

"A fascinating correspondent," said King Charles, startling both his queen and the duke, who had not heard him enter the room. "Yet we are troubled, not only by the sacrifice of my son's adherents, but by the perilous position in which we have placed this good woman."

"Nay, do not fret, my lord," Queen Isabella said, waving an airy hand. "She works for France—surely. Denis himself will protect her." Since her husband's velvet-and-ermine-clad back was turned to her, she allowed herself to roll her eyes at Burgundy in annoyance.

"My husband," she began in a coaxing voice, "now that your health has returned to you, perhaps it is time that you returned to our palace in Paris. Your people cry out for you, I am told. And you always liked the Cité better than Troyes, I know."

"We will consider such a course," Charles said.

Coulet smiled to himself. It must be irritating to the queen and her ducal lover, used to carrying on their affair with shameless abandon, to cope with Charles of Valois's rare lucid periods. During those all-too-infrequent hours or days, he was every inch a king, showing an annoying determination to manage the affairs of state and fully capable of having his cousin of Burgundy executed for adultery with the queen.

Coulet had much to tell Sir Adam the spymaster on his return to the English. He would be interested to hear that for the present, King Charles was again in his right mind, and that the guilty lovers were hoping desperately that the king would not hear that Isabella had appointed her paramour Governor of France. Burgundy was now plotting to capture Paris, which was in the hands of the Armagnacs. But Coulet would not tell Saker that Burgundy had no intention of sharing the city with his English "allies." The English would find that out soon enough.

Falaise, December 1417

Listlessly Elise scooped the slushy, melting snow into the pot, which she then hung over the fire so that the snow would melt. Gilles had kindled the fire outside their hut before joining Sir Adam in the woods, where the knight was overseeing the construction of a siege tower.

At least the snow provided plenty of water, so that she did not have to wait until the dwarf could fetch it from the little tributary of the Dives that ran by their camp. It was out of the question for her to go and draw it unescorted, Sir Adam had decreed, for in the forest around Falaise lurked French brigands eager to catch solitary English wandering away from the safety of their camp. Of course, he had said with a sardonic twist of his mouth, they might not find out that she was French before attacking her.

Elise had to acknowledge the wisdom of his words, for she had seen the hollow-eyed wretches peering from the thickets like hungry dogs, yet she could not quite bring herself to think of her fellow countrymen as the enemy.

When the water had heated, she would take advantage of the privacy afforded by the hut to have a bath. But then what? Even if she washed her hair, what would she do with the rest of the long day but wait for her husband, Harry and Gilles to return, cold and exhausted, to the shelter of the wood hut?

She had already visited the rude lean-to in back of the hut that housed Belle, and Sir Adam's war-horse, Alastor. Both horses had grown their winter coats, making them look fatter than in truth they were with the short grain rations. Elise had saved and halved a dried apple to share with them, and smiled now to recall how used the fierce Alastor was growing to her feminine presence—and that of her mare. When Belle came into season they would have to see about separating the pair if the white palfrey was not to become in foal with a colt possibly too big to deliver.

Perhaps she would make a stew with the hare that the dwarf had snared this morning. Sir Adam would thank her in his polite way for the warming supper she had fixed. He would respond to her questions about what had happened that day, though in truth there was not much to distinguish one day of the siege from another, and then he would fall asleep, like as not still in the quilted *aketon* and *braies* he had worn under his armor.

Which left her awake, staring up in the darkness as she lay next to the sleeping English knight who was her husband, and wondering how long the siege would go on. Would they still be here at Christmas? It was but a se'enight away, and the castle showed no signs of surrendering as quickly as the others had.

And would nothing have changed between herself and Sir Adam Saker?

Ever since the night at Alençon, when he had nearly taken her by force up in the minstrels' gallery and she had run into the darkness, eventually seeking a pallet for the night with the laundresses with some trumped-up story, matters had stood thus. Neither ever alluded to that night. They were not cold or sharp in their dealings with each other. Elise continued to perfect her English, and could now carry on a respectable conversation without resorting to too many French phrases, and Adam lauded her progress. But the more time passed since the night their marriage came so near to becoming consummated, the harder it became for either to know what to do about the impasse that yawned between them.

Three cannons roared now in unison, sounding closer than they really were. The explosion was followed rapidly by the crash of the huge balls into the stone of the besieged castle. Elise had grown used to the sound, no longer falling to the ground in terror, for just as at Caen, the English guns fired day and night. The French bombards no longer caused much anxiety, either, as they did not seem to have the range to reach the makeshift village of wood-and-turf huts.

Suddenly the sounds of footsteps pounding through the snow reached Elise, and she turned around in time to see a hooded figure run past, clutching a bag full of something. Distant shouts from the center of the camp reached her then, and the noise of pursuit, of many men sliding and cursing as they chased the fugitive through the slippery snow.

So the runner was a thief, one of the many *povres compaignons,* as they were called, hiding out in the woods. No doubt what he had stolen was food. Quickly Elise said a prayer that the young man would elude his pursuers. The figure had seemed fleet enough, but the snow would provide telltale tracks.

The cannons were silent at present, so she listened to the halloos echoing in the winter stillness through the woods around her. How like a pack of hounds they were, she thought bitterly, baying as they sought to pick up the scent.

And then the clamoring grew instead of fading, coming from the bottom of the hill, down by the icy stream. They had caught him! Her heart sank, and full of dread, she snatched up her woolen shawl and ran in the direction of the shouting.

She quickly became part of a crowd running down the hill.

"Come on! There's goin' t'be a hangin'!" A running man-at-arms yelled to another gleefully. "They've caught a frog thievin' in our food stores!"

"What...what are you saying? What is happening?" Elise pleaded, catching the man by the arm, heedless of the danger posed by her thick French accent.

"A hanging! You know—like this—" He raised a clenched fist above the back of his neck, and stuck his tongue out and made his eyes wild, as if he were choking. "They've caught a thief!" Fortunately for Elise, he was too excited to view the impending execution to insult the Frenchwoman begging information.

Her heart racing with outrage and terror, Elise ran on through the snow after him.

The thief stood at bay down by the partially frozen stream, his panting breath making gusts of steam in the cold air, his forehead beaded with sweat, his eyes glaring defiance. He had nowhere to run; at his back, on the opposite bank, two archers stood with arrows notched, ready to shoot; in front of him, three bared swords were trained on him, ready to spit him like a wild boar should he choose to die that way.

For die he would, it appeared. At one side, an English soldier had just finished tying a hangman's knot in a length of hemp, and stood ready to lower it over the brigand's neck; an oak tree stood nearby, with a stout branch conveniently high enough to execute the thief.

Men-at-arms moved in from all sides, restraining the thief, who continued to struggle as if avoiding the hemp noose would somehow stave off his fate. Elise had not seen the brigand's face, for he still wore his hood and his profile was turned away from her as he thrashed and writhed, but she felt his terror as acutely as if it were she they were about to execute. In another moment they would succeed in putting the rope around the Frenchman's neck, and then they would toss the other end of the rope over the tree limb and cheer as he was lifted off the ground, his face growing purple as he kicked and strangled to death, unshriven.

One of the soldiers, unsuccessful at pulling the rope over the thief's head, had succeeded in pulling off his hood, and for a moment Elise thought she was going to be ill. The only other man she had ever seen with hair of that same silvery blond hue, so pale it was almost white, was her brother.

"Jean!" she screamed, running forward. By the saints, was she about to see them hang her brother?

The man in the middle of those holding bared swords, Elise had seen, was the Duke of Clarence. He looked grimly satisfied as he watched the soldiers trying to subdue the thief.

Elise called his name as she ran forward. She had never liked Thomas of Clarence, always finding him eyeing her speculatively, never troubling to hide the lust in his eyes, but she could not let that matter now.

"Please, Your Grace! Mercy, please! Don't let them kill him!"

He looked around, surprised, his eyes still lit with the bloodthirsty zest some men exhibited at the prospect of watching another's painful death. She hated him at that moment, but buried the feeling, concentrating on saving the young man's life if that were possible.

The man was not Jean, though not many had that same white blond hair, she had seen with a glimmer of relief as she ran past him. He was but a youth, and a half-starved one at that. It had ceased to matter, though, that it was not her brother as she fell to her knees before the duke, clutching at his cloak with desperate fingers.

An angry murmur went up from the crowd around them, plainly afraid that the woman's pleading would cheat them of their spectacle. The hemp necklace now dangling obscenely around his neck, the young thief stared at her dully, despair etched on his pale features.

"What would you, Lady Saker?" the duke asked as he recognized the weeping woman before him. "The young whoreson stole a haunch of the king's own venison! Would you have me let him go free? By the rood, we'd then be overrun with the lazy buggers from the woods around here! Nay, His Grace himself would have this just execution proceed!'' With a gesture, he indicated King Henry, whom Elise had not seen before, standing on a slight rise, isolated from the throng around him. She saw no inclination to mercy in the austere face of the English sovereign.

And beyond him, with the woods in which he had been working beyond that, stood Sir Adam Saker.

Drawn by the noise, Adam had come upon the scene in time to hear Elise shriek, ''Jean!'' and to see her run forward, throwing herself at Clarence's feet.

She saw him now, and stood, brushing off her skirts, ignoring the duke's proffered assistance. Elise faced him across the snowy ground, her eyes full of pain. She would not plead with the king, who looked no more likely to extend clemency than Clarence, though with Henry it was more a matter of stern justice than the desire to please the crowd that the duke had. And Adam saw that she would not plead with him, either. No doubt she knew he had heard her recognize the thief as her lover.

She simply stood and waited.

''Very well, let us proceed,'' came the voice of the duke.

''Nay!'' Adam shouted. ''Stop!''

Clarence looked at him as if he had gone mad—as perhaps he had, Adam thought, to be pleading for the life of his wife's lover. He just knew he could not stand and watch Elise's agony as the Frenchman died.

"I would beg His Grace the king for his royal mercy," announced Adam, approaching the king. Henry just stood there looking at him, his gaze inscrutable. Adam did not dare look at his wife.

"Oh? Tell us, Sir Adam, why we should allow this young miscreant to escape the just penalty for his deed?" came Thomas of Clarence's scornful voice behind him. The crowd's murmuring had become an angry buzz.

"Why? Because the day of Our Lord's birth approaches, and He bids us feed the hungry, not hang them," Adam said. "Our royal sovereign's clemency is well-known. Who are we to blame the French for stealing when their bellies are empty? It is not the people who would frustrate our king's just pursuit of the French crown, but the greedy French nobles! Should we kill those who merely seek not to starve while the mighty struggle for the throne?"

He could feel Elise's eyes, and those of the captured thief upon him, while his gaze dueled with the king's.

And then he saw Henry smile ever so slightly.

"Sir Adam speaks eloquently on behalf of the French, especially for this poor thief. We say he shall go free, aye, and take the venison with him! This we do in memory of the Holy Season upon us!"

The young Frenchman, loosed from the soldiers' grasp, collapsed in a heap, sobbing blessings upon the English king and the knight who had intervened. Adam strode forward and extended a hand, helping the thief to his feet, and handed the boy the bag containing the haunch of venison.

"Here, take this, and don't be foolish enough to try such a foolhardy thing again," he said in French to the wonder-struck thief.

The youth looked around him as if he still could not believe that no one in the sullen crowd would restrain him, and then, fleet as a deer, he ran into the concealing woods.

The throng dispersed, cursing in frustration, but under their breaths, since it was the king himself who had decreed mercy.

Now only Adam and Elise stood there on the snow-covered hillside, their breathing coming in mists of steam, with the silence of the winter woods all around them.

"Thank you ... Adam ..." breathed Elise, as if she were afraid to speak and break the spell. "You spoke to save him—even when you thought it was Jean," she said in marveling tones. She meant: *even though you think Jean is my lover.*

Elise had not hesitated in the slightest, he had noticed, when she'd referred to Jean as her brother, but he realized all at once that it didn't matter. Just as he had learned to let go of his love for Anne, so he had learned to accept that at one time during her widowhood Elise had had a lover named Jean and feared to admit it to him. Maybe once Jean had been the center of her world, but he believed that it was over now. He trusted the love he saw shining in her eyes.

"I thought it was Jean, at first...seeing that pale fair hair, but it was not. He was but a lad, the thief, I mean—my brother is several years older."

She stepped forward and took his hand, holding it to her cheek and closing her eyes for a long moment.

When she opened them again he almost drowned in the emerald depths of her tear-glistened eyes.

"Can you have forgiven me for my drunken pawing of you at Alençon?" he asked her. "I was mad with jealousy, frustrated—"

Elise interrupted him with an upheld hand. "I love you, Sir Adam Saker."

"And I, you, wife." Trembling, he held her face between his two hands. "Elise . . . I want you."

Yes, her eyes answered as she gazed back at him. *Yes and yes and yes.*

Above them, on the hillside, a branch cracked.

"Come on, Saker, you may dally with your lady any time—we have a siege tower to finish, you know," came the Duke of Clarence's voice, a raucous crow's call shattering the splendid veil of silence.

Adam ground his teeth in frustration, thankful that his back was turned to the duke so that Thomas could not see his expression. "I come, my liege," he called, half turning, and then faced the rueful Elise again. "I will come to you at sundown," he promised.

Chapter Thirteen

Adam saw her smile over her shoulder as she turned and walked back in the direction of their dwelling, heard her footsteps crunching through the snow even after he turned to rejoin Clarence. *Tonight,* his heart sang. *Tonight she will be mine.*

"I rejoice to see things so cozy with your French bride," the duke said, pausing to let Adam catch up as he reentered the depths of the wood. "She must be accomplished in bed, judging by your besotted grin." Then Thomas of Clarence noticed his vassal's stiffened posture, and the chill gaze with which the taller man was favoring him. "Stay your hand, old fellow. I'm sorry if I offended you! I confess I'm jealous at the thought of what you have waiting in your hut compared to the cold comfort of mine. I regret if I interrupted anything back there. 'Tis just that I've promised my royal brother the siege towers will be ready for use on the morrow, and with a bit of hard work it might turn out to be the truth."

"Since, love, our minds are one,
   What of our doing?

Set now your arms on mine,
Joyous our wooing,
O Flower of all the world,
Love we in earnest—"

Singing as she entered the tiny hut, Elise looked around her, hugging herself in the chill air. It was no palace, to be sure, but this rude shelter would be forever enshrined in her heart as the place where she and Adam became one flesh. Still humming, she danced about the room, smoothing a wrinkle in the rough wool blanket that lay over their pallet, straightening the hanging blanket slung across a rope that divided the tiny room into bedchamber and dining area, where Harry and Gilles slept, for the illusion of privacy.

The door creaked open, causing her heart to skip a beat. It was too soon! She was not ready! But it was only Gilles who entered.

"Oh! I thought you were helping my lord with his siege tower," she said.

"I was, my lady, but as 'twas nearly done he bade me come to you and see if there was aught you needed," the dwarf said.

"Aught I needed—? Oh yes! By any miraculous chance, Gilles, could you obtain wine for supper this even? And could you bribe the king's cook for a fresh manchet loaf? Say I will trade him for any mending he has! After supper, could you bring in some hot water that my lord may wash? And, Gilles . . . is there . . . I mean, can there be any place else for you and Harry to sleep this night?"

She felt herself blushing, and turning away from her servant's discerning gaze, pretended great interest in the folding of a quilted arming tunic that Adam had left slung across the bed.

"So all is going well," Gilles said quietly. "I am glad, Lady Elise, truly. Yes, I believe I can obtain the wine and bread. And do not concern yourself—'twill not be too difficult for Harry and me to sleep elsewhere for as long as you say."

"Thank you, Gilles!" she said, twisting her hands together. Suddenly she had seen a shadow of wistfulness cross the wizened lines of the little man's face. How lonely Gilles must be, she thought. Because of an accident of birth there has probably never been a woman who cared for him, who could look on him as anything but a freak. All at once, love made Elise able to see the need for that magical emotion in the lives of others.

"Gilles...it is not wrong, is it, for me to love him?"

His black eyes met hers, and he smiled slightly. "No, my lady. I saw, too, what he did out there...to save that French boy."

"And he did it thinking he was Jean, and still determined to believe Jean was my lover, not my brother!" she told him, still dazed at the generosity of Adam's love.

"He is not a man who rejoices in injustice," Gilles said.

"Mayhap 'tis only that, but it makes me wonder, Gilles. Is it possible that loving me might convince him to serve the French cause?"

The dwarf sighed and looked troubled. "Anything is possible, I suppose. But I think, my lady, there you trifle with misery. Be happy if Sir Adam Saker loves *you,* and do not seek to change him from the man he is.''

Elise looked at him, sighing in her turn. ''You're probably right, my wise old friend. But how can I be happy in his arms, knowing that the Vixen plots to undo his king?''

''My lady, you seek to solve too much before the night has even begun. For tonight, think only of love.''

Supper was over. After bringing in the hot water, Harry Ingles and the dwarf had left for the night, Adam had retired behind the blanket-screen and was sponging away the sweat and grime of the day.

He came out in a long, hooded robe trimmed in squirrel and belted at the waist. His hair, black and glossy as a raven's wing, clung wetly to his head. He sneezed as he came toward her.

She couldn't stifle a giggle that was partly nerves. ''Oh, Adam! Come toward the brazier!''

He gave her a smile that sent her pulses racing. ''Nay, wife. 'Twas you that insisted I bathe, so 'tis up to you to warm me, I think.''

Opening his arms, he came to her.

In that instant, he filled her whole world. Her vision narrowed to just the sight of his intent face, all angular planes and shadows and eyes, brown with amber lights, which reached out to caress her seconds before she felt that first touch of strong, work-roughened fingertips on her face.

''You know,'' he said, his voice carrying hints of remembered frustration, ''before that titled ass began braying this afternoon, I was just about to kiss you.''

Her nostrils flared at his clean male scent. Elise gave him a tremulous smile, saying, "Then perhaps you should make good now on your intent, milord."

As he lowered his head, he said in a voice husky with passion, "Oh, I do intend to, Elise. Tonight I will give you all the kisses I should have been giving you all these weeks."

His lips were bare inches from hers.

"All of them tonight, Adam?" she said, touching her fingertips to her lips as if she could already feel them bruised with passion. "I shall have to wear a veil across my face, like a Saracen woman." Her eyes danced with amusement.

"Nay, my copper-haired spellbinder," he growled. "When this night is over mayhap you'll not be strong enough to leave our bed. And so I'll find you tomorrow even, just where I want you."

The promise turned her blood to liquid fire, just as his mouth touched hers.

He had intended it to be the merest brush of his lips against hers, just the pledge of what was to come, but they had waited too long for this moment, and now there could be no graceful, gentle beginnings for them, only clinging, breathless need. It was as if a bolt of lightning had shot between them, fusing them into one being made of wild, raging heat, a flame raging out of control.

Her lips opened immediately to his questing tongue as her arms rose to his neck. His hands stole around her, pressing her closer; when she showed no signs of resisting proximity to the sign of his need for her, his hands lowered to cup her buttocks, cradling her against his hips.

Elise's head fell back, her mouth drinking in long gasps of air, her eyes tightly shut as the wildfire raced through her.

"Thank Christ you are no maiden, Elise," he said on a ragged breath, lifting her off her feet and carrying her the few feet to the pallet. "I fear I would not be gentle enough for a virgin tonight."

She laughed shakily, half opening her eyes and revealing the emerald blaze within. "I was thinking much the same," she confessed. "I was feeling thankful that you knew me a widow, for by the saints, I don't think I could pretend to hide the hunger I have for you."

Then they were silent for a few moments, giving attention to removing Elise's clothes by the faint light of the single candle Adam had left burning by the bedside. They undressed hurriedly, for the brazier lent but scant heat to the cold hut, but it took torturously long to unlace the gown and pull it off over her head, then the warm woolen undergown, and finally her chemise. Adam's garment was a simpler matter, just a pull of the girdle about his waist, and then they were gloriously bare against each other, from neck to thigh.

That first touch of bare, soft breast against hard, muscled chest, and her womanly, rounded abdomen against the unyielding, flat planes of his belly was a shock so sweet it was nearly painful. With one accord they sank to the pallet, Adam leading, Elise following into his arms...and then Adam jerked away with an oath as his thigh landed on something hard. And hot.

"What the devil—?"

Elise recovered faster, remembering the thoughtful way the dwarf sometimes had of warming her bed with a heated stone. But this time the dwarf had used his procurement skills in a unique way. As she pulled the blankets aside, she found a large black cannonball that was still warm to the touch—as were the blankets spread over the pallet.

"I wonder if His Grace the king knows some of his ammunition is missing?" she asked, trying to stifle her laughter.

"Perhaps Gilles thought I might have to smash your resistance, after all?" he inquired innocently, but his eyes were alight with devilish amusement as he pushed the cannonball out of their way, then drew her down with him and pulled up the blankets before all the heat could escape.

Those were the last words they had breath for. After that his mouth was employed in kissing her, then in suckling her breasts, drawing each nipple into his mouth until the nipple was pebble-hard and she was gasping from the sensation rocketing through her. She found he liked her to do the same thing, and while she did that, her hands found their own diversion in exploring the hard, muscled warrior's body. She found ridges of scars crisscrossing his back; there would be time later to ask about those.

Adam groaned as she found and encircled his tense, rigid manhood with her fingers. "Ah, don't, love, for he is too eager to have you to trifle with him now." To console her for her loss, his hand left her breast, sweeping down over her quivering abdomen to the juncture of her thighs.

There had been no man since Aimeri, and after such a long period of chastity, Elise had thought that coupling with Adam would somehow be like losing her virginity all over again. And in a way she was right, for Adam Saker was nothing like Aimeri de Vire.

Had she ever felt this raging fire with her husband, this desire to be utterly consumed at the same time as she was consuming? She remembered gentle affection, courtesy, gratitude, a slight speeding of the heartbeat, from her marital bed at Château de Vire. She remembered fondness. And reticence on her part.

There was nothing reticent about her now. She was tossing her head wildly on the pillow, moaning, as he leaned over her and brought wave after wave of dizzying pleasure washing over her. She reached up a hand to pull down his shoulder, and moved her legs, inviting him in that age-old way to make the final, intimate invasion of herself.

"Are you ready for me, my wild vixen? Do you want me now?" he breathed, waiting, poised above her until her passion-glazed eyes opened to meet his. And then he entered her in one smooth motion, his path smoothed by the moisture of her need.

It caused a spasm of delight within her that nearly threatened his control, and so he lay still above her until she was used to the feeling of him in her before he started to move again.

"Please..." she protested his first easy strokes. "I need..." She did not know what.

"Oh, yes, my vixen," he breathed in her ear. "I know what you need, and I intend to supply it, that and more. But I have needed to feel this since the first moment I woke in your bed at Caen and saw you bending over me."

He was not sure if she heard him, for just then she clutched at his buttocks, simultaneously rotating her pelvis and pushing up against him, shattering his will to make her pleasure a prolonged, tantalizing torture.

He matched her movements, giving her exquisite pleasure right up to the final, shuddering, explosion of warmth within her. Only then did he increase the force and speed of his motions. Seconds later, he groaned and spent himself within her.

Chapter Fourteen

They lay in the pool of candlelight, their breathing quieting, the pounding of their hearts slowing after the fevered crescendo. Adam had rolled onto his back, pulling her into his arms so that Elise lay cradled against his chest, some of her hair spread out over the pillow behind them, some curling in fiery glory over her arm where it crossed his abdomen.

She felt precious and protected in Adam's embrace, and smiled as he kissed the top of her head. She felt utterly safe, completely loved. So this was what love was. She knew now that she had never known real love, true love, with Aimeri, kind as he had been. It had been more of a dazed gratitude that he, a knight and lord of a castle, had deigned to notice her, a mere burgher's daughter. She had been content to do her duty as a wife to Aimeri, fulfilling his manly needs whenever he came to their bed and began to kiss and touch her; she had even felt flashes of something akin to pleasure, brief as the flight of a shooting star, so transitory that she almost believed later that she imagined them.

She had most certainly not imagined her moment of climax a few minutes ago. She had uttered a cry, half moan, half scream, at the unexpected intensity of her ecstasy and a deeper joy as she felt him loose himself within her as if he had only been awaiting her completion.

Adam lay quietly, his breathing regular. She thought he slept. Aimeri had always fell heavily asleep after taking her, sometimes leaving her confused, feeling like a plate of rich food had been snatched away just after her first taste. Perhaps that was all there was for women, she had thought, and they were compensated by the joy of bearing their lords' children. But Elise knew now it could be different, that what she had felt in her first marriage bed paled in comparison with the effects of Adam's lovemaking. She couldn't wait to feel that explosive culmination again...how wonderful the nights ahead would be!

"You're smiling, Elise," he said suddenly, in her ear. "I can feel it."

The remark was both a comment and a question, and she grinned more broadly as she imagined shocking him with the knowledge that his wife was so wanton that she craved a repetition of his lovemaking already. She couldn't confess that! Even if he would not find it a mark of her base origins, what if he *couldn't* yet satisfy her? Men needed a period of...recovery, did they not? She had never been quite sure of how long that was, for even on their wedding night, Aimeri had not taken her again for hours, waking her in the middle of the night with his manhood erect and insistent against her, spreading her legs and entering her before she was even completely awake....

No doubt English ladies showed the proper reticence and demureness, never admitting their carnal appetites. She did not want to disgust Adam with the demands of his French wife!

"I...I was thinking what a babe of ours would look like, Adam," she said.

"You would like to bear my child, Elise?" he asked, in such a humbled tone that she was touched, and felt her love for this man swell within her.

She nodded against him, loving the touch of his warm, slightly damp flesh against hers.

"I'd like that above all things, a dark-haired son, then a copper-haired son, then a copper-haired daughter with your green eyes and fiery spirit to wind me around her little finger."

"What if our son has my hair? And spirit?" she teased.

He gave a mock shudder. "Then I shall probably need a stout rod for the vixen's cub, for our wills will doubtless clash! But I confess I would not have you great with child until we arrive home at Saker Castle," he told her.

"Why is it that a man is always proudest when he can show off his wife looking as if she had somehow swallowed a cannon ball?" she asked ruefully, nodding toward the former bed warmer.

"Nay, 'tis not that, silly wench," he told her, half-exasperated. "Given a choice, I would not have you bear our child on campaign, amidst all the danger and dirt. I should send you back to Caen, or on to England where I know you would be safe."

Elise wrenched away from him, and rose on her elbow in alarm. "No! Do not send me away, especially not to England! I could not bear to be parted from you, and live among strangers speaking a strange tongue! They would think me some foreign sorceress who lured you from your duty!''

''Elise! Elise! Calm down, my fiery vixen!'' he said, laughing at her seriousness. ''I merely said I *should* send you away, and only for the sake of your safety. But I won't, for I am a selfish man mad with love for my beauteous bride. I really should keep you from conceiving, though, love. If I come out of you, at the last moment—''

''No!'' she said, pulling him against her, and burying her face against the mat of curly hair on his chest. '''Tis how the peasants try to avoid getting with child! I would hate that, I think.''

''Ah, but there are other ways of pleasuring you, wife, ways that would not fill your belly, and you would not hate *them*, I think,'' he said, smiling down at her in the flickering light. He kissed her, drugging her with the mating dance of his tongue against hers. And then he rained kisses down her neck and onto her breasts again, not lingering there as he had before, but descending to her abdomen, where his tongue laved fire against the soft roundness there while his fingers played with the curls between her legs.

She could feel the inferno building within her again, but how? He moved down on the pallet, kneeling between her legs, giving her a smile of such incredible sweetness mixed with devilish mischief. And then she felt the intimate invasion of his tongue where only his hands and manhood had touched before.

She gave a soft shriek of incredulous, outraged surprise. ''Adam! You can't—''

He raised his head briefly, a pleased gleaming in those dark eyes. ''Can it be, my French wife, that this is a new joy to you? I thought the French invented love's arts. But let me show you what delight I can give you without spilling my seed within you—"

"It's not—" she began, intending to deny that the sensation was pleasurable. It couldn't be. It was *too* intimate, too... And then the waves of ecstasy took over and threatened to drown her beneath them, and she clutched his head as that warm, wet, skillful instrument stroked her to a pitch of delirium and she was writhing on the bed, tossing her head back and forth in an extremity of passion. The peak loomed in front of her, and she feared it, for surely nothing lay on the other side but death. One could not survive such a fall, could one? And still his tongue stroked, more and more until she knew she would go mad if she did not fall into the abyss. And surely such a wonderful death was preferable...

She was launched into thin air. Her heart had stopped, for she couldn't breathe, not that breathing was needful as she floated. As from a distance she felt Adam rise up from his position between her legs, and come over her. She had not the strength to open her eyes, but she felt him against her thigh, hot and hard and ready.

"I said that was just for your pleasure, vixen," he breathed against her ear as he guided himself home inside her. "But I find I lied, even to myself. I must be inside you, if only just until..."

She smiled as she heard him groan, his resolve not to risk getting her with child burning to ashes as love conquered caution and the hot flood of his need bathed her within.

In those last moments before sleep claimed her, still entwined with Adam, she thought in dazed amusement of how the English were reputed to be fumbling, clumsy louts in bed. They were incapable of satisfying a woman, so claimed her countrymen snidely. But no one who thought so had ever had *this* Englishman in her bed, at least....

They made love again just before dawn, tenderly this time, like lovers long accustomed to each other, and it brought sweet satisfaction to them both. Then Adam rose and began donning his arming tunic, while Elise was still struggling to light a candle.

"But where are you going? Surely you can stay here today!" she cried. "We'll send a message that you are ill!"

"Sick with love for my French vixen, you mean?" he teased with a grin. "I'm sorry, Elise, love, there's nothing I'd rather do than spend the day in dalliance with my seductive bride, but battles do not wait on belated honeymoons, I fear!"

"Battles? Is there to be a battle today?" she asked, terror for him lighting her face.

He could have bitten his tongue. He had meant not to mention it, and with any luck Elise would have stayed in the hut, ignorant of the day's events until they were over.

"The king grows weary of the siege and anxious to celebrate Christ's birthday with a victory," he told her. "The siege towers were completed yesterday, and today we will put them to use. With any luck we'll celebrate Christmas inside Falaise's walls, sweetheart—and you know that will mean less privation for Falaise's people, as well."

"But you're a knight! Surely that is work for men-at-arms, not knights!" she insisted, weeping.

His gut was wrenched by the sight of her with her face buried in her hands. Always before he had cared little for consequences, deeming death in battle honorable and preferable to old age. Now, however, Adam could not admit that there was nothing he wanted less after the night spent in passionate loving than to face danger and possible death. But he knelt by her, kissing her tear-wet cheeks and smoothing back the tousled, cinnamon tresses.

"'Tis not chivalrous to expect common soldiers to face danger by themselves, is it? They must be led by knights," he told her. "But you must not worry about me. After all, I'll be fully armored, and no siege-weakened soldier on the walls could—"

"Damn chivalry!" she exploded, emerald eyes blazing. "'Tis what got Aimeri killed! Oh, Adam, let's run away from this! You have no hatred for the French—you couldn't, not the way you saved that boy yesterday, and gave alms to the townsfolk in Caen! Why not go to the French court, where we could work for peace between the French and the English?"

Elise knew she should not have asked it of him, despised himself for her weakness that revealed itself in her sobs. 'Twas the fear of seeing his body, mangled and broken, as Aimeri's had been....

He stood, and his voice was cold. "You would un-man me, and make me a traitor—is that what comes of marrying a Frenchwoman?"

She flinched as if he'd struck her. "Nay, Adam, I'm sorry, 'tis just that I am so frightened of losing you, especially after last night. I love you so much...."

"I love you, too, Elise," he said, his gaze softening at the sight of her distress. He cupped her face between his hands and kissed away her tears. "No more tears, now. Give me some favor of yours to wear over my heart, and our love will be as a shield to me, sweetheart."

She gave him a tippet from one of her dresses, and watched as Adam tucked it solemnly down the front of his *aketon*.

He made her promise she would stay in the hut, safe and warm. "I would not like to think of you watching as I climb the siege tower and go over the walls," he told her.

Elise murmured her assent, her mind a whirling mass of fear, love and, yes—*anger* that this man she loved with all her being could not resist the siren call of danger, or the urge to put himself in jeopardy because a king would have Falaise as a Christmas present.

"I'll be with you this even, my sweet vixen," he said as he kissed her one final time.

Adam's use of his nickname for her was like a knife to her heart. She paced the earthen floor of the tiny hut after he left, wondering what he would say if he ever discovered what she was—a spy who had insinuated herself among the English solely to bring about their downfall and avenge the death of her first husband.

How could Sir Adam Saker ever believe that she truly loved him if he found out that she had been sending messages through Coulet about their destinations, troop strength, armaments, morale, the state of

King Henry's health? What a fool he would feel if he learned that his affectionate sobriquet was in fact her code name!

All at once a knock at the door interrupted her pacing. Clutching the blanket that had formed the "wall" of their bedchamber around her, she went to answer it, and found a man standing there amidst the swirling snowflakes, which coated his cloak and mustaches.

"They tell me to deliver this here," he said to her in Parisian French—accented English. "A message for milord," he added, taking a sheepskin-wrapped vellum from inside his cloak.

"Thank you," she said in English, puzzled, watching the man bow and lead his horse away.

Could it be a message from home, from Saker Castle? Instantly a vision of a gray stone citadel, high on a rock and surrounded by a moat, came to her, and she pictured arriving there with Adam and being greeted by his assembled family, his brother the earl, his sisters and, of course, Lady Anne. Strangely, the thought of meeting that golden lady who had once held sway in Adam's heart held no terrors for her now that she knew Adam loved *her*.

She broke the wax seal and unrolled the stiff vellum.

"To His Grace Henry, King of England, Esteemed Comrade and Claimant for the Throne of France, greeting," she read in French. At the bottom she read the bold signature, "Jean, Duke of Burgundy."

It was no missive from Saker Castle, then. But why had the messenger brought it here?

She brought the candle over to the crude bench and sat down, spreading out the vellum in front of her. *It was a private message meant for the King of England from John the Fearless.*

Painstakingly she deciphered the words, thankful that the Duke of Burgundy had trusted Henry's ability to read French, for her own ability to read English lagged behind her facility in speaking it.

She began to tremble as she gradually made sense of the message. The duke would like to assure his cousin of England that he looked forward to the day that Henry wore the crown of France, with himself serving as regent whenever Henry had to spend time in his "other kingdom across the Channel." Charles of Valois, the current "pretender" to the throne that was rightfully Henry's, was presently sane, but doubtless that state would not last; and the duke was sure he could persuade the frail Charles to return to Paris, "of which city the queen—who is agreeable to all that I propose—and I are presently taking steps to seize control from the damned Armagnacs and their leader, the bastard Charles who falsely calls himself 'Dauphin.'"

Elise dropped the vellum as if it were a snake. Her heart felt cold within her as disillusionment flooded her soul. She recalled Burgundy's face: fleshy, with cold, calculating, cynical eyes. Could he really be plotting to turn over the throne of France to Henry of England? She had known, of course, that King Henry believed the Duke of Burgundy to be his ally, but could it possibly be *true?*

Were all her perilous efforts, and those of countless others who did not want France merely an English possession, to be for *nothing?* 'Twas obvious that the Bavarian woman who was France's queen cared nothing about what happened to her son, coldly labeling him bastard and conniving with her lover for whatever advantage lay with the winning side!

And this duplicitous pair were the ones who had sent her out to spy! Sickened by the evidence she held in her hands, she rerolled the vellum and dressed.

Gilles was nowhere to be found. If only Coulet was in camp! She wanted to discuss what she had learned with the French courier, as a means of trying to decide what she should do. Surely she could not continue to send Burgundy information, now that she'd read proof that his only true cause was the one that held most advantage for himself! But Coulet, she knew, could not have returned from his latest trip to Troyes, where he had taken her last message to Burgundy and the queen.

Instead, Elise took the vellum to the king's quarters, where she was surprised to find King Henry, being armed by a slight but well-favored youth.

"Ah, Lady Saker, good morrow to you. You're looking well. You are acquainted with Owain Tydier, our minstrel? Owain doesn't mind occasionally doing double duty as our arming squire, do you?"

"Nay, Sire," the young man said, smiling diffidently at Elise.

"I have a message that was mistakenly delivered to our hut, Your Grace," Elise said, straightening from her curtsy and not waiting for the monarch to ask her business. "I mistakenly opened it, thinking it possibly ill news for my lord from his family... but as soon as I realized 'twas not so, I brought it to you, Sire!" she finished in a rush. She wanted to get away from that penetrating hazel gaze.

"Did you? 'Twas no mistake, really. Your lord often handles such...communications as a service to us,"

Henry said, still studying her. "You seem upset, Lady Saker? Is aught amiss?"

"No—yes! That . . . that is to say . . . I know my lord is with those attempting to storm the walls of Falaise today, and I fear for him!" she stammered.

She could not help the tears that began coursing down her cheeks again. It was not a lie; the disillusioning message had come so hard upon having to send Adam out to danger that she felt brittle as a frozen reed.

"Your wifely affection does you credit, Lady Elise. I see I did well to match you with Sir Adam. Pray to Our Lady for your lord—'twill protect him well, I vow. Be assured that Sir Adam Saker is the best of my knights. No harm will come to him, and if he should be captured, I promise you I will pay his ransom whatever the sum."

"Thank you, Sire," she said, kneeling to kiss Henry's hand and moved in spite of herself by the monarch's kindly voice and regal presence. She did not point out the fact that Adam might be killed before Henry could ever ransom him. Henry obviously cared about her distress, but he was making a promise fate might not keep.

Chapter Fifteen

She had really meant to obey him, Elise told herself. She had had every intention of doing as Adam had asked and remaining in the hut during the day, busying herself with preparing a hearty supper. When her knight returned to her, cold and aching with weariness—but triumphant, of course—she would have it ready to serve. And naturally she would be the final course, assuming he was not too tired to make love! If fatigue held sway, though, she would be well content to massage his sore muscles and then lie beside him, merely enjoying his warmth and nearness.

Putting herself in Adam's place, she could well understand that he did not want to be distracted by the thought of her watching him exposed to danger. When going into battle, a warrior had to clear his mind of everything but the task at hand—survival. If he let himself be distracted even for a moment, thinking of a watching loved one's anxiety as he faced the enemy's weapons, he was more vulnerable to a cleverly parried sword, a quick slash of a dagger or an obstacle that could cause him to go down in front of the waiting opponent.

Always before, she knew, he had had no one to be responsible to but himself. Disappointed about Lady Anne, he had not really cared if he survived or not, and that indifference had been strangely protective.

Let him forget all about me until it is over, she prayed.

But no one had told her that the waiting was so hard. Elise could hear the noise of the continuing bombardment as French *veuglaries* debated with English culverins and basilisks as to which kind of cannon could produce the most intimidating noise, if not damage. She could not tell, however, inside the hut, if the siege towers had been rolled into position yet. Surely she could pray more effectively for Adam's safety if she knew what was happening! If she just stepped outside the hut for a moment . . .

The trees and a portion of the rocky hillside on which Falaise was built were in the way, however, preventing her from seeing the portions of the wall under attack. She would just go to the edge of the camp, where the trees would still shield her from view, she thought, her footsteps crunching through the new-fallen snow. He would never know, and so it would not hurt him that she had disobeyed.

Thérèse and Angelique had not been able to resist, either, she saw as she threaded her way between the trees. Elise nodded solemnly to them as she approached.

"Here to watch the show?" Thérèse greeted her with lazy amusement. "Personally, I think they're foolhardy to take such a chance when eventually Falaise could be starved out, but—Elise, my dear, you look frightful! You're white as a shroud! What is it?"

"I . . . I'm just worried about Ad—about my lord," she answered, her eyes upon the scene before her. Which one of the siege machines would Adam be climbing?

"Nonsense! They'll either get over, or the Falaise defenders will beat them back! There'll be a few bruised pates, some injured pride, and then they'll go back to waiting them out—by the rood, Angelique, look—Elise weeping!"

"Don't mock her, Thérèse," said Angelique.

Thérèse was stung by the reproof. "Lady Pilcher to you!" she retorted, "or have you forgotten that weeks ago you were a harlot in Caen? I have not, I assure you!"

"I have not forgotten you were a burgher's widow, either, and no 'Lady.'" returned Angelique, unintimidated.

"Please, let us not squabble at such a time!" pleaded Elise. "But, Thérèse, you make it sound like a mere day at the tournament!" Elise cried. "Don't you worry about Sir George? If you won't concern yourself with him, have you ever considered what would happen *to you* if he were killed?"

Thérèse shrugged. "I'm not at all certain Sir George is even involved," she said. "He's not exactly the daring sort. But look, there's Sir Adam, Elise, see? Climbing up into that middle belfry?"

Three siege towers, or belfries, she saw as she shielded her eyes and squinted against the afternoon sun's glare, had been rolled up at evenly spaced intervals across the southern wall of Falaise. Each of the wheeled, four-staged towers was covered on the sides and top with water-soaked hides to help prevent the structure from being set alight as the men climbed from the bottom stage to the top. The goal of the men on it was to clear the wall-walks of opposition and drop the hinged drawbridge, allowing the belfry's inhabitants to land on the walls.

Solid ranks of French men-at-arms, bristling with pikes, halberds and short swords for close fighting, waited as the top deck of the belfry filled with knights, their swords drawn.

There was Adam, his back to her, his white surcoat with its black falcon emblem identifying him. He stood poised on the very top stage of the tower, blocked from jumping onto the wall by a life-and-death battle going on in front of him between an Englishman and a French soldier. It was obvious even from this distance that he was more than willing to take up the fight himself if needed.

"Look! The other two—" cried Angelique, pointing.

Rows of determined defenders were rushing the other belfries, going in low, while being covered by crossbowmen and swordsmen countering the attackers' thrusts, to push simultaneously at the high towers. Many of them were killed by crushing mace blows or lethal sword slashes as they bent to their work, but they were just as quickly replaced by others behind them.

Beside her, Angelique had dropped to her knees in prayer, Elise noted bemusedly, while Thérèse had already begun to run forward.

Shouts of dismay went up as the unwieldy towers swayed, the creaking of the lumber reaching Elise as her hands went to her mouth. Then, as she watched in horror, the siege towers were toppled backward, their human contents like so many helpless puppets falling amongst the wreckage of lumber and hides on the rocks below.

The English on the third tower frantically renewed their efforts, desperate not to allow a similar fate to befall them. Elise could see Adam fighting tenaciously, his sword flashing in the late sunlight, relentless in his efforts to land on the walls of Falaise rather than allow the belfry to be pushed over like the others. But there were not enough warriors on the top stage of the tower as skilled as Sir Adam Saker, and the bodies piled around him, both English and French.

Even as Elise began to scream, knowing what must happen next, the successful French rushed at the remaining belfry, and slowly, inexorably, it became overbalanced and fell with a resounding shudder.

Many of the Englishmen tried to cling to the makeshift vehicle in the terrified belief that it would save them or at least slow their descent; most of these were crushed beneath its wreckage of timber or by other armored bodies falling on top of them. Of those who did not die immediately, many lay where they fell, moaning pitifully, their backs broken, their limbs crushed.

Adam himself had been thrown free of the wrecked tower, and had landed on several of the bodies of those who had been slain on the top of the belfry.

I can't breathe, he thought with rising panic. *Is this my last conscious moment on this earth, before I am snatched away to purgatory to suffer for my many sins?* He couldn't remember what he was doing here, lying among these still bodies with the screams of the dying rising around him, mingled with the victorious shouts

from above him. He was aware only of the cold, and
the fact that he was unable to move. Then, painfully,
he was able to breathe again, as the air that had been
forced from his lungs when he landed rushed back in.
He felt a throbbing agony in his left shoulder and ribs
before he lost consciousness.

The king's physician bowed to Elise as he prepared
to leave the hut. "He should wake soon enough on his
own, but I would do nothing to hasten it, Lady Saker,
as he will be in pain from those broken ribs. In addition, 'twas a mercy I could set his shoulder before he
regained his senses, as 'tis a painful procedure indeed.
I shall leave you medicine against the pain—see that he
gets it when he wakes, and no oftener than twice a day
if he needs it."

"What is it?" Elise asked the cadaverously thin man
as he handed her a stoppered vial made of a murky-
hued pottery.

"A poppy tincture prized by the Turks," he replied,
in a tone which implied, *If you must know.* The look
of disapproval his face had worn ever since he had
heard her halting, French-accented English was un-
mistakable now. "Mind that you do not give him more
than the dose I indicated, even if he begs for it. It could
be lethal," he warned, wagging a finger at her. "And
someone must watch over Sir Adam as he sleeps, naturally," he added, addressing Harry and the dwarf,
who hovered near the sleeping knight.

Elise was hard put not to smile even as she longed to
tell the unfriendly man in no uncertain terms that Sir
Adam Saker was not the type of man to whine at pain.
"I assure you I will be most careful," she said, open-

ing the makeshift door and wishing the man would hurry through before any more cold air rushed toward the sleeping, injured Adam. "His squire and my manservant will, I'm sure, take turns with me sitting up with him. Thank you for coming."

She knew she had the king to thank for sending his physician; the man would have never consented to lend his services to a mere knight if Henry had not commanded it. She was touched by the evidence of the monarch's care for her husband, though perhaps part of it was due to guilt, for if Henry had not wished to hasten Falaise's submission by storming its walls, so many men would not have been killed and seriously injured today. King Henry had evidently learned his lesson; he had decreed that they would go back to the tedious business of waiting for bombardment and starvation to force Falaise's submission.

She was a fine one to be thinking of the guilt of others, Elise thought as she directed Gilles to warm up the thin stew left over from the night before. Adam had come so close to dying. 'Twas a miracle the fall from such a height had not killed him, but merely broken some ribs and dislocated his left shoulder; and yet she, the very woman who had rushed hysterically forward to him, heedless of the danger posed by crossbowmen on the walls above, was a spy for the French.

It could not continue. She could not divide herself into two beings, one fanatically devoted to revenge and the triumph of the French, the other committed to the man she loved, an Englishman, one of the enemy. While she still believed it was fundamentally wrong for the English to even be on French soil with their goal of attaining the French crown, she could not go on trying to undermine their efforts by her espionage. And she could not discount her disillusionment with Burgundy after intercepting his message to the king. She had no knowledge of the fugitive Dauphin Charles and his fitness to rule, but perhaps King Henry *was* more fit to rule over the French than the scheming Queen and her ducal lover. Those in the already-conquered portions of Normandy were already singing the praises of English rule, for taxes had been decreased and a relative peace reigned there.

Coulet would probably be back within two or three days, and she would tell him then—the Vixen would spy no more.

Adam woke shortly after Harry and the dwarf had eaten their meager supper. Elise had had no appetite, being much too concerned with watching her beloved sleep. To her great relief, reason shone in his dark eyes and was indicated by his first remark: "I suppose I proved I could not fly today, did I not?" which elicited chuckles from Harry and Gilles and a tremulous smile from her.

But evidence of the predicted pain also revealed itself in his pallor, the tight way he held his mouth and the barely suppressed groan as he tried to shift his position.

"Don't try to move by yourself," Elise said, rushing forward to assist him. "You've got several broken ribs, the physician said, and he's set your shoulder—"

"Must be why I'm wrapped up like a swaddled babe," Adam grumbled, indicating his left arm, which was tied to his chest along with the bands of cloth that bound his ribs. "Hurts to breathe . . ."

"Here, drink this," she commanded, holding the poppy potion to his lips.

"Noxious stuff," he commented, swallowing with obvious difficulty before sinking back against the pillows. "Now, Harry, tell me what happened after the towers were knocked over," he said to the hovering, anxious squire. But his eyes never left Elise as he listened to the youth's account. In minutes, however, they had glazed over and soon drifted shut as the medicine did its work.

"He won't wake before dawn," Gilles told her, seeing that his mistress was gray-faced with weariness now that her lord safely slept. "I will take the first watch."

"And I the second," Harry informed her from his bench seat.

To her surprise, Elise found herself agreeing to rest, and moments later, still clothed, nestling close to Adam's warmth on their pallet—not close enough, of course, to jostle him and cause him pain. She would just rest her eyes, she told herself, perilously close to tears of exhausted relief....

Adam woke when Harry and Gilles left the hut, intent on shooting some fresh game to nourish the convalescent. Quickly, before he was fully awake, Elise made him drink the potion before the pain of his injuries could claim him again. But she found that this time, far from making him drowsy, its effects enabled him to endure with giddy humor his wife's insistence on feeding him. "I do have *one* good arm, you know," he grumbled good-naturedly, but docilely drank down every spoonful of the broth she offered.

But her clumsy, self-conscious attempts to bathe him brought out the most amusement. "Saints, I could get accustomed to this, wife," he said, lying back with a look of bliss on his face as she sponged him with soapy warm water. "Nay, don't stop there," he directed, as her hand halted bare inches from the juncture of his thighs, where his burgeoning manhood gave evidence that it, at least, was quite recovered. "You must attend to *all* of me, if you would be thorough," he drawled, grinning at her discomfiture.

Blushing, she sponged that part of him that she had left untended, only to be rewarded by its further tumescence.

"Nay, but you are injured," she protested, her face scarlet as he reached out to pull her close. "T'will hurt you, Adam—" she stammered, trying to struggle without causing him worse pain.

"With this damned draft in me I assure you I'm *incapable* of pain," he told her breezily, then captured her mouth with his lips and her breast with his free hand until she was incapable of resisting further. "But it has left me capable in other ways," he added with a wolfish grin as he pulled her on top of him. "There are positions, you know, where I need move very little, and still have my base needs—and *yours,* sweetheart, satisfied quite nicely...."

Chapter Sixteen

When Adam finally slept, Elise left the hut for a few minutes. She was afraid that in her present mood, she would wake him with her restless pacing.

She felt recklessly happy and in love, but at the same time fearful and anxious that discovery of her role as spy would bring all this joy crashing down in ruins around her, much as the siege tower had done yesterday.

Perhaps she should distract herself by going to see Thérèse and Angelique. While telling them that Adam would recover, she could inquire if their husbands had been involved in the disastrous incident with the belfries. She had been much too distraught after seeing Adam fall to care about the fate of any of his comrades. Sir Ralph might have been there, and though Thérèse had been inclined to doubt that her phlegmatic Sir George was capable of brave acts, he might have been also.

Thérèse underestimated her kindly husband, Elise was thinking as she made her way over the rocky ground covered with the slushy, muddy remnants of snow. Actually, Sir George Pilcher was rather sweet.

Was there a way that she, Elise, could get the cynical Thérèse to appreciate him more?

"Hssst! Lady Elise!" came a voice from behind a tree.

It was Denis Coulet who stood there, she saw when she made her way around the thick-boled elm. He looked warily around to see if anyone had seen her join him, but they were quite alone.

"You're back from court already? You made good time," she commented in greeting. Her heart had begun to beat skittishly, and her voice sounded faint to her as she prepared to tell the courier of her momentous change of heart.

Coulet gave her a sidelong look. "Yes, well, John the Fearless was in a hurry for you to have these instructions," he said, taking a folded sheet of parchment from inside his cloak. " 'Tis good that you came out. I was wondering how I was going to encounter you 'accidentally.' "

"Actually, I was hoping to find you, too," she said, trying to make her voice friendly and casual. "I needed to tell you that I've been thinking—"

"Perhaps you had better read His Grace's letter first," Coulet suggested, his eyes narrowing slightly. "It might affect your 'thinking.' "

She had never liked him, Elise thought as her eyes left his face to concentrate upon breaking the seal on the parchment. There was something faintly...*reptilian* about the man, with his close-set, small eyes and pasty complexion. And he could not quite conceal the scorn he felt for Elise—or was it all women?—as if he thought working with her, a female, was somehow beneath him.

To our loyal supporter known as The Vixen, greetings:

While we commend you and continue to appreciate the assistance to the cause of France that you have rendered by your providing of information, we believe it is time to call upon you to render us a further service. That we ask this supreme act of daring of you is indeed a testament to our love and trust of you. Rest assured that your name will go down in the annals of history along with those of other great patriots such as the sainted King Louis. We have decided that the time has come to put an end to the threat posed by the presence of the pretender to the throne of France, Henry V of England. It seems unlikely that the dauphin's forces will be able to drive him out, and so we call upon you. You are in a unique position to accomplish this act, and should remember that your heroism will prevent the wasteful loss of life of countless Frenchmen who would otherwise perish in a long fight to preserve our freedom. You have told us that you are known to Henry of England, and are often present when he dines in state, and so we have sent with our courier a vial of fluid that you are to secretly mix with his wine. This fluid is colorless, odorless and tasteless, but produces sudden death about six hours later, which assures that suspicion will not fall upon you. While such an act would ordinarily be termed murder, the Bishop of Chartres has assured us that he will absolve you of any sin. In addition, we intend to reward you with marriage to a powerful count and lands in your own right. Without the arrogant Henry to lead

them, the English invaders will flee back across the
Channel like the curs they are. You are to render
us this service as soon as possible, so that the besieged people of Falaise—as well as all of
France—may celebrate the birth of Our Lord as
free men.

> John, Duke of Burgundy, servant of Their
> Majesties the King and Queen of France.

The parchment fell from nerveless fingers.

"Do you know what is in this message, Coulet?" she
asked the courier. "The duke commands me to kill the
king!"

"Shh! Don't say such a thing out loud!" Coulet
said, his eyes darting around to make sure no one could
have overheard Elise's hushed whisper, but they were
still alone. Then his gaze returned to her face, and she
could see that he had indeed known the contents of the
missive. "Think of it as executing a would-be usurper,
Vixen," he said, his face contorted in a smirk.

"But to suggest that I should *poison* Henry of England..." she repeated, horrified.

Then she saw Gilles making his way across the slushy
camp. He had seen her, for he raised his arm in greeting.

"I was told to remind you that when you were recruited you said you would do *anything*," Coulet
whispered in her ear, after she had turned to greet her
servant.

"Yes, but—"

"Wouldn't you like to be a countess, with a wealthy
lord and vast lands, not wife to some landless knight?

Of course you would! In two days, the king holds a banquet on Christmas Day for his nobles—'twill be a perfect time to do it! I'll hold the vial for now."

Aware of the dwarf's approach, she just stared at Coulet, amazed by his certainty that she would be so tempted by greed that she would follow Burgundy's orders. The courier strolled past Gilles, his face still wearing that hateful smirk.

"Do you come from my lord? Does he need me?" she asked the dwarf.

Gilles looked up at his anxious mistress, noting the wild, staring eyes and the way the folded parchment in her hand shook from her agitation. "Nay, my lady, I just looked in on him, and he sleeps," Gilles assured her. "What did Coulet want? I've never liked that man, you know."

"Nor I." Quickly Elise told the dwarf the contents of the message, the words tumbling out of her in gusts as tears began to flow down her pale cheeks.

"My lady, what will you do?" Gilles asked.

She put a hand to her face, wondering how much she should tell her servant. He had been with her from the beginning in her quest for revenge. "I...I can't do what the duke asks! 'Tis murder no matter how His Grace tries to dress it up as patriotism!"

"And there is no assurance that you would escape being blamed for the murder," the dwarf said shrewdly. "Remember, the duke and the queen know that you have no family, no one to question what happens to you. If you were caught they would only have to deny knowing you."

Of course! How could she have been so naive? "Gilles, I don't know what you will think of me, but I had already decided to cease spying."

"Have you made Sir Adam's king your own, then?" the dwarf asked.

"'Tis not that exactly..." she murmured, staring off toward the walls of Falaise. "King Henry can be severe—he would have permitted that French boy to be hanged that day, you know—and I still believe he has less right to the French crown than poor Charles of Valois. But he is a fair man, unlike the false duke and his royal trollop! By chance I was able to see a message from Burgundy and the queen to King Henry, all full of loving flattery—yet now he bids me assassinate the same man! Mayhap, since Charles seems hopelessly mad, Henry would be a better king. Do you think me disloyal, Gilles?"

"Nay, Lady Elise. If you'll forgive me, I think love has finally brought you to your senses," Gilles answered, smiling at her look of astonishment. "Sir Adam is not French, but I have come to know him as a good man, and I believe his love for you is true and enduring. And revenge has a way of taking the worst toll on the one bent on achieving it. You're a strong woman, my lady, perhaps stronger than you know, but this game of intrigue on behalf of France has too high a price. And you're certainly no murderess. Be happy with Sir Adam. But I worry about Coulet once you tell him of your decision. I don't trust him."

A *frisson* of unease traveled down her spine.

"I'll be careful, Gilles, don't worry." She bent down and kissed the dwarf on his wizened forehead, surpris-

ing him in his turn. "You're a wise man as well as a
good servant, Gilles le Petit. Thank you!"

She would see Thérèse and Angelique later, she decided. Right now, she would return to her campfire and
burn the despicable letter from Burgundy!

Chapter Seventeen

"Come to bed, love," called Adam from the "bed-chamber" side of the blanket in that deep, growling voice that always heated her blood and caused it to go coursing through her veins like a rushing river. "Whatever can you be doing out there so late?"

"Mending the rent in your *aketon* that was made when the siege tower fell," she answered.

"Blow out the candle and come keep me warm," he coaxed. "It can be done tomorrow, can't it? No one will be working until after Christmas Day, and you're probably just keeping Harry and Gippetty awake."

"Not even your bellowing aroused them, milord," she teased as she came around the side of the blanket. "Both have been snoring since shortly after supper."

"Good," came Adam's quick answer from where he lay on their pallet, the blankets falling down from his lightly furred chest slightly as he beckoned her to join him. "For I've a mind to enjoy you, wife. After all, 'tis all I've had to look forward to all day while lying here like an invalid!"

His shoulder and ribs still caused him pain, but she could tell he was mending fast; he was restless and inclined to be cross when told he should not be walking around outside in the cold. Still, it was good that the holy day of Christ's birth would ensure a truce, for Adam's injuries were still new, however much better he felt.

"I'll be glad when 'tis spring," Adam said, watching her quickly shed her shawl, then her woolen outer dress, then the underdress of softest wool and finally her chemise. "I would love to watch you undress slowly, sweetheart, tantalizing me as you remove piece by piece, then walk slowly toward me as God made you."

When he looked at her like that she felt quite warm, despite the chill December winds that leaked through holes in the mud chinking!

"You will like spring in Normandy, I think," she said. "'Tis lovely with all the apple trees in bloom...." She did not allow her musing to slow her task, however, and in a moment she was diving under the blankets and being pulled into the warm circle of his embrace.

Perhaps making love to her would tire him out, she thought as he began to kiss her, so that he would not hear her when she stole from his bed later.

Jesu, not my will but Thine be done, Henry of England prayed as he knelt in the darkness. *I wished for the submission of Falaise by the day of Thy birth to give Thee glory, but perhaps my motives were not pure enough. Perhaps, sinful man that I am, inwardly I wished to hear the praise of men for myself rather than all for Thee, and accordingly Thou hast denied me the victory as yet, though it seems Captain Olivier de*

*Mauny, cannot hold out forever. And Thou hast re-
turned that familiar thorn to my flesh. . . .*

Henry winced as another wave of griping pain spread
upward in his abdomen, causing him to grab at his
belly as if he could catch hold of the monster that bit
him inside. It was a creature well known to him, who
returned to torment him whenever he ate too well, or
drank his favorite Rhenish, or sometimes for no apparent reason at all.

He pressed the edge of his cloak to his mouth, determined not to cry out and wake his sleeping attendant. Perhaps if he strolled around camp for an hour
or so, conversing with the sentries, he would earn a
peaceful few hours' rest. . . .

Denis Coulet paced as he stood in the partial shelter
formed by three pines growing close together at the
edge of camp.

Damn the woman, why didn't she come? He'd been
told by the ugly little dwarf that his mistress needed
speech with him, and had virtually been ordered by him
to meet her here tonight, he thought resentfully. She
was to come at the hour of Compline, or as soon
thereafter as she could steal away with her lord none
the wiser.

*And here I am freezing my arse off while she's
probably got her legs spread for that English cur,* he
fumed as a cold gust of air found him, biting cruelly at
his fingers even though he had balled them into fists.
*She'd better arrive soon, full of apologies, and if she
knows what's good for her, she'd better tell me that
she's ready to do as the duke ordered her to at the
banquet tomorrow!*

He had a bad feeling about it, though. He knew
Lady Elise Saker didn't like him; that much was apparent in the unconscious way she had of narrowing
those green, cat's eyes she had when she looked at him,
of tilting that damned little nose of hers as if she
smelled rotten fish whenever she was around him. He
was accustomed to the distaste of women, and it didn't
matter to him, for he could buy the services of a whore
who had to put up with him for the sake of a coin.
'Twas all women were good for, anyway, even those
like Elise Saker, who fancied themselves ladies.

She'd begun to say, "I've been thinking." Trouble
never failed to follow when a wench told a man that.
Whoever encouraged women to believe they could
think had done the male sex a grave disservice!

And yesterday, when she'd read that Burgundy
wanted her to assassinate the king, she'd looked a little too horrified and disgusted to make Coulet believe
that she'd ever conquer those feelings enough to follow orders, even with the bait of a noble title and marriage.

'Twas what came of using a wench to do a man's
job, he thought irritably. Why didn't it ever occur to
Burgundy to offer *him* a title and marriage to an heiress? He'd see the job done quick enough! But somehow he knew it would never happen, for Burgundy
thought his sort unworthy of ennoblement and had already found his price: money.

"I'm sorry if you've been waiting long," came a soft
voice behind him.

He whirled. "It's about time, my fine lady! A moment more and I'd have left you here to get frostbitten
as I've done!"

"I *said* I was sorry," Elise Saker repeated, an edge to her voice. "I couldn't exactly leave to meet you before my lord slept, could I?"

"Very well," Coulet said grudgingly, eager to end the interview so he could seek his bed. "So now you're here at last. That dwarf said you wished to speak to me. Are you here to tell me you're ready to administer the poison?"

He could tell she was looking at him, but could not discern more in the moonless darkness. He heard her take a deep breath.

"No, I'm not. That is, I've called you here to tell you that I cannot commit murder, even of an Englishman. I will not kill King Henry, nor any other. And further, I cannot keep spying for Burgundy and the queen. I tried to tell you that yesterday, but you interrupted before I could and made me read that letter. Please tell them I'm sorry, but I've . . . had a change of heart."

"A 'change of heart,' Vixen?" he exploded. He had imagined she was going to be too craven to pull off the assassination, but to have suddenly grown a conscience about spying! "What brought about this *change of heart,* you pretty idiot? In love with your English knight's cock, are you? So smitten that you'd turn traitor to your country?"

"That's enough, Coulet," she cut in coldly. "You won't change my mind by insulting me. I won't murder, and I won't spy any longer. And yes, if 'tis any of your affair, I do love Sir Adam Saker. Love has nothing to do with nationality, I've found. I wish you well, Coulet, and do not fear I'll betray you—your secret is safe with me whether you choose to return to court or remain in camp."

"How very beneficent of you, my lady," he snarled. "Well, I hate to be the bearer of ill tidings, but you can't just quit such a task as if 'twere a garment you disliked sewing! Here's the poison," he said, pulling out the vial and forcibly closing her fingers around it. "Since you're so besotted by your English lover, perhaps you can be moved to carry out your orders knowing that I'll kill your lover if you don't kill the king!"

He heard her gasp, then, incredibly, she chuckled.

"*You?* Kill a powerful knight like Sir Adam Saker? You've lost your reason, Coulet!"

His fists clenched at his sides as rage swept over him in response to her cool scorn. And then he remembered Burgundy's words: *"If she becomes more of a liability than an asset, she can be dealt with. I am sure our friend here will assist us in that, should it become necessary."*

The foolhardy wench had signed her death warrant. Her protestations were meaningless. He couldn't trust her, not after she'd proved she cared more for her handsome bedmate than the cause of France! She'd betray him in a heartbeat if she thought it could make her rutting Englishman smile at her.

Deep in sleep, Adam turned on his side, causing needles of pain to shoot through him. By the rood, would he ever be able to lie on that shoulder again? Drowsily he reached out, intending to pull his wife against him, craving the comfort of Elise's sweet-scented flesh, her silken hair...

His hand encountered only empty space.

"Elise?" he whispered into the blackness of the room. No answer. Perhaps she had gone outside to answer the call of nature, though he'd told her to forget modesty and use the chamber pot rather than wander outside in the night. He sat up to wait, not wanting to fall back to sleep until she was safe beside him.

Five minutes later she had not returned. Had she become ill? The venison was fresh, a buck brought down just yesterday morning by a lucky shot from Harry's bow. But perhaps it had been overrich for her....

Ten minutes later she had still not returned, and he grimly threw on his clothes, determined to find her. They would have an understanding, his wife and he. If she was so ill as to leave the hut at night, he was to go with her. She shouldn't be out alone in a camp full of men. Oddly, it never occurred to him that she might be trysting with another man.

Warned by Coulet's twisted, hate-filled face, she still did not have time to reach the knife she had stuck in her girdle. Elise screamed as he sprang at her, his fingers curved to seize her throat. Though his hands failed to connect around her neck, he had been standing on a slight rise and the force of his full weight launched against her caused her to fall backward with him.

On the frozen ground they grappled in a deadly parody of lovers, both writhing as she fought him like a madwoman, kicking and biting, thrashing in her efforts to throw him off. If she could only reach her knife... But she dared not let go of his wrists, for he was trying to strike her head now. She knew that if

Coulet could knock her senseless, he would easily strangle her while she lay helpless. She kept screaming, wondering all the while how long her strength could hold out against the courier's; he was a slight man but wiry-strong.

He succeeded in wrenching one of his hands free, and while she bucked and struggled, struck her along her right temple, causing the world to suddenly be full of dazzling comets....

"What is the meaning of this?" a voice thundered from three yards away.

Denis Coulet cursed inwardly as his hands moved to seize her wrists. Depending who his intruder was, he might have to kill him *and* her before he could feel safe. He'd just have to catch the newcomer unaware by distracting him with some believable story.

And then he saw that the newcomer was the King of England.

"Elise? Is that you? What's happening? *Sire?*" Adam had reached the three pine trees just seconds later, from the opposite side of camp.

"I just arrived myself, Sir Adam," came the king's voice across the small space that separated them. "Fellow, we are waiting to hear your explanation."

"Oh Adam, Your Grace, thank God," breathed Elise, as Denis Coulet warily got up off her and stood facing the two other men. "He was going to kill me!"

"Why? Tell me, then say your prayers, you misbegotten cur, for you're going to die!" Adam said to Coulet as a red mist began to swim before his eyes.

"First, you'd better listen to what I have to say, *spymaster,* don't you think?" mocked Coulet. "I know

His Grace King Henry would be interested to learn that
the woman I was trying to subdue—so that I could arrest her and bring her to you, of course—is a *spy for
the French.*"

"Liar!" Elise screamed desperately, icy fear gripping her heart. Would Adam believe her? And why was
Coulet calling him Spymaster?

"What are you saying? You're insane!" Adam
shouted at Coulet. A part of him was aware, amidst the
craziness of the charges being hurled by this scoundrel
against his beloved, that the king had stiffened. A
glance at his sovereign confirmed that a cold, stern
mask had come over Henry's features.

"Oh yes, I've gotten your attention now, haven't I,
Sir Adam? The delicious little piece you've been bedding has been sending secrets to them, all the while I've
been spying on the French and reporting to *you.* She is
known as the Vixen to Burgundy and the queen of
France. Not content with spying, she's trying to curry
favor with them now by murdering the King of England! She's been promised absolution, lands and
marriage to a count if she's successful! See, here's the
poison she was going to drop into your wine at the
banquet tomorrow, Sire, on the very day of Our Lord's
birth! I had just wrested it away from her!"

"Liar!" Elise cried again. "I would never try to kill
King Henry! He—the Duke of Burgundy—had told me
to do it but I had just told Coulet I refused to do it, that
it was wrong! It's all a lie!"

"And what were you doing, receiving messages from
Burgundy, Lady Saker? Can it be true that you were
the Vixen?" asked the king, his voice silky, cold steel.

"I had wondered, as had Sir Adam as my head of intelligence, how Burgundy and his royal concubine seemed to know about my health, about where to address messages to me, when I had not communicated such to them," Henry went on. "Actually, we had begun to suspect an informer within our midst...but who? We never dreamed 'twould be the woman we had given our spymaster to wife who was the spy within our midst."

"I...I..." There seemed no point in trying to deny it. The king was already convinced. "Yes, Your Grace, I confess to keeping Burgundy informed...about certain matters. But my accuser is the very one who carried the messages!" she cried, pointing at the smirking Coulet. "And the very one who carried the poison and tried to bribe me to use it, saying he'd kill my husband if I refused!" She'd be damned if she'd stand accused by Coulet without exposing his true role in all this!

"She's the one who's lying," Coulet said disdainfully. "She's trying to wiggle out of serious charges by dragging me down with her!"

"I knew I could not fully trust my sometime ally, Burgundy, but to poison me?" Henry marveled. "We are grateful, Coulet, that you have brought this grave matter to light."

Henry might have been a stone statue, standing there, the personification of Doom, Elise thought.

Desperately she turned to Adam. His face was that of a stranger, his eyes inscrutable. "I was sending information, my lord—Adam!—but when we fell in love, I realized I had to stop! I could no longer continue to do something disloyal to that which you stood for! Please believe me!''

Across the whirling void that separated her from her husband and the king, she heard Henry's voice. ''Sir Adam, you know what happens to spies and would-be assassins. Put her in the gaol cell for the night, and set up a guard. We will deal with her after the morrow.''

Chapter Eighteen

Two men-at-arms, sentries with whom King Henry had been conversing before Elise's scream had brought him to the scene of her struggle with Coulet, came in answer to the king's shouted summons. They led her away to the windowless hut that served as the English camp's makeshift gaol cell.

The cell had few amenities: clean straw on the floor, a chamber pot, a cracked pitcher of water, a moth-eaten pair of blankets. There was no brazier, and the wind seeped through the haphazard chinking almost unhindered.

The gaol was empty of other occupants now, and had had few since the camp had been set up, all there accused of petty crimes: fighting, gambling, insubordination and the like. Lady Elise Saker was the first occupant who, it seemed, was in danger of decorating a branch of the huge oak that stood right in front of the hut.

Elise could not bring herself to care. She wrapped herself in one blanket—a difficult task since her wrists were manacled with a short length of chain between them, as were her ankles—and sat on the other, but she barely felt the cold. Drained by the anger and terror she had felt in the past hour, she could feel only a vague hope that the king would pass a sentence of death and end her suffering on the day after Christmas. It was too painful to live in a world in which hate was the only emotion Sir Adam Saker felt for her.

Coulet had followed the procession as she was led away, taunting her. "Now who's the clever fox, Vixen? Did you see the disgust on Sir Adam's face? Looks like your knight-husband took good advantage of your charms while he could, but now that you've been found out, he'll not care what happens to you!"

He seemed emboldened when she said nothing and her guards made no move to shut him up.

"Sometimes King Henry shows mercy to women, but I'd wager the most mercy *you* could hope for is life imprisonment! But don't think Saker will ever visit you! I'm sure he'd rather they hanged you—at least that way he'll be free to marry again without having to bribe a bishop for an annulment!"

Adam was the king's head of espionage. It was hard to picture him in the shadowy game of espionage, pulling the strings that sent agents, ignorant puppets like herself, to spy against the enemy—hard to picture him as anything less than the straightforward warrior he was. How ironic that among all the available Englishmen, she should have been attracted to him, and that neither of them had known what the other truly was.

Or had he perhaps known all along who she was, she wondered in despair, and had only been waiting until the time was right to expose her? In the meantime, as Coulet had jeered, he had had the convenience of a willing, available female. Had his initial reluctance to bed her been part of the elaborate pose, to lure her into a false sense of security?

She remembered her last sight of him, his eyes condemning, his mouth set in a hard, angry line. But she could not bring herself to damn him in her thoughts as she did Coulet, the Duke of Burgundy and the Queen of France.

Christmas Day dawned bleak and cold. Later in the day, while she forced herself to eat the thin, greasy potage brought to her by her gaoler, the sounds of revelry reached her from the king's quarters. Henry and his nobles celebrated Christ's birthday.

"Gippetty! So here you are! I've been looking everywhere for you!" Adam had finally found the dwarf after he returned to his hut at the end of the Christmas Day revels. Gilles le Petit was wrapping his few possessions into a bundle.

"I had supposed you would not want to see me, Sir Adam," Gilles said tonelessly, facing the knight. His face was even more wrinkled, if that was possible, and his eyes were dead and devoid of hope.

"Nay! Last night, after King Henry finally finished questioning me, I found you gone. You...you weren't leaving, were you?" he asked, gesturing toward the bundle.

The dwarf, who was thinking in his turn that Sir Adam looked very drawn and haggard, paused in his folding. "I did not plan to leave the English camp until it was clear what King Henry intends for my mistress."

"''Tis precisely what I needed to speak to you about. I'm afraid the king means to make an example of Elise—though he would normally show clemency to a woman. He's furious, Gippetty—I can't get him to believe that while my...Elise *had* been spying, she had refused to murder him, and had intended to do no more espionage! I tried to point out to him that the so-called 'secrets' that she had communicated to the French were nothing that had harmed us—the state of his health, the morale of the troops, the type of artillery we possessed and in what numbers..." His voice trailed off. "Henry can be vengeful just as often as he is clement."

"He means to...*hang* her, milord?" A tear spilled out of one of the dwarf's red-rimmed eyes onto his pale face.

"I think 'tis very possible. 'Tis why we have to see that she escapes tonight."

"*Escapes?* But she is guarded, Sir Adam!"

"So she is. But guards can be bribed—"

"Aren't you afraid of the king's wrath turning on you?"

"Not very much. Thomas of Clarence has already agreed to swear I was drinking all night with him, drowning the sorrow of having a French spy for a wife," he said with a flash of sardonic humor. "And I'm sure once Henry has a chance to cool down, he'll be glad I got her away before he could do something he'd regret later."

The dwarf heaved a gusty sigh of relief, his eyes brimming. "You *do* love her, don't you? I was afraid that you might not, after last night."

"Adam looked away from the gratitude he saw shining in the little man's face.

"Yes . . . yes, I do."

Midnight, Elise reckoned. Likely the last midnight she would experience on earth. Christmas Day was over, and in the morning the king would pass sentence. She had no doubt that once decreed, her execution would follow immediately, with only a few minutes' grace to confess and be shriven. Soon it would be over.

"Thank ye, sir," Elise heard her gaoler say to someone outside, and then she heard the sound of clinking coins. "Nay, I don't mind if ye tie me up. 'Twill save me gettin' in trouble later, like."

Moments later there was the sound of the bolt being shot back. Her stub of a candle had burned out an hour ago, so at first all she could see was the flame of the candle clutched by the figure who came into her cell.

Coulet, come to taunt her some more, or cheat the hangman by killing her now? No, the figure was too tall to be the wiry Frenchman. But her despairing mind refused to accept the other alternative as possible.

Even when she heard his voice, she thought it was only a damnable hallucination sent by the devil to torment her in her final hours.

"Elise, 'tis me. Where is your candle holder? I want to set this down."

Adam? Had he come to denounce her for her treachery, to let her know just how much he hated her before she was beyond his hatred? She heard the sound of him fumbling in the dark to settle the candle in the holder, then, unbelievably, she was in his arms.

"Elise, my darling! Are you all right? You're so very cold, sweetheart, like an icicle! Here, let me warm you...."

Dazed and still unbelieving, she felt him take off his cloak and place it around her, then he resumed his tight embrace, kissing away the tears that flowed unchecked down her cheeks.

"You shouldn't have come. Why are you here? Oh, Adam," she said through her sobs. She could die happy now, now that he had held her one final time. That was it, then. He'd come to say farewell, knowing this to be her last night. She could accept her fate, she told herself. And yet, some dying spark within her flared to life when she kissed him back. Suddenly she wanted so much to live.

"I...I love you, Adam," she said. "I'm so sorry for the pain I've caused you."

He held her face cupped in his hands. "Hush, now. None of that. You did what you must, I can see that. I love you, Elise, and I always will."

He meant he would love her after she died. "The king must be very angry with you, because of me," she said. "I deeply regret that. Marry again, soon—someone who will bring only honor to you."

"Marry again? I believe the Church frowns on bigamy, sweetheart," he said, smoothing her hair.

"You don't have to pretend, Adam," she insisted. "I know the king wants to hang me. And even if he's persuaded to show mercy, I don't expect to ever see freedom again. It won't be hard for you to get an annulment.''

"I think you're right—about the king's intentions, that is. That's why you and Gippetty was leaving the camp tonight.''

"Leaving? You mean escape? Is that why you're here? But y-you can't! Henry will be so angry he'll hang *you!*'' She sputtered. "I can't let you risk that for me!''

"Stop being noble, sweetheart, 'tis already arranged. Gilles is waiting at the eastern edge of camp with Belle and his pony. Go to Paris, Elise—I'll find you there later, after Henry's wrath has cooled, and I've secured a pardon for you.''

"My wonderful, chivalrous darling, the king isn't going to forgive me, not if you wait ten years! He thinks I was going to *poison* him!'' By the light of the single candle she could see him smiling fondly at her protests as if she were a dear but fretful child. "I have to make you see, Adam! If you persist in this foolishness, King Henry will never favor you again—he may even ruin you!''

Serious now, he looked deeply into her eyes. The candle made deep shadows in the angular planes of his face. "I don't think 'twill come to that, but I don't care if he banishes me from England forever, Elise. His favor means nothing if I can't have you. Didn't you hear me say I would always love you.''

"Ah, God, you mean it," she said, weeping against his chest.

"Of course I do. Poor darling, you must have been so frightened. But 'tis all over now. Come, we should get you going—"

Behind him, Adam heard the bolt being drawn back. 'Twas the dwarf, he thought, come to see what kept them.

"I don't think your little French spy is going anywhere—nor are you, Saker."

Adam inwardly cursed the close quarters of the cell. Drawing his sword to slay this vermin was going to be difficult without endangering Elise, but he had wanted Coulet to die, and die as painfully as possible, ever since Elise's arrest, and doubly so after he realized that Henry wasn't going to listen to him when Adam insisted that his courier was obviously a double agent.

"Coulet!" Adam exclaimed as he recognized the other's voice. "How very stupid of you to interfere when I want you dead more than I want my next breath—" Adam wondered if Coulet had brought witnesses with him—if so, the game was up before it truly began; if not, the courier was incredibly cocky. He'd know in moments which it was.

His hand went to his sword, but before he could draw it from his scabbard the smaller man jumped at him, his long-bladed dagger naked and ready to stab upward into Adam's chest.

Coulet's only advantage lay in surprise, and he knew it. He would have to wound Adam mortally in the first moments of the struggle, or the larger man would eventually overpower him and use Coulet's own dagger on him. The Frenchwoman's witnessing their struggle was not a factor. Manacled, she was in little position to help Saker, and even if anyone could hear her screams, she dared not raise the alarm.

Coulet was vaguely aware that Elise had backed against the wall, her hands raised to her mouth in terror. He was going to enjoy slitting her throat after he killed Saker—though perhaps he would rape her first if there was time.

He probably would have failed, even with the advantage of surprise, if it had not been for the empty bowl that had held Elise's supper, which had been left out in the middle of the floor. Adam backed into it, and it was enough to cause him to lose his balance for a lethal second. He went down heavily, groaning as he landed on the recently injured shoulder and ribs, and Coulet fell on top of him, his dagger poised.

He aimed a vicious slash at Adam's chest, which Adam only managed by his upflung forearm to deflect upward to his left shoulder, where it nevertheless sliced deeply into muscle. The additional message of agony to Adam's brain momentarily dazzled him with pain so intense that he almost blacked out. Coulet raised his hand again, and this time the bloodstained dagger would not miss.

But the double agent reckoned without Elise's fury and determination that this little worm of a man was not going to kill her beloved. Moving as quickly as her manacles would allow, she had seized the metal chamber pot—which happened to be empty, as her gaoler had emptied it when he brought her supper—from the corner of the cell and moved behind Coulet. With a shriek of rage, she struck downward with the pot against the back of Coulet's head.

He had moved just a trifle before the impact, enough that the heavy metal pot missed the more vulnerable back of his skull, striking the side of his head over one tender ear. Disbelieving that Elise had dared to act, his ears ringing with pain, Coulet heaved himself off Adam and turned to face his new attacker before she could hit him again.

Before he could harm Elise, however, and while Adam was rolling, intending to yank him off his feet, Coulet suddenly uttered a grunt of surprise and staggered. Then, a look of incredulity coming over his face, he fell headlong, a dagger buried to the hilt between his shoulder blades.

"I thought you might possibly be needing some help to get her away, so I came to check. A good thing, eh?" said Thomas of Clarence, striking in from the open doorway to kneel beside the dead man. After pulling his jewel-hilted dagger from the corpse, he casually pushed him off Adam.

"Your Grace, I will be forever grateful," Adam said, finally remembering to breathe.

"Nonsense, I merely finished what your brave spit-fire of a wife started," the duke murmured. "Had she not acted I would have been too late to save you, my friend. Now I think we had better hurry and strike off the lady's chains and get her away from here in case anyone else has heard the noise. Then we will get someone to stitch you up without talking about it, Saker," Clarence finished, pointing to the blood-soaked top of Adam's tunic.

"But the body—" Elise pointed out, shuddering.

"We'll see that it's not found until the wolves have gotten it," Thomas of Clarence said cheerfully. "No one will miss the vermin, anyway."

Five minutes later, her arms and legs wonderfully free of manacles, Elise made her way through the silent camp with Adam and the duke. Gilles, already sitting his pony and holding the reins of Elise's palfrey, was waiting in a grove of trees just inside a narrow break in the palisade that ringed the camp.

"*Mon Dieu,* I was so worried that something had happened to prevent you from coming, my lady!" he said in a harsh whisper, then caught sight of Adam. "But what has happened to milord? He looks in pain, no?"

"She'll tell you about it as you ride, Gippetty," Adam said, pain making his voice abrupt. "Right now the most important thing is to get your mistress far away from here before we are discovered. Here—take this purse. You'll be needing money."

"Yes, Sir Adam! You know I will do it!"

"Adam—" Elise whispered. What words could she say to convey her love for this man, who had risked his life to free her of her torment at parting from him? "I can't bear to leave you here! I think you should just come with me! Why stay and risk your part in this being found out?"

"I...can't," he managed, setting his jaw against the burning pain. "My...place is here...for now. Besides...can't ride like this...hold you back..."

"For God's sake, get going, Lady Saker!" commanded the duke in a harsh whisper. "Can't you see he won't be upright much longer?"

With a sob, not daring to put her arms around his neck, Elise gently drew his face down to hers and pressed a kiss to his lips. "Goodbye, my Adam. I will love you always."

"Go to Paris, darling," he said softly, his eyes gazing deeply into hers. "I will come for you there."

Hours later, as the first rays of dawn struck their path, they reined in their horses at a fork in the road. Gilles was surprised when Elise took the one that bore northeast, rather than the eastern one, marked in crude lettering, Paris.

"My lady," he called, spurring his pony to catch up with her, "shouldn't we be taking the other road? Sir Adam told you to go to Paris, did he not?"

Elise's eyes filled with tears. "Yes, but we are going to Rouen, Gilles. He hasn't thought this through, don't you see? It's over for us, it must be! If we stay together he'll be disgraced—he'll lose the king's favor, any chance he might have at lands and a title of his own! I—I can't let him do that, Gilles—he'd grow to resent what I cost him, and then his love would turn to hate! No, Gilles, we go to Rouen. We'll find my brother there, and the money Adam gave us will support us until I find work. I . . . I'll try to forget him." Without another word she spurred her horse forward.

"As if you could, my lady," Gilles said to himself, before following.

Chapter Nineteen

Rouen

Elise took an appreciative sniff of the aroma of roasting pork as she turned the haunch roasting over the fire. She felt the warmth of the flames heating her face.

It was so good to be warm again—really warm, as one could never be in a drafty, makeshift hut, or by a campfire. It was wonderful, also, to cook food that had been purchased in a market rather than bought from her sullen countrymen—or stolen, when necessary—plump poultry and haunches of venison, beef and pork, eggs, dried apples, bunches of onions braided together, beans, even precious spices. She loved the savory smells coming from the hearth these days, and Jean had told her that her face had lost the pinched and hungry look it had worn when she arrived with Gilles ten weeks ago.

She gave an involuntary shiver as she recalled their flight across war-torn Normandy to Rouen. Afraid that the English were pursuing them, they had shunned hostels and abbeys and dared only a small fire at night for cooking and warmth. Vulnerable, a woman attended only by a dwarf, they had kept to themselves, as afraid of being set upon by roving French brigands as by English soldiers. They had only breathed easily when they had crossed the Seine to Rouen just before New Year's Day.

It had not been difficult to locate Elise's brother. Her inquiry at the western gate into the city had caused the watch to send a messenger scurrying off to fetch Jean Jourdain, Captain of the Artillery. Minutes later she saw a horseman trotting down the narrow street toward the gate.

The man wore a breastplate over a knee-length tunic and a *sallet* helmet, one cut longer in the back. Dismounting, he swept off the latter, revealing a thatch of hair so blond it was almost white.

"Jean?" Now she had begun to tremble with uncertainty. Despite her determined words to Gilles when they had headed for Rouen rather than Paris, she was not at all sure she had made the correct choice. After all, there had been a coolness between her brother and herself ever since her marriage to the French knight, and no communication had been possible once she had left the Château de Vire. Now that she had come so far, what if Jean turned her away, totally indifferent to her fate?

His face, when he straightened, had been full of a wary pleasure.

"Elise! But what are you doing here in Rouen?" She could see his eyes taking in her dirty, travel-stained appearance, and the presence of Gilles, who stood holding the reins of their weary mounts.

Fortunately, she had been able to indicate with her eyes that she would prefer to postpone discussion of the events that had brought them here until they could do so privately. Elise did not wish to recite her tale in front of the curious soldiers who had gathered around them. That night, however, over supper at a nearby tavern, she had told him everything, beginning with her visit to court to offer her services against the English to the point at which she, accused of intent to murder the King of England, had escaped the English camp with the aid of Adam and the Duke of Clarence.

Jean's face had grown more and more troubled as she recited the saga, especially when she admitted that she had fallen deeply in love with the English knight she had married originally only to gain information. He had glanced often at the silent Gilles, sitting next to them, as if hoping he would contradict his mistress.

"Am I...do you think I am a very horrible person, Jean? Completely irredeemable?" she had asked, breaking at last the silence that stretched between them.

Jean had reached across the rough-hewn table for her hands and clasped them in his. "My poor, brave sister, how you must have suffered," he had said. "Did you think I would turn you away? Of course I will find you a place and you will stay in Rouen so I can look after you!"

So complete was her relief she had almost begun to weep, but Jean spoke again. "But what of this English knight? You are truly wed?"

Elise had nodded, a tear streaking down her cheek. All the pain she had kept at bay during the journey claimed her now. "Yes—but he'll have to forget me. It...it would never work...now. His only chance is to disavow me entirely, don't you see? He'd lose any favor of the king, any chance of advancement."

"As if I care about that cursed Englishman's retaining the king's favor," Jean had growled. "It's just as well you'll never see him again."

Elise had changed the subject before he could say anything more.

"Are you pleased to be Captain of the Artillery? I'm so proud of you, Jean."

He'd looked happy for a moment, then he had looked down at his hands and seemed to be struggling for the right words. "Naturally, what man would not, in my position? But I have to tell you, Elise, that I would rather have achieved it on my own, not merely because my sister was Burgundy's spy. *Peste!* Now I've hurt you."

"I'm sorry, Jean. I . . . I was just trying to help."

"You did, little sister, and I'm grateful, really," he said, awkward in his apology. "Now it is my turn to take care of you."

Jean had found her a small, comfortable house in the northwest part of the city. It was near the castle, his headquarters, which made it easy for him to take supper with her almost every night, doing the few chores for her that Gilles could not. When he was not on duty, he often slept there, in front of the fire.

At first, she and her brother were uneasy together, remembering the estrangement between them since she had become Lady de Vire. Soon, however, it was almost as if the rift between them had never been. It was wonderful to grow close again to the elder brother who had once been so dear to her, who had carried her on piggyback rides and shouldered the blame when she had broken her mother's favorite crockery bowl. She shared memories with him, and listened fondly as he told her how his commander, Guy le Bouteiller, trusted him with great responsibility.

But she didn't tell him she was carrying Sir Adam Saker's child.

Elise had only grown certain of it herself after missing her monthly flux for a second time. The first time she had ascribed it to the lingering fatigue that seemed to dog her steps after their perilous winter journey to Rouen. She had slept much, and her stomach had been strangely queasy when cooking the rich meats her brother relished. But now she found herself retching each morning the minute she lifted her head from the pillow, and she realized that passion-filled nights with Adam had resulted in a new life.

She could not seem to be sorry, though doubtless her state would bring its own complications in time, and she dreaded telling Jean. But the babe growing within her was all she would ever have of Adam, and she would treasure the little boy or girl and make it her whole world.

The thought made her smile and touch her belly, which was hardly rounded yet beneath the dress and apron she wore. There would be time yet before she had to share her precious secret with her brother, but already Gilles was looking at her oddly. She knew she would have to tell her shrewd little servant the truth soon, if he had not already guessed. And she would have to see how far the seams of the two dresses she had brought with her could be let out, she thought with a rueful grin, in the bodice as well as in the waist, for already her breasts were fuller and strained the material.

"Ah, what's that good smell that assails my nose as I pass by, dear lady?" came a voice through the door.

Elise inwardly cursed the window that she had unshuttered to let in the March sunlight and fresh air.

"'Tis my brother's supper, Captain Blanchard," she said levelly, facing the burly figure who had advanced into the room without waiting for an invitation.

Alain Blanchard, Captain of the Crossbowmen, was a big man, heavy-boned and handsome in a bluff, hearty sort of way, with slightly bulging blue eyes and drooping golden mustaches that partly concealed a full, sensual mouth. He had become aware of her when Elise visited once at the citadel, and quickly made it his business to discover that she was Jean's sister rather than his leman. From then on he had found frequent excuses to stop by the stone house near the castle, usually at times when Jean was not expected to be there.

"And when do we sup, my lovely Lady Elise? For I must have some of that roast pork, I must indeed, and while we wait for Jean, I will tell you how I have helped keep this city invulnerable to the English dogs."

He had made no secret of the fact that he found her attractive, and had begun dropping hints that he would even like to wed her—a distinct change for him, Jean had said dryly, for Blanchard had an eye for the ladies and usually had a mistress or two about the city. Elise could tell that Jean did not like his fellow captain, though he did not say so in so many words. Perhaps he thought he should not discourage her? *As if I were free to form any kind of honorable relationship, even if I liked this arrant braggart, which I do not!*

"We do not sup until much later, Captain, and I fear I have not invited you," she said firmly, turning back to stir the contents of a pot hanging over the fire.

Blanchard roared with laughter. "So tart and feisty! No wonder you survived your capture by the English!"

Elise was still wondering how much her brother had told Alain Blanchard about her time with the English when she felt Blanchard's hands on her shoulders, pulling her back against him.

"I like a woman with spirit, my beautiful Elise," he said, lifting her thick braid to drop a moist kiss on the back of her neck, while his other hand stole around to fondle her breast.

Immediately she wrenched free of him, snatching up the poker from the hearth. "I am not *your* beautiful anything, Captain Blanchard—"

"Please, call me Alain," he said in coaxing tones, still not convinced he had failed with her. His charm always worked with women. "You need not fear my intentions. I have been known as a devil with the wenches, yes, but you, *you* I would honor as my wife, *ma chère* Elise."

"Captain Blanchard," Elise reiterated, still gripping her weapon, "hard as it may be for you to believe, I want nothing to do with you. I do not look to marry, and I want nothing but to be left in peace."

"My lady, did you have need of me?" Gilles had entered silently from the back entrance. He had been sharpening knives out behind the house, and still—coincidentally?—clutched a long butchering knife.

Blanchard's high-colored face grew purple with fury as he stared at the servant, then back again at Elise.

"So—you think you're too good for me now that
you've been in a knight's bed, do you? Yes, Jean has
told me you were a widow of Agincourt, and were
forced to wed an English knight when Caen was taken,
only to be widowed again when he fell in battle."

Thus far, it was the story they had agreed upon, but
Blanchard wasn't finished. "What he hasn't told me,
though, I can fill in for myself! I'll warrant you've been
a whore for the English, haven't you? Yes, naught but
a whore, and the time will come when you'll be glad to
come to me on your knees! But you'll lie down for me
then without the benefit of a priest's blessing, *Madame* Elise!"

He turned on his heel and left the house, slamming
the door and leaving Elise white-faced with fury.

Chapter Twenty

Louviers

"Come on, let's go find a tavern and have a drink. I need one after witnessing that," Thomas of Clarence said grimly, turning from the gibbet with its dangling bodies.

"What are we celebrating, Your Grace? The execution of the Louviers gunners for doing their duty? Or merely the successful conclusion of another siege?" Sir Adam Saker retorted.

"Adam, my lad, you've grown as sour as an old crone, and about as much joy to drink with! How about celebrating the fact that you're back in good graces with the king, after saving his life? Did some angel whisper in your ear, and tell you to knock him down just in time to save him from the stone one of those poor sods shot at him from the walls? You certainly can't do any wrong now, as far as my royal brother is concerned!"

Adam shrugged, dismissing the lucky chance that had caused him to sense the direction of the shot and throw his sovereign to the ground. Henry had risen afterward, shaken to see how nearly he had missed certain death, and had vowed vengeance against the Louviers gunners, a vengeance he had achieved today, after the town had surrendered, by hanging every last gunner.

"If it hadn't been for your intervention in the winter, my liege, I might not have been around to serve the king. I'm mindful that you not only saved me and my lady from that knave, Coulet, but provided an alibi to shield me from the king's wrath when he discovered my wife's escape."

"Not that he believed it," Clarence said with a snort. "But it prevented him from venting his spleen on you before he'd had a chance to reflect. Now, of course, he has even more cause to be glad he didn't clap you in some convenient dungeon. Your star is definitely on the rise, m'boy."

"I am ever my sovereign's loyal servant," Adam said with heavy irony. "Lead on to the tavern, Your Grace." Perhaps he could drink enough strong wine that when he finally sought his pallet this even, he wouldn't dream.

His dreams were always the same. Elise, her flame-cloud of hair spread out beneath her, gazing up at him with love and passion . . . her eyes the green of emerald or jade, depending on the light and her mood, her hands, touching him, pulling him closer, her voice, sighing in his ear or whispering his name in that enchanting French-accented voice, *Ah-dom* . . . by the Mass! If only tonight he would not wake in the still of the night, reaching for her. . . .

He entered an establishment called La Tête du Loup in the duke's swaggering wake, but his mind was not on the sullen charms of the blowsy tavern wench, nor on the potent *ozey* she brought them. He was picturing Elise enjoying the summer sunshine in Paris. Was she thinking of him at this moment? Was she wakeful in the night, too, and did her body long for his touch as his longed for hers? Had the coins been enough to purchase her comfortable lodging? Would he find her easily when he finally went to Paris?

"Now that Louviers is ours, we should be at Rouen's gates in a month," the duke was saying. "And after Rouen, welladay! Nothing will lie between us and Paris!" He snapped his fingers, then grinned as Adam looked up, his previously unfocused gaze sharpening. "Ah, now I've got your attention! Paris is where you sent her, isn't it? Your secret's safe with me, and don't worry—we'll find a way to get Henry to accept her by then."

"Am I so transparent, then?" Adam found himself smiling in response to his liege's infectious optimism. "But I think Rouen will be rather a tough nut to crack compared to these other cities."

"Possibly, especially now that Burgundy's dropped his pose of working with Henry and has invested the city against him. But no one can stand against Henry's fanatic determination for long."

Rouen. Rouen and then Paris, at last.

Rouen

A warm July breeze caressed brother and sister as they strolled past L'Église de St. Ouen.

"You know, Elise, I believe Rouen is every bit as magnificent as Paris. Only consider, this church is only one of seventy here, and the merchants are famous for sparing no cost for their houses and guildhalls.''

He saw a worried expression furrow his sister's brow under her heart-shaped headdress.

''But Jean, how can you be so sure that Rouen can hold off the English? Don't forget, I've seen them besiege several Norman cities!''

Jean made an elaborate dismissive gesture. ''Bah! Argentan, Alençon and even Falaise are not the capital of Normandy! 'Tis the wealthiest city in France, sister, *and* the best defended, now that the Duke of Burgundy has taken it over! Why, Le Bouteiller has fifteen thousand militia, two thousand of them artillerymen at my command! The walls not only have dirt embankments behind them, but no less than sixty towers, each with three cannon aimed at all three angles—''

''Stop! Stop!'' Elise said, laughing, holding up her hand as if to ward off an attack. ''I'm quite dazzled by your figures, brother! 'Tis just that one can't ignore the facts—no city in their path was held out against the English yet, and I've told you how much Henry wants Rouen! Once this city is his, nothing stands between him and Paris!''

Privately, Jean was just as worried as his sister, but now that Elise was some six months gone with child, he felt he had to put a carefree face on matters. How could he admit to Elise, whose ripening figure now revealed her coming babe, that he lay awake nights, wondering if he had done the right thing to welcome his sister to Rouen? Even when she arrived it had been common knowledge that the enemy's eventual target was the Norman capital. If he had refused to accept her, would she have gone on to Paris as her English husband had told her, and be safe now, at least until Henry turned on Paris?

But no, he had been too joyful to see her after so long, too touched that she had sought him out, and now his affection for his sister might result in her being trapped in a besieged city! Would she have to experience starvation or, possibly worse, face the renewed wrath of the English king?

He had been hard put to conceal his dismay when she had finally admitted her pregnancy only a month ago. He had been teasing her about how well her new life in Rouen—with plenty of good Norman food—was agreeing with her, judging by the way she'd had to make herself new, looser gowns, when suddenly she had burst into tears and confessed she was with child by her English husband and expected to be delivered in the fall.

Jean could see that Elise thought he was disgusted by the thought of his sister bearing a half-English child. Perhaps she still thought so, although he had insisted it was just that he hated to see her bear her child without its father.

She had only smiled then, a madonnalike upcurving of her lips that suddenly made her more beautiful than ever before. "But you'll be there to be its devoted uncle, will you not, dear Jean? I'm sorry if it distresses you, but I cannot regret this coming babe." And then her green eyes had grown misty and faraway, and he knew she was thinking of the English knight who was forever lost to her.

Jean kicked at a loose cobble. If Elise could be safe he'd even be happy to know she was in England with her Englishman! By Saint Denis, no woman expecting a babe should have to face the horrors of a siege! He knew there was no chance that Henry's forces would turn aside from his beloved adopted city, and that they were every bit as formidable as his sister claimed.

Once, he had relished the idea of aiming Rouen's vast array of cannon at the English and proving that this city, at least, would not lie down and tamely submit to Henry of England! However, because of Elise's presence in Rouen, he now secretly hoped that le Bouteiller would surrender.

He felt a sudden tugging at his sleeve.

"Jean! In here!" whispered Elise suddenly, pulling him into one of the many cookshops that lined the streets.

"What is it? Are you hungry again, with supper just finished?" he teased, once they were both inside. Elise's frequently ravenous appetite had been a source of jests, once he was aware of its cause. But his sister did not look amused at present.

"No, I'm not hungry. 'Tis merely that I saw Captain Blanchard strolling down the street toward us, and I didn't desire to meet him."

"Has he been bothering you again? I'll run him through, I swear it!"

Elise laid a restraining hand on his sleeve. "Nay, he's not come to the house since that day I raised the poker at him, but sometimes I see him in the streets, Jean. He...he just *looks* at me...in that bold way he has...as if I were a strumpet for hire. I'm certain he noticed I was *enceinte*...and I heard him laugh as I walked on."

"That damned lecher! I won't leave him for the English to kill if he doesn't leave you alone. But Elise, mayhap you should stay in, now that the babe grows so big. Send Gilles on your errands.''

"I won't be driven indoors during the warmest time of the year while I can still get around,'' she insisted stubbornly. "'Twill be all too soon I'll be too big to do more than waddle around the house. Don't worry, I'll take Gilles wherever I go, when you're not there.''

"Very well, my willful wench of a sister. Just be careful and continue to avoid him.''

"I hear and obey, brother,'' she agreed with suspect meekness.

Jean wasn't fooled. Elise would do exactly as she pleased. She'd had to be responsible for herself for too long, with only minor assistance from that odd little dwarf. He supposed it was too late to expect her to be docile and submissive, but in truth Jean was proud of his sister's feisty nature.

He wasn't fooled, however, by her brave, breezy approach to the coming challenge of motherhood without a husband at her side. Jean often heard her footsteps on the floorboards overhead as she paced in her room late at night, or heard the rope mattress creak when she tossed restlessly in her bed. He saw the haunted pain in her eyes when she daydreamed about her English knight.

Jean was only just becoming reacquainted with Elise after years of separation, but he knew instinctively that after the babe was born, Elise would not settle for the attentions of some other, lesser man. He was glad that his sister did not find the bluff, hearty Alain Blanchard attractive, but it seemed sad that if Saker never reentered her life, there would be no room for any other lover, either.

* * *

Gilles ran back from the marketplace one morning in late July as if all the fiends of hell pursued him.

He found Elise sitting on a bench in the small, fenced-in private garden in back of the stone house, basking in the sunshine as she applied decorative stitching to tiny garments.

"My lady! The news is all over Rouen! Pont-de-l'Arche has fallen!"

Elise felt an icy stab of fear. "But how can that be? It's held by Burgundy's troops—and it's on the far bank of the Seine! Jean says they burned every boat anywhere near the city to keep the English from getting across, and that the crossing itself is protected by a fort with heavy cannon!"

"But it was done, Lady Elise. 'Tis said the English constructed little boats of leather and wicker, and then built a bridge on top of them!"

"Pont-de-l'Arche lies between Rouen and Paris...." Elise mused aloud. "That means—"

"We are cut off, my lady," the dwarf finished for her.

It was true. Honfleur, at the mouth of the Seine, above Rouen, had fallen in February. Pont-de-l'Arche was but several leagues downriver from Rouen itself. The noose was drawing tighter around the proud, prosperous capital of Normandy.

"Lady Elise, within days Rouen itself will be under siege. The gates will be closed, and no one will be able to get in or out. Farmers will be unable to bring in their produce from the countryside. Mistress, you must get out while you can! Do as Sir Adam suggested—ride for

Paris. I'll go with you and protect you, I swear it," Gilles promised.

Elise was moved by the earnest devotion lighting his features. Gilles was so good to her, never thinking of himself. He was indeed a guardian angel. And he was probably right about what she should do. But the torpor brought on by the growing babe and the summer sunshine made it hard to be very concerned about anything beyond the garden walls. Her world had narrowed so that the only thing that really mattered was the child. Adam's child.

"But Gilles, I am far too heavy to travel now!" she said with a light, self-deprecating laugh. "Even if Belle would consider such a heavy burden, I fear I just couldn't consider it. I do appreciate your faithfulness, though. I wouldn't blame you a bit, Gilles, if *you* wish to take your pony and go while you can."

Her servant ignored her suggestion. "If we left tonight we could still get out by the southeast gate. We'd travel in easy stages. Please, my lady, do as your lord wanted you to—"

"I'm not leaving, Gilles," Elise insisted in a voice she normally reserved for difficult merchants, thinking that would be the end of the matter.

But the dwarf had obviously anticipated her obstinance, and took another tack. "Lady Elise, Clarence was the commander who took the fort," he told her. "That means Sir Adam himself is but a few leagues away. If you won't go to Paris, let us go to him and seek his protection for you outside Rouen. He would do it, my lady, you know he would! Even if he had to do it secretly! He loves you, and would want you and his babe to be safe above all things!"

Mention of Adam almost undid Elise's carefully held control. Adam, her love, the father of the being who even now kicked at her ribs, a child he didn't even know existed. How wonderful it would be to present herself to him, even large and ungainly as she looked now, and know that he would die before he would let any harm befall her and his child.

Exactly. He would give up his own life to save hers. He almost had, in rescuing her from the king's wrath and Coulet's treachery. Even assuming Henry had believed the alibi given him by the Duke of Clarence, Adam had put in peril any chance of prospering in the service of the king, any chance of advancement. If he was discovered aiding his traitorous French wife, no one would be able to protect him this time. Perhaps Adam had already forgotten her, and that was best. If he still thought of her occasionally, let him think she was still in Paris until it was too late. Someday he would see her for what she must be to him—a mistake he had once made and would not make again.

The tiny garments lay forgotten at her side. Elise felt the stinging of tears in her eyes as she looked up from where her hands were spread in an unconscious gesture of protection over her belly.

"I can't do that to him, Gilles. I love Sir Adam, I always will, but for his own good, he must be allowed to go on without me."

The dwarf's face crumpled in protest, and Elise held up a peremptory hand. "I mean it, Gilles. No more."

When Jean joined them for supper that evening, he had heard the news, and added his pleas to those of Gilles that Elise flee for safety while she could.

"There's going to be a *siege,* sister, and no easy capitulation as at those other Norman cities. Food is
suddenly going to grow very scarce, especially with all
the refugees within the walls who have fled the English
advance! I've even heard talk of putting them out and
concentrating on feeding Rouen's own first!" At
Elise's look of alarm, he hastily added, "Of course, as
my sister, you would be exempt from such action, but
I still think you should go, Elise!"

Jean, however, met with no greater success at per-
suading her than Gilles had. Elise was unconvinced
that the Rouennais would consider such an unchris-
tian action, or that if worse came to worst, that the
citadel would try to hold out against the English. They
would see the handwriting on the wall and surrender,
and then she had merely to stay within the cottage so
that Adam would not chance to find her. If Rouen was
conquered, the English would soon go on to Paris, for
Henry's bride awaited him there.

In any case, Elise was adamant. She would stay in
Rouen, come what might.

Chapter Twenty-One

Resigned to his sister's stubborn refusal to leave, Jean wasted no further energy in argument. After withdrawing a purse of saved coins from a hiding place in the citadel, he gave the coins to Gilles and directed the dwarf to spend every sou buying up foodstuffs, especially flour. Prices had already risen as rumors flew around the city, but it was still possible to buy even poultry and swine as local farmers sold their stock before fleeing eastward.

Still six weeks or more from her confinement, Elise was tormented by the summer heat, even when she stayed within the relative coolness of the stone house. Plagued by swollen ankles and the periodic cramps of false labor, she was able to do little more than sit and long for the evening to bring partial relief from the sun's rays. Somewhat to her surprise, Gilles had not taken advantage of her permission to leave Rouen, and now he prepared the simple meals she was too weary to cook.

They ate less than before, ever mindful of the coming siege, but the dwarf would not let his mistress reduce her portions very much. The babe needed it, he said, urging her to drink the milk from the cow he had purchased and brought home after dark recently; it wouldn't do to have too many know they had it, Gilles said.

The dwindling peace did not last more than a fortnight. Rouen awakened on the first of August to find that the English had surrounded the city.

Now Jean, as Captain of the Artillery, was expected to remain at the citadel night and day, even though the English seemed more inclined to try to starve Rouen out than to batter her with cannon. He kept messages of encouragement coming to his sister, though, through Gilles.

Frantic at the confirmation of his darkest fears, the dwarf renewed his pleas that Elise seek out Adam for protection. Did she not see that there was nothing else to do, he asked, now that Rouen was blockaded?

Did *he* not see why she could not do that? she would retort, until finally, one hot August day, she stamped her foot and forbade her servant to mention it again. He had been free to leave, she reminded him; he still could, if he felt it was worth the risk.

When she awoke the next morning, the dwarf was gone, as was his pony from the small barn out back.

She shrugged, fighting back tears, and said a prayer that Gilles le Petit would be safe. She had heard terrible stories of atrocities perpetrated by Irish kerns, mercenaries who had joined the English encampment around Rouen. Dressed in little more than tunics, they killed indiscriminately from the backs of their ponies as they foraged the countryside. *Please, St. Denis, do not let Gilles fall into such hands.* Perhaps his diminutive size would aid him in escaping the enemy.

Elise learned that a woman nearby served as the neighborhood midwife, and she had already met her, a cheerful, apple-cheeked woman named Clothilde. She lived on the far side of the square, within sight of Elise's house, in a dwelling thronging with children of her own. It was comforting that Clothilde lived so close; confidence-building that after giving Elise a brisk, businesslike examination, the midwife had said she should bring forth her child with a minimum of fuss.

Anxious to keep the midwife's goodwill, Elise did not tell her that the father of the babe was an English knight; Clothilde had somehow come to the conclusion that she was the widow of a common Burgundian soldier, and Elise was content to let her go on thinking so.

One afternoon she was surprised to receive a visit from the midwife.

"Nothing yet, Clothilde," she greeted her neighbor, after making her way slowly to the door and inviting her in with a gesture.

"Nay, I thought not," said the woman cheerfully, as she entered the hall, "since ye had not sent for me, but I'd been thinkin', my girl. Since you're all alone here, with yer brother defendin' the city and all, why not do yer lyin' in at my house? Nay, 'tis no trouble—I could watch over ye better *and* keep my brood free o' trouble easier that way, d'ye see? Ye could stay with us from the first pang up until ye've recovered from the birth and could cope with the babe and all."

"But however would you make room for me with all your children?" asked Elise, amused at the woman's enthusiasm, "and how could I pay you? I have very little money...."

"Nor do any of us, *ma petite*," Clothilde said, waving away her protest. "But I thought as how you had that cow in the shed with yer horses, and how good it would be for my babes to have some milk, that with the blockade and all..."

So that was it. Gilles's cow had not been very "secret" after all. But how could a creature that lowed whenever she needed milking remain a secret in a hungry city? The midwife had seen a way to feed her children at the same time as she helped Elise bring her babe into the world, and why not? Doubtless they would all have to find ways to help one another survive the siege. Elise resolved to surprise the midwife by also bringing some of the food she had hidden beneath a loose stone in the hearth, but some would have to remain there for after her confinement.

And so the bargain was struck. Elise would go to stay with Clothilde when her labor began, while one of Clothilde's older boys kept watch over the stone house, tended the cow and Elise's palfrey and kept Jean informed.

The pains began gradually one night in the third week of September, waking Elise from an uneasy sleep with their nagging grind in her lower back, a dull ache that spread around her flanks to her swollen abdomen in periodic waves that left nausea in their wake.

She remained in her own bedchamber until dawn, not wanting to wake Clothilde's household by demanding entrance in the middle of the night. Then, as she walked the short distance across the square, her water broke, so she arrived at the midwife's house with the first rays of the sun, the bottom of her skirt drenched, with moisture trickling down onto her feet.

Her labor began in earnest then. Doubling over with the force of the first real contraction, she waited outside the house, listening to the woman run to the door in response to her pounding. How was she ever going to survive several hours of this? she thought dizzily. And then Clothilde was there, opening the door, exclaiming sympathetically over Elise's white face.

Shooing away a host of children of various ages and stages of undress, the midwife ushered her to a bedchamber that had been cleared of other occupants. After Clothilde assisted her to undress, Elise gratefully headed toward a straw-filled mattress covered with clean linen.

"Nay, that's for after," Clothilde informed her. "Ye must walk now, if ye want to have this babe afore midnight tonight."

"Midnight?" gasped Elise, as the next pain washed over her.

"Oh yes, most times the first birth takes very long, days sometimes, but walking hastens matters," the midwife said with exasperating cheerfulness. "And yon is the birthing stool, for when the babe comes," she added, pointing to a low chair with a large hole cut in the seat, and leather grips for her hands on the arms.

She had dim memories of such a piece of furniture at Château de Vire, which her sister-by-marriage had already used twice before Elise left, but Elise had not been present for the births. She had not begun her duties as nursemaid until the wetnurse had first given them suck. Then Elise had been invited in to coo over her niece and nephew while Bertrice de Vire was lying in smirking's triumph in the great bed—the bed that had been Aimeri and Elise's.

Oh, Adam, where are you? Elise thought later that afternoon. She would give her soul to have him at her side at this moment, walking with her, holding her up when she faltered, encouraging her to keep walking when the ripping agony threatened to swamp her, promising her that there would be an end. She was unaware that at the height of her pains, she had called out his name more than once, causing the midwife to regard her curiously, for "Adam" was not a French name. But Clothilde was used to women in travail crying nonsense.

By suppertime Elise could no longer walk, and after somewhat crossly telling her children that their meal would be a little delayed, Clothilde at last gave her charge permission to sit on the birthing stool and push.

Her son was born just at dusk, several hours short of the predicted midnight, with a head of raven-dark hair making its way first into the world.

"'Tis a boy, Elise, a fine boy, small but well formed, and with a good set o' lungs, as ye can hear for yerself," Clothilde told her, briskly wrapping the infant in his first swaddling clothes before putting him to his mother's breast.

"His name is Thomas," Elise murmured. It was a good name for a half-English, half-French boy, for it was used by both nations. No one but Adam or Gilles could have appreciated the irony that it was in tribute to the royal duke whose intervention had helped saved her life. Pleased that the babe's coloring favored his dark-haired father, and guessing that the cloudy blue eyes would soon turn dark like Adam's, she fell asleep.

"You'll make a fine monk, Lucien," Adam told the young man from Brittany as he put the final touches on the tonsure he had shaved.

"My thanks, Sir Adam," the Breton replied, rolling his eyes ruefully at the pile of tow-colored locks that lay at his feet. "I had no idea when His Grace of Brittany sent me to serve his ally that I would be required to go to such lengths."

"Ah, 'twill grow back in no time," Adam reassured him, "and you'll be suitably rewarded for performing an invaluable service. We need to get a man inside St. Catherine's Abbey, so we can gain control of the Paris road, and that requires a Frenchman. I don't think the monks would believe that my squire, here, is a monk from a brother house in Brittany—his French is still dreadful. And they certainly would be too suspicious of an emissary from an English monastery at this time."

Harry, standing by the entrance of his master's tent, grinned good-naturedly. "I told Sir Adam I was perfectly willing to try it, though I'm just as glad to keep my pate covered," he said, rubbing the top of his red head meaningfully. "But I speak French like a native, now that Lady Elise—"

"Lucien will be too polite to disagree with you, I'm certain," Adam snapped. Suddenly aware that his master's foul humor had been pricked by the careless reference to his wife, Harry quickly found something to do outside the tent.

Adam himself wondered if he was cross merely because he had been plagued with feeling so ill at ease about Elise of late. For months he had taken refuge in pleasant visions of her safe in Paris, waiting for him; now these images seemed clouded with feelings of foreboding.

Or was his bad mood also caused by the necessity of once again trusting a Frenchman to be a reliable agent? His experience with the treacherous double agent, Denis Coulet—not to mention the shock of finding out that Elise had been a spy—had made him wary of putting his faith in Frenchmen, however good their reasons were for aiding the English.

Could he trust Lucien, one of a handful of Bretons who had thrown in their lot with the English as mercenaries, after the treaty signed by their duke and King Henry? He would have to, he supposed. The ring around Rouen could not be complete until the English controlled the road to Paris that ran right by the fortified abbey. The English needed an agent in St. Catherine's who could be counted on to let in a sufficient force by the postern gate to wrest control from the militant monks. Adam had managed to obtain a black monk's robe, sandals and rope belt, but as he had said, the monks at St. Catherine's would hardly trust a monk with an English accent.

"Shall I go then, Sir Adam?" the Breton mercenary-turned-monk questioned, standing near the tent flap.

"Yes, I suppose you're as ready as you'll ever be. Go with God."

Lucien turned, raising his hand as if blessing his spymaster, then gave a cheeky wave and was gone.

With the agent sent on his way, Adam thought he'd change from his wool tunic and join the Earl of Salisbury's work force nearby as they toiled to clear the roads approaching Rouen. The city's defenders had left felled trees and boards with protruding nails on the roads to slow their enemies' progress; these entanglements were obvious, but the caltrops, small four-pointed metal devices that always had at least one point sticking up out of the dirt, were the real hazard. A fellow knight's war-horse had stepped squarely on one, driving the metal point straight up into the tender frog area of his hoof, and had been lamed. Adam certainly did not want to see that happen to Alastor.

And perhaps an afternoon spent in hard work would make it possible to sleep tonight without waking dreams of Elise.

"Sir Adam, you have a visitor," he heard Harry say as he was in the middle of pulling the fur-trimmed woolen tunic over his head. Now who could that be? It was too early to expect his courier back from Paris.

He pulled the tunic back over his head, not wishing to receive a visitor in just a shirt. He was astonished by the sight of the small figure standing in front of him.

"Gippetty! What do you here?"

Chapter Twenty-Two

"I am come from my mistress. She needs your help, Sir Adam," Gilles said, peering up at him.

"You have come from Paris? Why, what is the matter? Is she not safe there?"

"She would probably be, if indeed she were there, milord," the dwarf said wryly, "but as she would not listen to either of us, she is in Rouen, and has been ever since she left you."

"In *Rouen?*" Adam repeated, thunderstruck. "Whatever is she doing in Rouen? I told her—"

"To go to Paris. Yes, I know. *She* knew. But she insisted that you must forget her, for your own good. You would have no chance of advancement, and might even lose your knighthood and be outlawed if you insisted on remaining loyal to her." He repeated it as a lesson learned by rote. "And so she went to Rouen to her brother, Jean, and he found her a place to live."

"But she can't stay there! We have cut off the city. King Henry won't be satisfied until they starve or submit!"

The dwarf nodded tolerantly until he finished. "Everyone in Rouen knows that they are under siege.

Don't you think I begged her to leave? I argued, I cajoled, I threatened, Sir Adam. But there are limits beyond which a servant cannot go. Finally, she became too big to travel—"

"What are you saying, 'too big to travel'?" Adam shouted, a horrible thought taking shape in his mind.

"She is carrying your child, and will be brought to bed of it any day now," Gilles le Petit said matter-of-factly.

Adam whirled from him, grabbing a pewter plate from the table and throwing it against the wall where it rebounded with a ringing clang and fell with a thunk into the rushes. "How convenient! She goes where she had always planned to go, meets her lover and gets with child, and now she needs *my* help to escape from the consequences of her folly!"

"You damned fool of an Englishman! Can't you count?" shouted Gilles, every bit as loud as Adam for all his diminutive size. "There is no lover, and never was! The babe is *yours*, you fool! Count back on your fingers if you must! Is it not a fact that you lay with her just before Christmas? *And now it is nearly nine months later,* and the babe will soon come. It is *yours*, Sir Adam," he repeated.

Adam sat down heavily as the truth of it struck him, his eyes unfocused, his shoulders slumping. "So Elise is trapped in a blockaded city, where food will soon be nonexistent, about to give birth to my child. Gippetty, I must get her out!"

The little man raised his arms heavenward. "Thanks be to God, I have gotten through your thick skull, milord! When can you leave? I will show you where she is!"

"Nay, just tell me where she may be found and I will go alone. Your size makes you too noticeable, my small friend. Besides, you look none too well fed yourself. I'll tell Harry to bring you some food. Just stay out of sight until I return."

"Oh, thank you, Sir Adam!"

"'Tis naught, you certainly look as if you need it—"

"Nay. I don't mean for food, though of course I'm grateful," the dwarf said, coming to kneel in front of him and taking Adam's hand to his lips before he could stop him. "'Tis that I can see that you still love my lady." Gilles's eyes were liquid with tears.

Adam's heart thumped painfully within him. "Yes, I love her, Gippetty, I really do. Always and forever."

The king received Adam immediately, thinking he had some reconnaissance report to present.

"Nay, Your Grace, though I have today sent our agent Lucien the Breton to infiltrate St. Catherine's. What I have come to tell you is that I must go into Rouen myself. I must . . . there is something I must see that cannot be reported to us in words," he finished, hoping for once Henry's all-seeing hazel eyes did not penetrate to the truth of his motives.

The king sat back in his camp chair, clearly surprised. "But is it truly necessary that *you* go, Sir Adam? When you agreed to become the head of our espionage network, we said we hoped putting yourself personally at risk would not be required. And now you come and tell us you *wish* to go behind the lines?"

"It . . . it is necessary, Your Grace," was all Adam trusted himself to say.

Henry made a tent of his fingers, studying Adam. Adam forced himself to return the level gaze steadily.

"Do you go immediately?"

"Yes, Sire. As soon as I may exchange my garments for some more . . . shall we say, nondescript?"

Elise had never been so exhausted, or so happy, as she was in the days immediately following Thomas's birth. She had not imagined there could be as perfect an infant as little Thomas Saker. He cried briefly, he nursed, he slept, all in an endlessly repeating cycle that left her tired but content. Her world had narrowed to the confines of Clothilde's noisy but happy household; if Thomas's stomach was full, and he was dry and warm, she was content. It no longer seemed to matter that outside, Rouen's citizens felt the rising panic of a coney as the snare tightens around its neck.

"Ah, the wee darling," cried Clothilde, gazing in delight as Thomas suckled at midday. "Such a handsome boy already! Was your late husband swarthy like that, did you say?"

"I didn't say," Elise said, keeping her eyes on Thomas's raven's-wing black hair so that the midwife could not see the pain within. "But yes, yes, he—was."

"Ah, ye miss him, do ye not?" Clothilde clucked sympathetically. " 'Twill get easier in time, though yer heart may ache a bit as the boy grows to look more and more like him. But he'll be a comfort to ye."

Elise nodded, already feeling the ache. She had not known it would hurt this bad, to want to share this little wonder with Adam and know that she had made the choice not to. She hadn't realized how much she would want to say, "Look, love, he has your eyes, but I think 'tis my nose. See, love, how fiercely he wrinkles his face just before he cries!'' It would almost be easier if she were, in fact, the widow she claimed to be. Then her heart would stop reminding her that Adam was probably just outside the city, and would move heaven and earth to get to her and the babe if he but knew they were there.

Elise realized she had been happy in this house. Clothilde and her large brood showed her more genuine caring than her brother- and sister-by-marriage ever had, even right after Aimeri's death! The children, all eight of them, had made a pet of little Thomas and competed with one another to hold him and amuse him, almost as if they were not familiar to the point of boredom with infants from caring for one another. The middle girl, in a supreme sacrifice, had even contributed her rag doll to the cause of Thomas's pleasure.

Clothilde never mentioned her own husband, who after giving her eight children had taken up with a trollop on the other side of Rouen, though apparently he brought her a few coins from time to time. No one in the household, however, seemed to notice the lack of him, and they had lived comfortably enough on the money Clothilde earned with her midwifery.

Satisfied, the babe stopped suckling now and released the nipple, his small body already relaxing in slumber. Elise, sitting on a daybed in front of the open window in the main room, had begun to set him down beside her when she heard a knocking at the front entrance. The midwife went to the door. Probably 'twas some distraught husband, saying his wife's time had come and Clothilde was needed.

"Elise, you have a visitor," Clothilde called.

It must be Jean, she thought, raising her hands to lace up her bodice. It would be pleasant to see him, though it was a shame the babe had just dropped off to sleep. Thomas was such a good baby that his proud uncle had rarely seen him awake, but Elise was glad her brother could take a few minutes' rest from the responsibilities of his position.

Perhaps she could talk to him about helping her move back to her own cottage across the square. As much as she liked this kind, energetic family, she longed for the peace of her own place. Clothilde had urged her to stay for a month, but Elise was not sure if she really needed to, or if Clothilde wanted to ensure the continued advantage of the milk cow. No matter, she would tell the midwife she could use as much milk as her family needed.

"A beautiful infant, *Lady* Elise," said a voice, not Jean's.

Her eyes flew up to behold the beefy face of Alain Blanchard, smirking now as his avid eyes watched her shaking hands complete the lacing of her bodice.

"Well met, *madame.*"

"Blanchard! What are you doing here? How did you find me—did Jean tell you?" she asked, angry at the flush of embarrassment she felt creeping up from her neck. She couldn't imagine her brother informing this hateful man of her location, but it might have slipped out accidentally.

He laughed hugely, enjoying her discomfiture. "That closemouthed prig? Of course not," he retorted. "He said you'd gone to stay with friends since his duties kept him at the citadel so much of late. But I'm no fool—I saw you prancing through the streets, bold as brass with your growing belly, and one night I followed him when he came here. Aye, and even saw the proud uncle holding up his—what, madame, a nephew or a niece?—before they shuttered the window.''

" 'Tis a boy,'' she admitted through clenched teeth. "But I fear you must excuse me, sir. I do not feel up to having visitors. The birth of the babe has tired me, and I must rest when he does.''

"Nay, 'tis not lying about you need, but fresh air, my fair one, to restore the roses to your pale cheeks! Faugh! The air stinks of onions in here, and worse!'' he announced, indicating the cloths drying on a line in front of the fire. "Just come for a stroll with me.''

"I am not going anywhere with you, Blanchard.''

He leaned close, and she could smell the wine fumes on his breath.

"I think you will, Elise, or I'll tell your friend that her houseguest is naught but a whore for the enemy, and her brat a half-English bastard. Then you'll not only be unwelcome here, but anywhere in Rouen, I'll warrant.''

Elise winced, hoping Clothilde was not pressed against the door of the other room, eavesdropping. "Thomas is more trueborn than you will ever be! But very well, a stroll around the square, naught more. And I am bringing the babe,'' she added, thinking Blanchard would be less able to attempt mischief if she carried Thomas.

He scowled, but could not argue without admitting dishonorable intentions. "Very well, bring him.''

"Ah, what a good idea!'' Clothilde exclaimed when Elise went to tell her. " 'Twill do you good, some sunlight and a stroll with a handsome man! But take your shawl, dear, there's a breeze." The midwife's pleased voice reassured Elise that she had not been eavesdropping.

It had been good to get out, despite her companion. Elise had not realized how stale the air inside the crowded house had become, nor how she'd missed the kiss of the sunlight on her cheeks, or the sight of the blue sky. There was a feeling of autumn in the air. Even baby Thomas seemed to appreciate the change, for he smiled in his sleep.

They had nearly completed the circuit around the square. Elise had been able to check on the house Jean had rented for her, at least from the outside; the lock still held in their absence. Now, as she and Blanchard drew near to the midwife's house, Elise looked back across the square, longing to be living there again, if only there was no threat of Blanchard calling uninvited. Perhaps she had better remain with Clothilde after all!

Then she looked again, shielding her eyes with her hand. "There's someone over at my house," she murmured, stopping Blanchard.

A man, clad in breeches and a short hood over his shirt, had just approached the house, and was knocking at the door. With his back to her, all Elise could see was that he was tall. Probably just someone asking directions, or for food, and yet for all his humble clothing he did not carry himself like a beggar. Then he left her doorstep and tried to peer through a crack in the shutters, and she caught a glimpse of an aquiline nose and lean, high cheekbones.

"Adam?" she whispered aloud, her companion forgotten. Her heart began to pound as she became more certain that it was indeed Adam Saker across the square. Then she realized she had spoken aloud.

"'Adam'?" Blanchard repeated, following her eyes. "'Tis not a French name, I think . . . ah, can it be that your English lover seeks to rescue you from this besieged city?"

She was not quick enough to prevent the shock and fright that flashed across her face and confirmed his suspicions.

"I see that I am right. 'Tis brave of him to come, my beautiful Elise, but foolish. After all, he might be caught and executed for a spy."

"Nay...I was mistaken," she said, striving to sound casual. "I thought 'twas someone I knew, but 'tis likely just a beggar. Thank you for this outing, and—" She had to get rid of Blanchard, and then catch up with Adam before he left the area!

"I don't believe you. In here, *madame,* right now, and be silent if you would have your babe remain alive." He yanked her into the narrow passageway between Clothilde's house and her neighbor's and drew the dagger at his belt. He clutched her, still holding the babe against him with one arm, while the other held the dagger poised a bare two inches from Thomas's soft body. There was no way she could struggle free without risk to the babe.

He peered around the building at the man across the square.

"Very good, *madame.* Now you are to go into the house without looking back, and do not come out no matter what happens, if you want your child." Roughly he pulled the shawl up over her distinctive hair, then shoved her out of the passageway.

Trembling with rage and fear, she walked over to Clothilde's house, looking neither to the right nor the left, achingly aware of the imminent danger for Adam, and that there was no way she could warn him.

The door was slammed behind her. Then, through the open window in the main room, she heard Blanchard's hoarse cry: "The watch! To me, the watch! An English spy! I have found an English spy! Don't let him get away!"

Chapter Twenty-Three

Where can she be? Adam went back to the door and pounded on it as if the very intensity of his knocking could cause her to appear when it had not before. He was certain he had followed the dwarf's directions exactly, and the small gray stone house certainly matched the description Gilles had given him.

He was deep in thought as to what to do next when the cry went up from across the square. A burly man across the square was pointing straight at him! Simultaneously the meaning of the French words, *un espion*, sank into his brain, and without conscious thought he began running.

How had the man spotted him? he wondered dazedly as he dashed down one of the narrow side streets that led off the square. His russet breeches, shirt and the short hood that covered his head and shoulders were the same sort worn by any French peasant. What telltale clue had revealed his Englishness beneath the anonymous disguise?

Looking back over his shoulder, he saw that his spotter was in hot pursuit. He stopped thinking about anything but escape. Adam had never been in Rouen

before; he knew nothing of it but the map he had
studied in Henry's quarters and the crude drawing
Gilles had made. Now, as he concentrated on merely
outdistancing his pursuer, landmarks were forgotten
and the narrow cobbled streets lined by tall old buildings became a sinister maze.

Adam felt no panic as yet. He was lean and agile
compared to the thickset, already panting Frenchman,
who was wasting precious energy bellowing for the
watch. Surely he could outrun him long enough to lose
him, especially if the other man was unsuccessful in
summoning help.

Behind him, he heard a trio of men coming down a
street that intersected his, calling out questions.
"Halte-là!" Adam heard a new voice call. There was
an end to that hope!

He had come in over the wall by cover of darkness
and hidden his grappling hook and rope under a pile of
refuse near the wall, but it was not an escape route that
could be taken in broad daylight with men close behind him baying like a pack of hounds. Even if he
could lose them, the men-at-arms patrolling the walls
would sight him and put a crossbow bolt through his
back before he could even drop to the ground on the
other side. He would have to wait for nightfall—but
first he had to evade his pursuers and find a hiding
place.

He plunged down one street after another, realizing
he was running deeper into Rouen and becoming
hopelessly lost. Once, when he looked over his shoulder again, he ran straight into an elderly man, knocking him flat. There was no time to be chivalrous; calling
an apology over his shoulder, he ignored the indignant

burgher's curses and hoped his pursuers would be delayed by the man's sprawled body.

The lucky accident helped; he heard them stop to assist the graybeard, all shouting questions at the old man at once. Fortunately for Adam, the burgher was deaf as a post, and their queries delayed them vital seconds. Once they resumed the chase, they were not far behind, but they'd lost sight of him.

His lungs burned as he tried to draw breath. His sweat was at once hot and chilling as it trickled down between his shoulder blades. So this is how a roe deer feels chased by baying hounds, he thought, hearing more voices calling out from nearby streets, joining the pack. "A spy! An English spy! He's dressed in humble russet, but too tall and muscular to be a peasant!"

Coming to the end of a street, he was offered the choice of turning right or left. The symbolism of turning right appealed to him, but he thought he could smell the river that way. Therefore, that way was south, away from where he'd come over the wall and hidden his rope. He was not sure, but he had no time to debate. The "hounds" were not far behind. He turned left.

The street he had chosen twisted and turned, winding past houses and shops, but offering no side streets leading off it. He rounded a bend and suddenly realized it was a blind alley!

Trapped! He heard them behind him, though the bend hid him from their sight as yet. In a moment, they would come around it and be on him, fists flying, making the hours before they hanged him from the battlements a foretaste of hell.

Desperate, he ran up to a door, praying it was not locked, and when it gave at his shove, he slipped inside.

He heard a gasp as he stood there, panting.

"Who's there?" a voice quavered from the far side of the room, over by the hearth where a single log burned smokily. As he peered through the dim light, his eyes made out a white-haired woman huddled in a chair by the fire.

"Who's there?" she called again. "I'm blind—take what you want, fellow, but please don't hurt me!"

"I mean no harm, goodwife," he said softly, praying his accent would not cause the old woman to run screaming for the door. "I'm just a beggar who got caught stealing a capon from a merchant's pantry. I dropped the bird, but they won't give up! Of your mercy, good woman, please don't give me away—they'll cut off my hand for sure."

Outside, he heard his pursuers run past the house and stop, puzzled, calling to one another: "Didn't he come this way? I'm certain I heard him turn this way! You, Jacques, take Hébert with you and take the other turning, while we search these houses and make sure he's not hiding within—"

"Please, *madame*, they will be knocking on your door in a moment! Is there somewhere I can hide? God will reward you for your mercy—"

"Down there," the woman indicated, pointing to a trapdoor near the hearth. Lifting it, he found it led down into a cellar, and while he stood poised in the cool darkness just beneath the trapdoor, he heard the old woman scoot her chair directly over it. Moments later, there came a pounding at the door, and she called permission to the watch to enter. Adam prayed a silent blessing on the old woman's head as he heard her denying that anyone had entered her dwelling in the past few minutes.

The blind old widow had listened to Adam's grateful thanks, then insisted on sharing the pottage she had simmering over the fire. Soon afterward she had fallen into a snoring slumber in her chair by the hearth, leaving Adam hours to ponder his narrow escape and wonder if he would yet manage to leave Rouen alive.

There was even a moment or two, as the afternoon deepened into evening, when he wondered if he had been recognized as a spy because Elise had seen him and raised the alarm. Had he been a fool to believe that the Frenchwoman he loved could love him more than her country?

Then he cursed himself for a doubting idiot, crazed by fear. Elise would not do such a thing. He trusted what the dwarf had told him. His beloved had come to Rouen because of the very unselfishness of her love for him. Elise believed that the price of loving her was more than Adam should have to pay.

But where was she?

"I believe it is best that you move back to your own house, *madame,* as soon as may be," Clothilde said to Elise that evening after her children had gone to their beds and Thomas slumbered in his cradle. "While I do not believe you are to blame in any of Captain Blanchard's accusations, my neighbors heard what he said of you when he returned after failing to capture the Englishman. I have my children to think of, after all."

Elise nodded dully, knowing the midwife did as she must. "I am grateful for all you have done for me, Clothilde. I shall move my belongings in the morning."

She felt numb. The fear she had felt while watching Adam flee from the square had threatened to overwhelm her until the captain returned to the midwife's house hours later, frustrated and angry that the spy had eluded them. He had denounced Elise from the doorstep, drawing a curious crowd who had eyed Elise afterward with angry suspicion.

Tomorrow would be time enough to worry about living alone, now she was branded as "the Englishman's whore." Now she could only thank God that Adam had apparently escaped.

"So you went to the house the dwarf told you about, and there was no sign of her?" Thomas of Clarence repeated, passing Adam a cup of mulled wine that he had just stirred with a heated poker. The spicy smell rose to greet Adam's nostrils, but he didn't notice; he was nearly too tired to lift the cup to his lips.

Adam nodded, lying on his side on the camp bed. "Aye, and the next thing I knew the hue and cry had gone up and I was running for my life." He went on to tell the duke how he had hidden in the old woman's house until it was safe to go back over the wall the way he'd come. "By the saints, I don't know how I gave myself away, Your Grace!"

"You don't think your Frenchwoman—"

"I've thought of it," Adam cut him off, "but nay, Elise did not play me false. Sooner would I believe that someone here in camp betrayed me, and I don't really believe that now that Coulet is dead. But what haunts me is this—if she's not there, where *is* she? Where did she go?" He set down his cup, and seized the duke's hands. "Your Grace, you must intercede with your royal brother and obtain permission for me to go back into Rouen. I must search till I find her! Unfortunately, the king saw my bedraggled state as I returned to camp, and I was forced to tell him just how close I had come to capture. Now he refuses me permission to try again! No reconnaissance information could be that important, he says, and of course I dare not tell him I am seeking my wife, a woman he believes to be a spy and assassin!"

"If Henry's made up his mind to forbid you to go, then you must accept that," Thomas of Clarence said, but eyeing the distraught knight, he kept his tone gentle.

"But, Thomas," Adam argued, dropping the title as he did on rare occasions, "Gippetty said she's carrying my babe! She's probably given birth by now! How can I rest, not knowing whether they live, or if she died in childbed? How can I leave them there to die of starvation?"

"If you didn't find her there, Saker, then she must have gotten out of Rouen," the duke said reasonably. "She probably realized the sense of the little man's words right after he left, and did likewise. Yes, I'm sure that's it!" he added, seeing Adam's doubtful face. "She seemed like a resourceful woman, your Elise. I imagine she made it to Paris somehow, or some safe refuge, and is even now seeking a way to inform you."

Adam sipped his wine, unconvinced. Surely, if Elise had died, he would feel it, deep in his soul, and he felt no such desolation. Give me a sign, he begged, not sure whether he was pleading with God or Elise.

Chapter Twenty-Four

As autumn waned, the English army settled into the business of a siege. The mighty cannons were silent; Henry meant to wear Rouen down, not batter her into submission.

The French garrison made frantic sorties from the walls in an effort to break through the blockade. Adam laid aside his role as spymaster, spending day after day in full armor with the rest of the knights on the alert, ready to beat back the French, who sometimes stormed out a thousand strong. Henry's army was always successful in forcing them back inside the walls, but not without cost. The French set mantraps as they retreated to catch unwary English; those who were captured were thrown—alive—in weighted sacks into the Seine, or hanged from the battlements in full sight of the English.

"May Our Lord damn him to the hottest corner of hell," Henry growled, glaring at the jeering hangman, who was completing one such execution on the walls on a gray, cold day. "Though I vow hell will seem like a summer pleasance after I get through with him."

It was torture to watch helplessly, knowing they could do nothing to save their captured countrymen save to avenge their deaths by executing French prisoners. The knights and nobles standing with the king ground their teeth in anguish, staring at the swaying body dangling from the high gibbet.

The hangman, flanked by other Burgundian men-at-arms, had not bothered with the traditional black hood. Suddenly Adam realized that the mocking, beefy blond man was the same one who had chased him through the streets of Rouen, and said so.

"Who is he, Adam? We would know his name," said King Henry, startling Adam out of his dreams of vengeance.

"I know not, Sire," Adam said, not taking his eyes from the hated figure on the walls. "Only let me go back inside the city, and I will not only learn his name but rid the world of him—I promise 'twill be done excruciatingly," he said with a grim smile.

"Saker, you're like a harper with one string," commented Thomas of Clarence, though he understood why his vassal wanted so much to return to Rouen.

"Nay, we cannot allow it," Henry said. "We would not want to risk losing you, Adam, and the damned Burgundians would just select another executioner, in any case. Our retaliation will have to wait."

Then, without warning his men about what he was going to do, Henry cupped his hands and called up to the Burgundian. "What is your name, hangman? Tell me if you dare!"

The big, bluff fellow seemed to find this hugely amusing and led the chorus of guffaws from the walls above.

"Why, Harry," he called down from the ramparts. "Are you in need of a hangman? Do none of the men in your army have the *ballocks* for it?"

Adam saw the king go livid at the vulgarity and disrespect. A vein stood out under the chestnut hair as Henry called back, "Nay, but we would render you just payment when we enter the city!"

The threat seemed to bother him not at all. "It seems a safe enough risk to tell you—'tis Alain Blanchard, Harry! Just ask for the Captain of the Crossbowmen—*if* you ever enter!"

Adam had felt his own fury rising along with his sovereign's, and could hold back no longer. Pulling off his *basinet,* he shouted, "I'm afraid I have a prior score to settle with you, so unfortunately there'll be nothing left for His Grace, *King Henry of England and France,* to hang when I get done with you, Blanchard!"

The figure on the walls shifted his gaze to Adam. "Why, 'tis the timid hare I chased through the streets weeks ago! Elise's former lover! I believe your name is Adam, is it not?"

Adam felt all eyes on him. A red mist of rage filled his brain; his heart began to pound. "*Sir* Adam Saker, if it's any concern of yours, knave!"

Blanchard shrugged in elaborate unconcern. "'Tis of no import to me, cur. But perhaps you would like to know that 'your' Elise served—quite ably, mind you—as my mistress for a time and that she died in childbirth only recently. My son died with her, more's the pity!"

There was a stirring behind him on the walls as another figure came forward, but Adam had eyes only for Blanchard. "Lies, all of it! She is not dead, nor would she ever have let you touch her! The babe Elise carried was mine!''

Adam felt Henry's eyes boring a hole in his back and knew he would have some explaining to do later, but he was so far gone in fury that he did not care.

"Ahem, royal brother," spoke up Thomas of Clarence from a little behind them. "Perhaps Your Grace should withdraw now, and quickly. The fellow behind yon blowhard on the walls is carrying some sort of handgun, and I don't know its range, but I feel you should take no chances."

The man carrying the long stock of wood with the metal fittings on its end was dressed similarly to Blanchard, as if he, too, were in command, but there seemed to be some sort of disagreement between him and Blanchard. The big, stocky man seemed to be ordering the other to shoot his gun, while the other refused.

All at once, Blanchard wrested the long weapon from the other man and screeched a command that brought a soldier with a lit piece of tinder. While the soldier placed the burning brand at the touchhole, and Blanchard took deliberate aim, the English hastily fell back, convinced at last of the danger.

The shot landed just inches from King Henry's foot.

Henry flushed, but affected not to notice, knowing he would be well out of range before the captain could fire again. With lordly unconcern, he gestured to Adam as he strolled back to his pavilion, a motion that gave no hint of the angry questions Adam knew he would face. It didn't matter, not when his heart was busy denying the echoing words of Blanchard: "My mistress . . . died in childbirth. . . .''

* * *

"I'm glad you have come, Jean," Elise said, putting down the carving knife she always carried with her to the door now and letting her brother inside. She smiled wearily. "I made a stew from the last of the cow, and I'd not eat it alone."

They had slaughtered the cow weeks ago, having no choice after she had gone dry. With the animal's usefulness as a furnisher of milk ended, there was no point in Clothilde's children guarding her, and sooner or later someone would steal her for meat. Doubtless that was what had happened to Elise's pretty palfrey, Belle, who had disappeared even before that. Elise had no longer been able to buy hay for the cow, and there was not a blade of grass or a weed left in her yard thanks to the poor, desperate citizens of the blockaded city.

Jean glanced at the "stew," in which there was precious little meat. "Nay, I won't take what little food you have left," her brother told her, "since we still have rations, meager though they are, at the garrison. I'll just sit at the table and hold my nephew while you sup, sister."

"Thomas is sleeping, the saints be thanked," Elise said, going to the pot over the hearth. "He's been so fussy lately, poor lamb. Worry probably does not sweeten my milk."

Jean frowned at the ladleful of stew, which was all she'd put into her bowl. No wonder her clothes hung so loosely on her! He wondered how she was still managing to nurse the babe. Doubtless Thomas's suckling sapped much of his sister's reserves of strength. "Give yourself more than that, Elise. You're much too thin."

She pushed a wayward strand of hair back under her coif before replying. "This has to last as long as possible, Jean. There is no more meat after this. And why should I be any different from the rest of the people of Rouen? You look like a scarecrow yourself. But enough of that! What news, brother? Does our gracious duke come to relieve Rouen?"

He looked haggard in the flickering firelight. "Burgundy has sent word that he'll be here four days before Christmas."

"Surely 'tis good news? Is that why the church bells rang out across the city today?"

Jean nodded. "That's the reason, but there's no use in premature rejoicing. What good are Duke John's promises, Elise? Nay, I'd sooner rely on the English taking a sudden notion to withdraw, or Guy le Bouteiller having sense enough to surrender, though neither seems likely."

"Can Rouen hold out until Christmas?" Elise wondered aloud. The feast commemorating the birth of the infant Jesus was more than three weeks away.

"I don't know," he admitted grimly. "On my way here a starving young girl barely old enough to have breasts accosted me and offered herself to me for a hunk of bread. I'd be the first, she swore on the body of her mother, who had died only yesterday! I haven't seen a cat or a dog in the streets for weeks, and I hear rats are gourmet fare now. The poor are making a soup of dock leaves! And the citizens of Rouen have begun rounding up those who came as refugees and putting them outside the walls, Elise!"

"I had heard rumors of it," she admitted. "But surely King Henry will give them aid, or if not, will let them pass beyond the lines?" If worse comes to worst, I'll let them put us out, she thought. *I'll let the king do what he will to me, but I cannot let Thomas starve.*

"Nay, I've seen what happens from the walls," Jean said, his face haunted. "They're put out into the ditch beyond the walls, but when they would climb up and out, toward the English lines, the soldiers herd them back at pikepoint!"

She paled. "So Henry shows no mercy either? Will the Rouennais force me out, a woman with a babe?"

He sighed. "Those pitiless bastards don't care whether a woman has a newborn babe or is about to give birth! But I have let it be known that you are my sister, and that should suffice to protect you," Jean said, hoping it was true. *Ah, why did she ever come here?* He debated with himself whether he should tell her about seeing her English husband from the wall today. He remembered how, even from a distance, he had seen Sir Adam Saker wince at Blanchard's taunts that Elise had been his mistress and that she'd died in childbed. If only he could believe King Henry wouldn't wreak his long-delayed vengeance on her, that she'd be safe, he'd force Elise out beyond the walls himself!

The babe awoke and began to wail, and as Elise went to tend him, Jean gazed at the smoldering log in the fireplace. There was little fuel left, either. Soon Elise would be forced to burn what little furniture she had, and then what would she do?

"Blanchard hasn't been back to bother you, has he?" he asked as Elise began to nurse the babe.

"Nay, why fight me when he can have any of the poor young maids out there selling their honor for bread?" she said in an ironic tone that did nothing to make Jean smile. "In truth, though, Jean, he did come back once, and I kept the door bolted. Finally I had to threaten to use the butchering knife on sensitive parts of his anatomy if he didn't go away and leave me in peace! He must have believed me, for I haven't seen him since. Don't worry, Jean, he's just a blustering bully," she said lightly.

"Yes, but be on your guard, sister, for men such as he love to show their strength against the weak. However, I'd not care to be Blanchard if the English ever enter Rouen—they've seen him enjoying the role of executioner of their countrymen too much!" Jean omitted telling Elise about the threats Blanchard had made to him after he'd refused to shoot King Henry. His sister already had enough to worry about.

Elise did not hear from Jean for a week. And then one morning, as the snow fell in big wet flakes and the wind whistled through the streets, Blanchard returned.

"You'd be well advised to let me in, unless you wish me to announce what I have to say to the entire square," he told her as she peered through her shutters at him. "Hold your knife if you must, but I think you'd better listen to me this time." Something about the big man's ominous tone had already convinced her to open to him even before he added, "And there's no use hoping Jean will come. Le Bouteiller has him in a dungeon cell for a few days, cooling his heels for refusing to fire on King Henry when he had a clear shot."

Elise, knife clenched in her hand, gazed warily at Alain Blanchard as he swaggered through her doorway with at least part of his former bravado. Even he had lost flesh, however. The formerly rosy cheeks were pasty and slightly sunken beneath the gold beard. She noticed that he was clutching a small bag.

"I come to make you an offer, *madame,* the last you'll hear from me, if you say me nay. But you're skin and bones, Elise—I don't think you'll listen to your pride if it means starving to death."

He opened the bag, letting her see within, where the carcass of a pheasant, its feathers still gaudy in death, lay curled up inside.

"Where...where did you get it?" she breathed, licking her lips in spite of herself.

"I have my sources," he said with smug mysteriousness, staring avidly at her. "Think of it, *ma chère,* roasting over the fire, its skin crisping, its flesh succulent.... And I can get more—if you'll stop playing the haughty lady with me and become my mistress, Elise. Why should you and the babe starve for your coldness? Damn my eyes but you're beautiful, Elise de Vire! Even skinny as a starveling cat, you still make me want you."

Her empty stomach rumbled protestingly, as if it had seen the bird.

He grinned, sure of victory. "We could pluck it and start it turning on the spit while we seal the bargain, my copper-haired beauty."

It was the very smugness of his smile that stopped her thinking how good the fowl would taste and forced her to remember what it would cost her. "Nay, I'll wait for the duke to relieve Rouen," she told him. "I know he's on the way. Good *day,* Blanchard."

He laughed without mirth. "Don't count on John of Burgundy. He's camped at Pontoise, only a day's march away, but he's quarreled with the Armagnacs, and swears he won't move except to withdraw.''

She stared at him, wishing she didn't have to believe him, but she saw the truth in his bleak eyes. Blanchard had been the duke's man as much as her brother was, but she could see Blanchard had lost faith in the fickle noble just as Jean had.

"Get out," she breathed, speaking before she would allow herself to think any more about what she was giving up—the chance to live without hunger for a few more days, at least.

"Do you know what you're doing, Elise? Refuse me now, and I'll send the Committee of Rouen, I swear it," he told her. "You know, the ones who are looking for 'useless mouths' to eliminate from the city? You and your bastard will join the others in the ditch, and none of them will care that you're a lady—the ones who still live, that is."

"Send whomever you like. But begone now," she said dully, refusing to cry until he'd slammed the door behind him.

Chapter Twenty-Five

"Sir Adam! Harry told me what that *coquin*, that scoundrel, Blanchard, said! *Mon Dieu*, it is terrible!" The dwarf's monkeylike face was awash with tears, his eyes reddened from weeping. In his distress he had obviously forgotten what the knight had said about keeping out of sight.

Adam, whose mind had been on the very uncomfortable audience he had just had with the king, was startled at the ravaged visage of Gilles le Petit. He stopped and put a hand on the little servant's shoulder.

"Yes, but I don't believe a word of what he said, nor should you," he told Gilles.

"No, of course she would not for a moment have allowed that *salaud*, that *bâtard*, to touch her, but to have died giving birth to your child!" Gilles burst into a torrent of weeping.

Now Adam knelt in front of the dwarf and placed both hands on his shoulders, shaking him gently. "Gippetty! *Listen to me, Gippetty!* I don't believe that, either! 'Tis a lie!"

Gippetty opened tear-flooded eyes wide. "You don't..."

"No, indeed I do not." Adam did not let his eyes leave Gilles's. "He but said it to taunt me, and he will pay dearly, I promise you. But I think I would feel it, *here*—" he said, placing his palm flat over his left breast. "And I do not—so therefore she is alive."

"Alive? But where—?"

"I believe she got out of Rouen, Gippetty, and is safe somewhere, waiting. We must trust Our Lord to help us find her, eh?"

The dwarf dragged the back of his hand across his face. "*Oui,* sire. I see that faith is not just a quality of the French," he finished, smiling slightly. "But Harry told me, too, that Blanchard's taunts got you in dreadful trouble with the king."

Now Adam's lips curved in rueful memory. "His Grace is not best pleased with me, 'tis true," he admitted, "now that that knave has babbled the truth among the lies, that Elise was in Rouen all this time. King Henry's no fool—he could guess that my harrowing expedition into the city was no reconnaissance mission at all, but an attempt to find my outlaw bride! He expressed his royal displeasure at being deceived in no uncertain terms!"

"And does he... punish you?" the dwarf asked apprehensively.

"Nay, except to forbid me in the most severe terms to try such a foolish trick again." Adam sighed and stood up. "I think he knows I am already being punished by having to live with the uncertainty of not knowing where Elise is, or if I will ever find her again."

* * *

Two days after Alain Blanchard's visit, Elise was awakened by a pounding on her door. She jumped up, still half asleep and tangled in the blanket, causing the babe to set up a fretful wail beside her.

She could not have said what time it was. She slept whenever the babe slept now, husbanding her meager strength. And what was there to do, after all, but think about food and pray for deliverance?

When she cautiously opened the door, the fragile rays of a December sun were streaming over the building opposite, illuminating it and the group of men standing in front of her doorstep.

A jowly burgher stepped forward, unrolling a parchment scroll. "Madame Elise de Vire?"

Shivering in the cold wind that whipped around her bare ankles, Elise nodded, and clutched the blanket-wrapped infant to her. There would be no advantage in informing them that she was actually Lady Elise Saker.

"You are not a native of Rouen, and came to this city less than a year ago?" It was a mere formality; the committee obviously knew the facts already.

Behind the half dozen richly clothed burghers she could see a company of men-at-arms, each carrying a halberd, surrounding a handful of dispirited-looking men and women—other refugees, she realized, about to be put outside the walls. She could also see clusters of neighbors, whispering behind cupped hands, their faces guilt-ridden and sympathetic. Among these was Clothilde, her children huddled around her, pointing at Elise. But it was the figure standing alone, a little to the side of these groups, who caught her attention while she replied mechanically to the questions being put to her. It was Alain Blanchard, so smirkingly gleeful and self-satisfied that she was tempted to hurl the dagger she carried at her belt at him.

"Then, *madame,* having confirmed that you are indeed no lawful citizen of Rouen, and since there exists a state of emergency in this city that makes it impossible for undeserving vagrants to be fed out of charity, we must ask that you come with us to be escorted out of Rouen."

She had meant to accept the sentence meekly when it came, but the sight of Blanchard's smug face and hearing herself referred to as an "undeserving vagrant" finally shattered her self-control.

"Charity? I never sought charity from anyone, unless you would call the aid my brother rendered me out of love 'charity'! And for the past few weeks I have been starving just like the rest of this unfortunate city! And do you *know* my brother, good sirs, Jean Jourdain, Captain of the Artillery? Would you indeed banish the sister of one of Rouen's chief defenders to the mercy of the ditches?"

The burgher's face blanched, but he nodded. "Alas, I fear we have no choice. You have a few moments to dress as warmly as possible, and then we must require you to come with us."

She had run out of firewood days ago, and had had to wear several layers of clothing to keep warm, so all there remained to do was to grab up the fur-lined woolen cape and a pile of dry swaddling. Little Thomas, having heard his mother's harsh, upset voice, resumed his fretful wail.

The band of about-to-be-refugees had just been herded out of the square when the sound of running feet and shouted cries to halt reached them. Elise turned around and spotted Jean, his face flushed, trying to regain his breath enough to speak.

"I've just this moment heard what you mean to do with my sister. I must forbid it! She is innocent ... of any wrongdoing!"

"Sir, none of these people are guilty of aught except not being citizens of this beleaguered city," explained one of the committee. "'Tis merely that there is no food to feed them, and—"

"Then by your definition *I* am no citizen, either!" Jean shot back. "How is it you let me defend you, you ungrateful wretches who would put her out to starve? I say she stays!"

At a low command from Blanchard, the men-at-arms moved forward, their weapons at the ready to intervene.

Elise stepped forward, laying a restraining hand upon her brother's shoulder. "Jean, let them do as they must, and do not interfere. Do you not see, it is my babe's only chance?"

"But you will starve out there, Elise, if you do not freeze to death first!" he shouted, nearly weeping in his anguish. As if to punctuate his words, snow began to fall in big, wet flakes.

She forced herself to be calm, not trusting Blanchard. "Brother, we are starving within the walls, and have no fuel to burn for warmth, so there is little difference. But outside the walls Adam may find us, if he is there."

"But King Henry—"

"I care not what justice the king metes out so long as my babe lives," she told him, her gaze locking with his sorrowful one.

"He'll pay for this, I promise you," Jean muttered, with a meaningful glance at Blanchard.

"Leave him to the English," she insisted. "Go with God, brother—and if allowed to surrender to the enemy, do it. The English can be merciful."

Chapter Twenty-Six

Elise stirred in her sleep, pulling the fur coverlet around her and felt the deliciously soft mattress beneath her, and her husband's warm presence at her side. Thomas was snug in his cradle, smiling as he dreamed baby dreams of warm milk and his mother's green eyes and soft hands. in a little while he would wake and before he whimpered loud enough to wake her beloved lord, she would rise and put him to her breast where he would suckle himself back to sleep. . . .

Just then a large, inquisitive raindrop found its way inside the cloak Elise had pulled up over her face and startled her to full awareness. Then she felt the cold, hard mud beneath her, and the rain dropping in icy plops on the moisture-saturated cloak. She remembered that she was not safe in a castle somewhere with Adam but lying in the great ditch that surrounded Rouen, in the company of hundreds of others labeled by the citizens as "useless mouths to feed."

It had been the day before Christmas when she was expelled from the town. The wet snow had turned to rain as she and the rest of those turned out reached the ditch, and the rain had not stopped since, only varied its intensity.

On the next day, the Feast of the Nativity, the English had lowered food into the ditch, the first food some of the ditch inhabitants had seen in weeks. There was enough for all, though many were too weak to rise and get any. Others seized more than their share, pointing to this one or that one who had died and had no further need for it.

She had tried calling out to the soldiers lowering the food that she was the wife of Sir Adam Saker, an English knight, and wished to be taken to him, but they seemed not to understand her.

There had been no food offered after Christmas Day, and she grew steadily weaker. She made no further effort to speak with the English soldiers who came near. They seemed universally deaf to all pleas coming from the ditch.

There was a constant undertone of moaning in the ditch, as folk prayed for deliverance and cried from the pain of their empty stomachs and frostbitten limbs. She had seen more than one babe brought into the world in this hellish pit, leaving a relatively warm womb and entering a world of cold misery, hauled up in a basket to be baptized by an English priest, and lowered again to its waiting mother. Of course babies had to be raised to be christened, she reasoned; there was no God in this ditch.

She touched her babe beneath the cloak, reassured by the racing pulse still palpable in his chest, though it seemed fast and thready compared to before. He stirred and cried out at her touch, and Elise shifted him to her breast, marveling that there could yet be any nourishment there. But he seemed too tired to nurse, releasing the nipple after only two weak pulls.

Oh, Adam, please help us, she thought drowsily, dimly aware of a dangerous languor stealing over her, knowing that she must not give in, for to give in was to die. But what else was there to do?

She slept so soundly, and with such a faint rise and fall of her chest, that the starving man thought her already dead. He began to pull off the sodden, fur-lined woolen cloak from around her body, exposing the huddled infant in her arms—also dead, he thought, and crossed himself.

If the thief had not exposed the wet, dark red of her hair at that precise moment, the little man walking above, staring down into the ditch, might have seen only a shapeless, mud-spattered form and gone on. But first he noticed the hair, and even though it looked very little like the fiery copper glory that had adorned Lady Elise Saker in better times, it was enough to make him look twice. Then he spied the gaunt, heart-shaped face and recognized that his long, terrifying search was over.

"Harry! Harry Ingles! *Grâce à Dieu,* I've found her! Hurry! Bring the pallet and get down here!"

His shout startled the thief, causing him to scuttle off between the reclining and sitting refugees with his prize before he could be stopped. But the dwarf didn't see anything except Elise as he scrambled down the steep side of the ditch.

"Get Sir Adam! No, never mind, stay here, I'll never be able to raise her without you, you great redheaded

ox!'' Gilles cried, almost hysterical in his joy and relief. ''We'll take her to him!''

''I don't know, Gippetty,'' murmured Harry, kneeling at the woman's side and staring at her dubiously.
''She looks more dead than alive, and the babe too—
nay, he lives right enough,'' Harry corrected himself
when a gentle nudge elicited a whimper. ''But for how
long without a mother?''

Gilles bent over and felt at her neck for a long moment, terrified that what the squire had said might be
true, but at last he felt it: a slow, faint ripple of a pulse.
''You great fool, she *is* alive, but she won't be if you
want to stand around and doubt all day! Here, let's lift
them onto the pallet—gently now, and then spread
your cloak over them, and let's get out of this ac-
cursed ditch.''

In the end they decided the most sensible course was
to carry her to Sir Adam's tent and then go and fetch
the knight. Here they very nearly came to blows, for
while both recognized that the gravely ill woman and
her babe must not be left alone, each wanted to be the
one to tell their master that his beloved Elise had been
found alive.

Finally, common sense won out as Gilles realized
that with his skill, *he* was the best one to stay and watch
over Lady Elise, while Harry, long-legged and fleet of
foot as a young deer, could reach Adam more quickly
than could the bandy-legged dwarf.

Adam was at the king's side when Henry had his first
meeting with envoys from Rouen regarding terms of
surrender. The encounter was not going well. The
gaunt-cheeked envoys were trying to bargain for the

most favorable terms. Henry, though, irritated to the point of fury by the long, costly siege and guilt-ridden because of the hundreds of people starving in the ditch, was determined to show these stiff-necked burghers they had nothing with which to bargain. They were absolutely at his mercy, and the sooner they acknowledged it, the sooner serious negotiations could begin. Under the circumstances, it was easy for Adam to slip out, unnoticed, in response to his squire's beckoning.

Harry's cautiously radiant face told him the news before the redheaded youth could open his mouth.

"You've had word of her? Elise is alive, and sends word?"

"Nay, not a message. The dwarf found Elise herself, Sir Adam, in the ditch—and your babe! But sire, hold—" for the knight was already poised to run "—she and the babe are more dead than alive, near frozen to death, and she does not waken—"

"But she lives? She breathes?" Adam begged hoarsely, tears standing in his eyes as he clutched the squire's shoulder with the desperation of a drowning man.

"Aye, Sir Adam, she yet breathes, and the babe, too. Gippetty may have found her just in the nick of time."

"And they're in my tent?"

Harry nodded, and Adam waited no more, though the squire called after him, "Sir Adam! The babe is a boy! You have a son!"

For a long time Adam just knelt by the cot, watching the sleeping woman and baby. Tears coursed down his face, as he stroked her alabaster cheeks and smoothed back her hair, and stared at the tiny scrap of humanity lying next to her that was his son.

She was so thin—both of them were. The flesh was stretched so tautly over her once-rosy cheeks that he fancied he could see the skull beneath. Elise's arms were little more than sticks. When he pushed the blanket down slightly, Adam could see that her collarbones stood out sharply from her upper chest. And the babe, whose face should have been plump and pink, was pinch-cheeked and sallow. But he is *my son,* Adam exulted, seeing the raven black hair and the promise of an aquiline nose much like his own. So small, so fragile. He looked at the dwarf.

"Oh, Gippetty, will they ever wake? Did we find them only to watch them die?"

Gilles turned back from the brazier he'd been tending, his face sympathetic at the misery in Sir Adam's voice.

"Now it is *you,* Sir Adam, who must have faith. She will wake when she is warmed through, I believe, and the babe as well. But if I might make a suggestion as to how that may be accomplished more quickly..."

After listening to Gilles, Adam began removing his clothes.

Surely she had died and was in heaven, Elise thought. It would be too cruel of God to let her wake again only to feel the chill mud beneath her and the cold rain falling on her. As yet, though, she felt only dry and safe and warm—so warm, especially at her back, that if she didn't know better she could swear the bare skin of her back was touching the warm flesh of another human being. *So Adam and I used to lie abed at Falaise, a lifetime ago, curled up like two spoons, his chest against my back, our limbs entwined....* But that was impossible, wasn't it?

Against her breast, the babe stirred, nestling closer to his mother. Elise slept again, after deciding that if such dreams were common, heaven was a lovely place.

She awoke again to the sound of harsh male voices, shouting in anger over her head.

Chapter Twenty-Seven

"She has been condemned, not only as a spy, but a would-be murderess as well! And you *dare* to suggest to us that this woman should not *pay* for her crimes now that she has fallen into our hands a second time?"

Elise's heart sank within her as the words penetrated the deepest recesses of her brain. She could feel Adam's answering anger. Now not only would she pay the price of the king's continued wrath, but Adam would also pay. She tried desperately to intervene, to speak before he could ruin himself, but as yet her muscles would not obey her commands.

Henry of England, swathed in his ermine robe, had drawn himself up to his full height, every inch a regal Plantagenet. His voice vibrated with anger, his hazel eyes were terrible in their fury. A lesser man would have quailed before him, as lesser men always had.

Even though he was not royal, however, Sir Adam Saker was no lesser man. And the suggestion that this unconscious, gravely ill woman lying on the camp bed should have to face any punishment after what she had just been through enraged him past diplomacy.

"Don't you think she has paid *enough*, Sire? Just look at her! She's been slowly starving to death ever since our army surrounded Rouen, she and my son, a suckling infant! 'Twas Coulet who was the double-dealing traitor, not my wife! She refused to kill you when she had the chance!"

Henry had just burst into the tent a moment ago. He had been well aware, after all, that Adam had left the meeting. Curious about the look of dawning joy on Adam's face, and becoming suspicious, he had followed the knight as soon as he could. Now he watched as Adam placed himself protectively between Lady Elise and him.

"And what of the petty information she passed on to the faithless Duke of Burgundy?" Adam continued, unaware that he was shouting every bit as loudly as Henry had. "She had already informed Coulet that she would be an agent no more when he tried to force her into murder! Think, my king! Is it likely she would have *poisoned* you, if she would not *spy?* Did any of these facts prevent your ultimate triumph here? The burghers are beginning to sue for peace—'twill be a matter of days before Your Grace and they come to terms! And then the road lies essentially free to Paris— and the French throne—and we both know it, Sire! 'Tis my humble opinion that you can well afford some royal clemency in the matter of my French wife, Your Grace, since you have been granted triumph over Rouen!"

Ah, now you have burned your bridges, my beloved. And who will care for our son if Henry claps you into prison for treason? I was counting on you— for even if he lets me live, he will never let me be free, my foolish love.

"You are bold to the point of foolhardiness, Sir Adam," the king ground out.

Eyes of darkest brown met hazel ones and locked, neither man revealing by so much as the flickering of an eyelash that he would ever give way.

I must say something, must deflect the king's fury.... Her mouth opened, but no words could force their way past the parched vocal cords. Her eyelids seemed weighted down by stones. Elise managed a feeble flexing of her hands, but it went unnoticed by the two men.

Finally, Adam spoke again. "You offered me a reward of lands when I saved your life at Louviers, Your Grace, and I said I wanted naught, that I was merely doing my duty. I have changed my mind, Your Grace, as you urged me to do that day. I will claim my boon—not lands, but a pardon for my beloved wife."

"Nay! He'll never..." *grant such a thing,* her mind finished. *You dare too much, my Adam!* She could not deny, however, that her heart was warmed by what he was willing to sacrifice on her behalf.

Both men jumped, startled by the hoarse sound of her voice, a voice Adam had begun to think he would not hear again this side of the grave.

"Does she wake?" Henry asked.

Adam was afraid to hope. "'Tis but delirium, I fear...she dreams...." But he knelt by the bed, unable to take his eyes off her. The sound was the most encouraging sign that she had shown since being found.

The king sighed. "We would have given you a demesne whose breadth would make your brother appear the veriest pauper by your side, and a title to match it."

Adam shook his head. "What are lands, if I cannot have this brave woman, who has given me a son and fought so hard to preserve his life?"

"Done, then." Henry's gaze shifted to the woman lying so still on the bed behind Adam, and the knight could see the king's eyes widening as he took in Elise's emaciated appearance, and that of the undergrown babe. He looked back to Adam, his expression saying clearly, *Have you traded an estate for a dying woman and child?* "She is a brave woman, Sir Adam. I shall send over both my physician and my chaplain."

"Thank you, Your Grace. I—" He stopped suddenly as Elise stirred, her eyelashes flickering.

And then she succeeded, at last, in opening her eyes.

For a moment she could see nothing; the candle-light was blinding to one so weak. Then, as her gaze focused, her vision was filled with the sight of Sir Adam Saker, his face just inches from hers, his dark eyes wet with tears, and she was blinded all over again by the love she saw shining there.

"Adam..."

He would have given up his hope of heaven to have heard her say his name again in that piercing-sweet French way, *Ah-dom*. He saw how difficult it was for her to force out the word.

"Elise! Ah, don't speak, love—'tis enough that you have opened your eyes...."

Gently, he put an arm around her and laid his face on hers, and she could feel the warm tears fall onto her cheeks. His arm tightened across her back as if he still feared the king, or someone, would try and wrest her from him.

Just then the infant Thomas, warmed by several hours' slumber against his mother in the brazier-warmed tent, decided to protest both his empty stomach and the embrace of the stranger. He broke into a wail that surprised Adam so much that he fell onto his backside, his mouth hanging open.

"He has the sound of you, I think—already protesting injustice," the king jested, to hide the fact that he, too, was moved to tears.

But neither Adam nor Elise was paying any attention. They were both too busy rediscovering each other, and their son. After a moment, Henry of England recognized the futility of remaining and soundlessly departed.

He returned the next day, accompanied by Clarence, to make sure that the laundress who had recently given birth had arrived and was acting as temporary wet nurse until Lady Saker should be strong enough to resume the task.

Sure enough, Rose Watson, formerly of London and married now to one of the king's archers, sat in the corner of the tent, holding the contentedly suckling babe, while her own infant, already fed, slept in his woven-rush cradle at her feet. But it was the sight of Sir Adam Saker, knight of the realm, carefully spooning broth into his wife's mouth, that brought the grin springing to life across the royal face.

"You make an excellent nursemaid, Adam. Remind us to call upon you should we fall ill," Henry gibed, but his tone was kind. When Adam would have laid aside the cup and spoon in order to rise and make his bow, though, he stopped him. "Nay, she needs the nourishment more than we need your reverence. We but came to see that Rose was able to be of assistance...."

"We are...grateful...Your Grace," Elise Saker, swathed in blankets, managed in hesitating English.

"Yes, thank you, Sire," Adam added, wondering why the king had returned.

He had to wait to satisfy his curiosity, however, for now Thomas of Clarence stepped forward. "I'm so pleased to see you safe, Lady Elise," he said, "but I must confess I am come to check out a rumor."

"A rumor?" Elise asked as Adam assisted her to sit up against the pillows.

"'Tis noised about that your son—" his gaze took in both Adam and Elise "—bears the same name I do. Coincidence, madam?" He inched closer to the laundress, as if seeking the answer from the suckling child. "A handsome child, Adam, Lady Elise," he murmured. But Adam saw his eyes stray to the laundress's exposed blue-veined breast.

"Yes, your grace, 'twas in your honor," confirmed Elise, too French not to notice Clarence's distraction. "After all, you helped us—" She halted, coloring as she realized she was incriminating the duke before his brother the king. But Henry appeared not to have taken heed. "We rejoice to see you and the child recovering, Lady Elise," said Henry formally. Though she searched, she could see no trace of condemnation remaining in those eyes. "And we have thought much through the night, Sir Adam. While it touches our heart that you were willing to give up any right to a reward other than pardon for your lady wife, it is not necessary that you do so. With so much of Normandy regained by us, who are entitled by ancient heritage to possess it—"

If a man tells himself something long enough, he begins to believe it, Elise thought. After all the heartache and bloodshed, he has convinced himself that Normandy and all France belong to him.

"—and since Lady Elise is of Normandy and might become homesick if wrenched from her land, we are creating you Comte du Lessay, your principal seat being in the Cotentin."

Elise saw the color leave Adam's face, then flood back as the dark-haired knight struggled for words.

"I . . . I don't know what to say, Your Grace! Truly, I had not looked . . . for any other reward. . . ."

The king smiled, amused at Adam's dazed expression and reading nothing more into it than bedazzlement at his good fortune.

"Please . . . forgive me, Your Grace, and Adam, but I must speak," Elise interrupted.

All three men—Henry, Thomas of Clarence and Adam—turned to her, obviously wondering what she was about to say.

Elise's heart pounded. Would she undo any goodwill Henry might have regained toward them? "Your will is mine, my dear lord," she said, staring straight into Adam's puzzled brown eyes, "but I would have you know what is in my heart. If after listening to me you would accept this honor from His Grace, then I will rest content. But I would prefer that you decline it."

"What? Refuse a title and a rich county?" This from the Duke of Clarence, thunderstruck. The king's gaze became impassive.

"Why, love?"

"Yes, why, Lady Saker?" echoed the king. Seeing her hesitate, he added, "Having gone this far, do not fear to be candid."

"I...I can tell that you are willing to accept it for my sake, Adam, thinking it would make me happy to stay in my homeland, but in truth, I would rather you have the smallest, meanest of knight's fees in England than the entire Duchy of Normandy."

Darting a glance at Henry, she could not read his hooded gaze, but she caught the flash of relief in the black depth of Adam's eyes, and plunged on. "I have experienced war in all its horror until I long only for peace. I believe your sovereign will indeed conquer France—as mayhap it is, indeed, his right. But there are those in France who will always attempt to gainsay him, jealous of land they will continue to call theirs— the Armagnacs, the Burgundians. I would know that wherever you are called to serve your king, my Adam, there is a part of England—even just a chamber in your brother's Saker Castle—that is safe haven from war, as I fear France will never be."

It was a long, honest speech, and at the end of it she cast her eyes down, fearing to see the reaction she had caused.

"Well said, *madame*," breathed Clarence, moved beyond his usual cynicism.

"Your will is *mine*, my green-eyed vixen," said Adam, smiling. "I love you, Elise."

Now everyone turned to the king, who had not revealed his opinion as to Adam's refusal of his generous gift.

"You drive a bargain as hard as any tinker, *madame*," said the king wryly. "We can see you will be a valuable asset in keeping Sir Adam from making foolish decisions. Very well, then, we have just today had word that Reginald, Earl of Rothley, has died, leaving only a cloistered nun, his aged sister, as heiress, and she, of course, has no desire at her great age to leave the peace of the convent and take up again the cares of the world. Therefore I am granting you the Earldom of Rothley." He turned to Elise, asking, "Will *that* agree with you, Lady Elise?"

She ducked her head again, color flooding her pale cheeks. "*Oui,* very well, *mon roi,* if my lord is content."

"Sir Adam?"

"Aye, Sire. It pleases me very well, for the lands march with those of my brother. I am overwhelmed with Your Grace's goodness toward me."

"Yes...well, I do have a condition." All eyes turned toward him. "As soon as Rouen surrenders, Sir Adam—ahem, that is, *Lord Rothley*—you have our leave to take your bride home and let her recover in England. Let her get to know your family—she'll learn that the English are not all bad."

It was said with a twinkle in his eye, and Elise managed a smile.

"But we would have you return soon, my lord. Soon we will be in a position to obtain our heart's desire—not only France, but the hand of the Princess Katherine of Valois in marriage. It would mean much to her if a countrywoman of hers could be one of her first ladies-in-waiting."

It was an incredible honor for a Frenchwoman who had spied against this very monarch to be offered a position as attendant to his queen, and Elise knew it. But she could not forget what she had just endured, and how many hundreds of suffering folk were still enduring it.

"I, too, have conditions, Your Grace."

"Conditions?"

Henry gaped; Clarence chuckled. Adam looked concerned, but made no move to silence his wife.

"Mon roi, I will accept the position with pleasure if you will end—immediately—the suffering of the folk in the ditch. They never should have been left there, and they need food and shelter at once. As do the starving people in Rouen."

Henry paled and looked away. Obviously it was a matter that had already troubled his conscience. As well it should! thought Elise.

"Had we sent *you,* Lady Elise, as our ambassador, this war would be over already!" the king marveled. "But you said condition*s, madame?* What else can there be?"

"My brother, Your Grace." Now Elise allowed the tears she had been struggling to hold back to flood her eyes, and she clasped her hands together. "He is Jean Jourdain, Captain of the Artillery. He...he is a good man. When Rouen surrenders, as it soon must, I would beg Your Grace's mercy toward him."

A half smile played about the king's thin lips. "We promise you, Lady Elise, as long as he surrenders, your brother has naught to fear of us. And now we will take our leave, Lord and Lady Rothley. If we stay we will end up bargaining away our crown!"

Chapter Twenty-Eight

Elise placed her sleeping son in his cradle, smiling as Thomas stuck his thumb in his mouth and resumed sucking. She stroked his soft, pink cheek, saying a prayer of thankfulness for the way his tiny body had filled out in the past fortnight. He was still smaller than he should be, but he was catching up quickly—especially, she fancied, now that she had regained her strength and was nursing him herself.

Evening was drawing near, and she wondered when Adam would return to the Carthusian monastery guest house. They had been moved there to aid her recovery, but since King Henry made his headquarters there, it was also convenient for the king.

Her husband had been gone since early morn, for today was January nineteenth, the appointed day of Rouen's surrender. At noon today, she knew, the English army had entered the city and accepted the capitulation of the garrison. The king, having already done as he had promised by feeding and providing shelter for the desperate refugees in the ditch, had reiterated his pledge not to harm any soldier who was willing to surrender. Her brother had said Rouen *should* yield; now she awaited word that Jean had done so and was safe.

Elise was anticipating her husband's return for another reason, too. She picked up the bone comb from the nightstand and began to comb out the braid she had worn all day. Freed from confinement, her long tresses fell past her shoulders in ripples of fiery copper.

She opened the door to their chamber and peered down the corridor of the guest house. The torches set in the walls revealed no one. When would Henry dismiss Adam from his duties? Nervously she smoothed the folds of the emerald silk gown she had worn at their wedding. Would the sight of it make Adam realize that she was ready to resume the physical side of their marriage?

He had been so kind and considerate in the past two weeks, placing no demands on her, knowing she was too weak and tired to do other than snuggle gratefully against his warmth at night. He had asked nothing of her but that she regain her strength. She sensed that he would wait for some signal that she was ready.

But Elise had seen the glowing look in his eyes as he complimented her on the color returning to her cheeks, and the regained luster of her hair, and she knew he hoped it would be soon. Tonight she would not disappoint him!

Suddenly she heard voices in the corridor, and before she could run to open the door, he was there.

Unthinking in her excitement, she ran into his arms, only to notice as he held her close that he was not alone. Standing diffidently behind him, watching as the new Lord Rothley embraced his wife, was her brother!

"Jean!" she cried, leaving the circle of Adam's arms to hug her brother. He was hollow-eyed and gaunt of cheek, but he smiled and pretended to reel under the force of her joyous greeting.

"Oh, Jean, I am so glad to see you safe! My lord, what means this? How are you able to bring him to me? I had heard the garrison was to be marched outside the gates and made to leave! I did not think I would actually get to see Jean—"

"Hold on, vixen! How will I tell you if you keep chattering?" Adam said, smiling to see the happy reunion. "That is indeed what happened to most of the garrison. But those who were willing to swear allegiance and serve King Henry are allowed to remain, and—"

"You have pledged fealty to King Henry?"

Jean nodded. "As did Guy le Bouteiller. 'Twas not an easy decision, of course, but both of us feel King Henry is a better ruler than the poor mad creature who currently holds the throne of France—or devious Burgundy."

"And so my brother and my husband are now comrades-in-arms? Ah, this is too wonderful for words! We must celebrate! Sit down, both of you, and I will pour the wine!"

She had planned a lavish supper for Adam and herself, and now, with the addition of Jean, she was glad. King Henry had bade her make free with the fresh supplies he received from England via his boats coming down the Seine, and so she had both a ham and a haunch of roast beef to carve from, as well as a cameline meat brewet and freshly baked bread.

"In sooth, sister, I had not thought to see this much food again this side of heaven," Jean said with an appreciative sigh. "Even the garrison was starving, having given away much of our stores to the poor citizens."

For a while there was no talking, just eating, but Elise saw that Jean ate sparingly, afraid to trust his shrunken stomach. But she kept his wine cup full, and was gratified to see his gray pallor being replaced by a healthy flush.

The babe awoke as they were eating their sweet wafers. Jean, expressing a desire to become reacquainted with his nephew, picked him up from his cradle and held him for a few moments before passing him to Elise to be fed, marveling how well he looked considering what he had gone through. Obviously, Adam had already told Jean how the dwarf had found her and the infant in the ditch. She was glad—it was not a time she wanted to relive by telling of it.

There was, however, a matter she must know, for her own peace. She had turned aside to suckle Thomas, but now she looked over her shoulder at Jean and Adam, sitting companionably together with the flagon of hippocras between them.

"You have not mentioned Blanchard," she said. "What became of him?"

She saw Adam's face darken; he got up and stared at the glowing coals in the brazier as if they contained the answer.

"Dead, but unfortunately not by my hand," he growled. "Damn Henry, I told him he was mine!"

After a hasty glance at the Englishman's closed face, Jean picked up the story. "Blanchard was missing when the garrison surrendered, and a search of the citadel did not reveal him. Having met Lord Adam, I mentioned to him that the scoundrel might be hiding in the house I rented for you, for he had boasted to others of seizing it after you were banished. I offered to show a contingent of soldiers the way."

"And did you find Blanchard there?"

Jean nodded soberly. "Cowering in the cellar like a trapped rat. I must admit, it was a pleasure to drag him in front of the king. But when the king saw Lord Adam among the group, he insisted he wanted your husband and none other to escort Archbishop Chichele into the city. 'Twas almost as if he wanted him out of the way! By the time Lord Adam returned, Blanchard had already been hanged by the king's order."

Elise winced in spite of herself. It was over—she would never see that sneering, lustful face again. Then she saw the rigid set of Adam's shoulders as he turned away from them.

In the past few days she had told him much about her life in Rouen, and especially how Blanchard had tried in vain to coax, then coerce, her into being his mistress, and how he had finally been instrumental in having her put into the ditch. Adam, in turn, had told her about Blanchard's taunts to him from the walls—though he added that he had not believed them. So Adam had had a very personal reason for wanting to be the one to end Blanchard's life, but Henry had robbed him of that privilege.

Male pride! She would have to tread carefully here, she knew. Placing the satisfied baby back in his cradle, she went to face him.

She spoke in English, for what she said was meant only for Adam Saker's ears. "I know you wanted revenge, my love—both for my sake and for those unfortunate Englishmen who fell into his hands—but I'm glad 'twas not you that killed him. If you had been the one to execute him—not in the heat of battle, but in cold blood—would there not be a danger of becoming even a little bit like him, my love? *He is dead, and we are alive,* and we have many reasons to rejoice. Tonight, I would not have you remembering war."

Something in the green eyes fastened so entreatingly on his told Adam more than Elise's earnest words could.

Tonight, I would not have you remembering war. He swallowed, drinking in the love she offered him. His pulse began to race.

Behind them, Jean cleared his throat. "Excuse me, but I think I shall retire now, my lord, Elise. Thank you for supper, and you, Lord Adam, for your good offices with the king today. I . . . I am honored to count you as family, as well as my friend."

"The feeling is mutual," Adam murmured, but his eyes hardly left his wife.

"We'll see you on the morrow, Jean," Elise said absently, then opened her arms to her husband as the door closed behind her brother.

It was a homecoming for them both. Adam pulled her into his arms, feeling the still-too-slender form fit itself against the hard planes of his body. He caught the heart-shaped, upturned face between his two hands as his head dipped to drink from her lips.

She felt so tiny, so fragile in his arms. He must go slowly, gently, remembering how recent her ordeal had been. But when her lips opened at the first pressure of his mouth on hers, and he felt the soft lushness of her milk-swollen breasts against his chest, he felt his resolve weakening.

"Here, I will play tiring woman to you, love," he said, hearing the shaky huskiness in his voice as he loosed her enough to unfasten the tiny buttons down the front of the silk gown.

His voice was not all that was shaky, he found. No wonder there were tiring women! There must have been two score buttons down the bodice, and all of them too tiny for his trembling, battle-callused fingers to easily undo. And then, when his hands would rather fondle what was hinted at through the thin woolen undergown, there were buttons on each sleeve, as well! He was torn between frustrated laughter and curses by the time he had freed them all, and too aware of her bright, amused gaze. Then, after the undergown, there was the chemise, and finally she was naked, and somehow— much more easily—he was, too, and they were sinking down on the camp bed together.

And when he would have loved her tenderly, considerately, she raised herself over him.

"Nay, I am no ghost, Adam! I am alive!" Elise insisted, smiling tenderly and yet with a mischievous glint in the now jade, now emerald green eyes that changed in the flickering light. She rained kisses all over him, on his brow, down the angle of his jaw, over his nipples, lingering on the flat belly, which quivered as she laved her tongue lower.... Straddling him, she rubbed against him, feinting at sheathing his hard manhood within her, coming so close and then gliding away, until at last he had had enough of her teasing and turned her over onto her back and buried himself within her. And she smiled and answered him thrust for thrust until he could contain himself no more.

Later, as she blinked at him in sleepy satisfaction, he gazed at her naked, love-warmed body, unable to get enough of looking at the woman who had been lost to him for so long. The candlelight illumined her ribs, still prominent underneath the breasts that suckled his son. "By the saints, Elise, I'm going to enjoy feeding you every delicacy I can find between here and Saker Castle, and then I'll have our old cook make all her specialties. You should taste her mortrews, and her apple tarts are a delight fit for heaven. And then there is the meat tile that she makes of veal, chicken, bread and almonds, and her *blancmange,* and stewed eel, and meat pasties—"

"Hold!" She laughed. "I will not show well against your brother John's wife if I become fat as a pig!"

He sobered, wondering if he heard a note of uncertainty underlying her jesting.

"Elise, you know that you have naught to fear about Anne—about my feelings for her? I loved her once, you know, but 'twas not the same once I met you. I love her now only as a brother-by-marriage ought to."

She nodded. "Perhaps 'tis like that I once felt for Aimeri. It gleams but palely compares to what I have with you."

"Ah, I cannot wait to arrive at Saker Castle and show you to them, Elise! Not only to John and Anne, but to Cecily and Amicia—perhaps we will also be able to visit Mary-Claire in her convent as well. They will love you just as I do!" He saw her shiver slightly.

"What is it, love? Have I overwhelmed you with talk of family? I promise you, we will have ample time to be private too—I mean to inspect well our new property of Rothley before we return to the king's service!"

She sat up on one elbow. "Nay, it isn't that. I once longed to hear you say that they would love me too. But you were just Sir Adam Saker then. They will be so proud that you are now an earl! Won't your brother resent that you have thrown away your family's chance to make valuable alliances—English alliances—by marriage to a Frenchwoman, and a penniless one at that?"

"John's not like that," he told her. "None of them are. I suppose we never forgot that the family began as mere falconers to a king. And even if they didn't love you for your own sweet sake, I'd tell them how you begged me to turn down the chance to become a French count for 'the smallest, meanest of *English* knight's fees!'" She smiled, but he saw the faintest of doubts lingering. He would contrive to kiss them away, until he could show her the truth of his words.

Chapter Twenty-Nine

Calais, January 1419

The breeze rippled over the merchantman's deck as it waited at anchor, causing the canvas overhead to snap as if in anticipation of the short journey across the Channel. Picking up a little force, a gust nearly stole the headdress that Elise wore, but since her hands were free, she was able to clap one of them atop her head, feeling the veiling in the back rustle at the wind's passing.

Adam, Lord Rothley, was not so fortunate; his hands were full with his squirming son, and so the wind was free to steal his stylish sugar-bag hat. Before he or Elise could prevent it, it had flown capriciously off his head and landed in the harbor, to be picked at by diving gulls until the velvet became waterlogged and sank beneath the surface of the brown water.

Little Thomas cooed, finding it all very funny, and laughed with delight as a gull flew near and cried harshly.

Adam smiled ruefully over at his wife. "See that? I suppose it means I was never meant to wear aught but a mail coif and my *bacinet* helm! None of fashion's pretensions for the likes of me!''

Elise smiled back at him, secretly preferring the way her midnight black hair was free now to be ruffled by the harbor breeze. She hadn't told him how much she disliked the hat, which reminded her uncomfortably of the black one Burgundy was wont to wear. She smiled, too, at the sight of Adam holding his son, gazing fondly down at his son as the infant pointed a chubby finger at another dipping, soaring gull. Would the babe first call them *birds,* or *les oiseaux?* It didn't matter. He would grow up speaking both languages equally well.

It was wonderful to see how at ease Adam had become in recent days with his son. At last, as the child gained weight and lost his pallor, Adam had been convinced he would not shatter if held—even inexpertly— by his father. Now Thomas found his father's face just as familiar and loved as that of his mother, and cooed and smiled when Adam held him.

Eager to win his spurs in upcoming conflicts as the king strove to reach Paris, Harry Ingles would be staying with the army until Adam returned to France. But Gilles le Petit had elected to go to England, and in the squire's absence would serve Lord Rothley as well as his lady. Therefore, this would be his last sight of Normandy for a while—though actually, this port had been English for centuries, being the only possession King John had not lost along with the rest of England's former lands in France. Gilles had insisted he did not mind leaving France—had even said he was eager to see England—but Elise had caught him looking pensively out over Calais as if searching for something. And there was that wistful look she often saw on his face when she found him gazing at at her and Adam.

The ship bobbed at anchor as if eager to be away, but she would not leave for an hour. The tide was not yet right.

And then Elise saw her—standing on the docks, selling oranges and limes to the sailors of many nations, who believed in the fruits' efficacy in preventing scurvy during long voyages. A tiny little woman whose basket was almost as big as she was, a dwarf, just like Gilles.

Elise gave a discreet tug to Adam's velvet-clad sleeve to gain his attention, then indicated the woman with a nod of her head. She glanced meaningfully at Gilles.

"Ah, there's a fruit seller!" Adam said, picking up his cue. "'Twould be nice to have some fruit for our voyage, would it not, my lady? Mayhap it comes from Spain, or even from Africa. Go down there, Gippetty, and buy us some, please," Adam commanded, handing the dwarf some coins and giving a secret wink to Elise.

"Very good, milord," said Gilles, very proper now that he was the servant of an earl and his countess— and then he saw the fruit seller.

The transformation of his face, and the look of lively interest on the face of the little woman as she saw a man coming toward her who was just like herself, though an inch or two taller, made Adam and Elise smile.

"I believe, as a countess, I have need of a maidservant, Adam," Elise murmured, laying her head against his shoulder as she watched the two small people conversing on the dock below. "Do you suppose the fruit seller would be willing to come to England with us?"

Adam grinned. "I'll wager she would, as long as Gippetty is a part of our household, my matchmaking lady!"

She gazed up at him, her green eyes alight with happiness. "I would have everyone find what I have found with you, my Adam."

"Ah, vixen, there is none like you! I love you," Adam said.

* * * * *

Harlequin® Historical

WARRIOR SERIES

The WARRIOR SERIES from author
Margaret Moore

It began with A WARRIOR'S HEART (HH #118, March 1992)—the unforgettable story of Emryss Delanyea, a wounded Welsh nobleman who returns from the crusades with all thoughts of love put aside forever... until he meets the Lady Roanna.

Now, in A WARRIOR'S QUEST (HH #175, June 1993), healer Fritha Kendrick teaches mercenary Urien Fitzroy to live by his heart rather than his sword.

And, coming in early 1994, look for A WARRIOR'S PRIDE, the third title of this medieval trilogy.

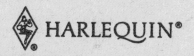
HARLEQUIN®

THE TAGGARTS OF TEXAS!

Harlequin's Ruth Jean Dale brings you
THE TAGGARTS OF TEXAS!

Those Taggart men—strong, sexy and hard to resist...

You've met Jesse James Taggart in FIREWORKS!
Harlequin Romance #3205 (July 1992)

And Trey Smith—he's THE RED-BLOODED YANKEE!
Harlequin Temptation #413 (October 1992)

And the unforgettable Daniel Boone Taggart in SHOWDOWN!
Harlequin Romance #3242 (January 1993)

Now meet Boone Smith and the Taggarts who started it all—
in LEGEND!
Harlequin Historical #168 (April 1993)

Read all the Taggart romances!
Meet all the Taggart men!

Available wherever Harlequin Books are sold.

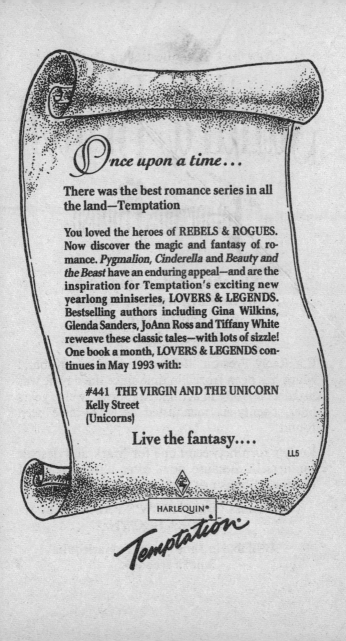

_O_nce upon a time...

There was the best romance series in all the land—Temptation

You loved the heroes of REBELS & ROGUES. Now discover the magic and fantasy of romance. *Pygmalion, Cinderella* and *Beauty and the Beast* have an enduring appeal—and are the inspiration for Temptation's exciting new yearlong miniseries, LOVERS & LEGENDS. Bestselling authors including Gina Wilkins, Glenda Sanders, JoAnn Ross and Tiffany White reweave these classic tales—with lots of sizzle! One book a month, LOVERS & LEGENDS continues in May 1993 with:

#441 THE VIRGIN AND THE UNICORN
Kelly Street
(Unicorns)

Live the fantasy....

LL5

HARLEQUIN®

Temptation

Where do you find hot Texas nights, smooth Texas charm and dangerously sexy cowboys?

Crystal Creek

AMARILLO BY MORNING

Show time—Texas style!

Everybody loves a cowboy, and Cal McKinney is one of the best. So when designer Serena Davis approaches this handsome rodeo star, the last thing Cal expects is a business proposition!

CRYSTAL CREEK reverberates with the exciting rhythm of Texas. Each story features the rugged individuals who live and love in the Lone Star State. And each one ends with the same invitation...

Y'ALL COME BACK...REAL SOON!

Don't miss **AMARILLO BY MORNING** by Bethany Campbell. Available in May wherever Harlequin books are sold.

Following the success of WITH THIS RING and
TO HAVE AND TO HOLD, Harlequin brings you

JUST MARRIED

SANDRA CANFIELD
MURIEL JENSEN
ELISE TITLE
REBECCA WINTERS

just in time for the 1993 wedding season!

Written by four of Harlequin's most popular authors, this
four-story collection celebrates the joy, excitement and
adjustment that comes with being "just married."

You won't want to miss this spring tradition, whether
you're just married or not!

**AVAILABLE IN APRIL WHEREVER HARLEQUIN
BOOKS ARE SOLD**

JM93